Dark is the Wood

Dark is the Wood

ENCHANTED TALES WITH DRAGON SCALES

BOOK ONE

KRISTIN WARD

Also by Kristin Ward

Romantasy - Enchanted Tales with Dragon Scales

Dark is the Wood

Treacherous is the Tower

Celtic Mythology Dark Fantasy - Daughter of Erabel

The Girl of Dorcha Wood

Blood of the Lost Kingdom

A Storm of Wrath & Ruin

Legion of Shadows

Dystopian

After the Green Withered

Burden of Truth

Science Fiction - Fantasy

Rise of Gaia

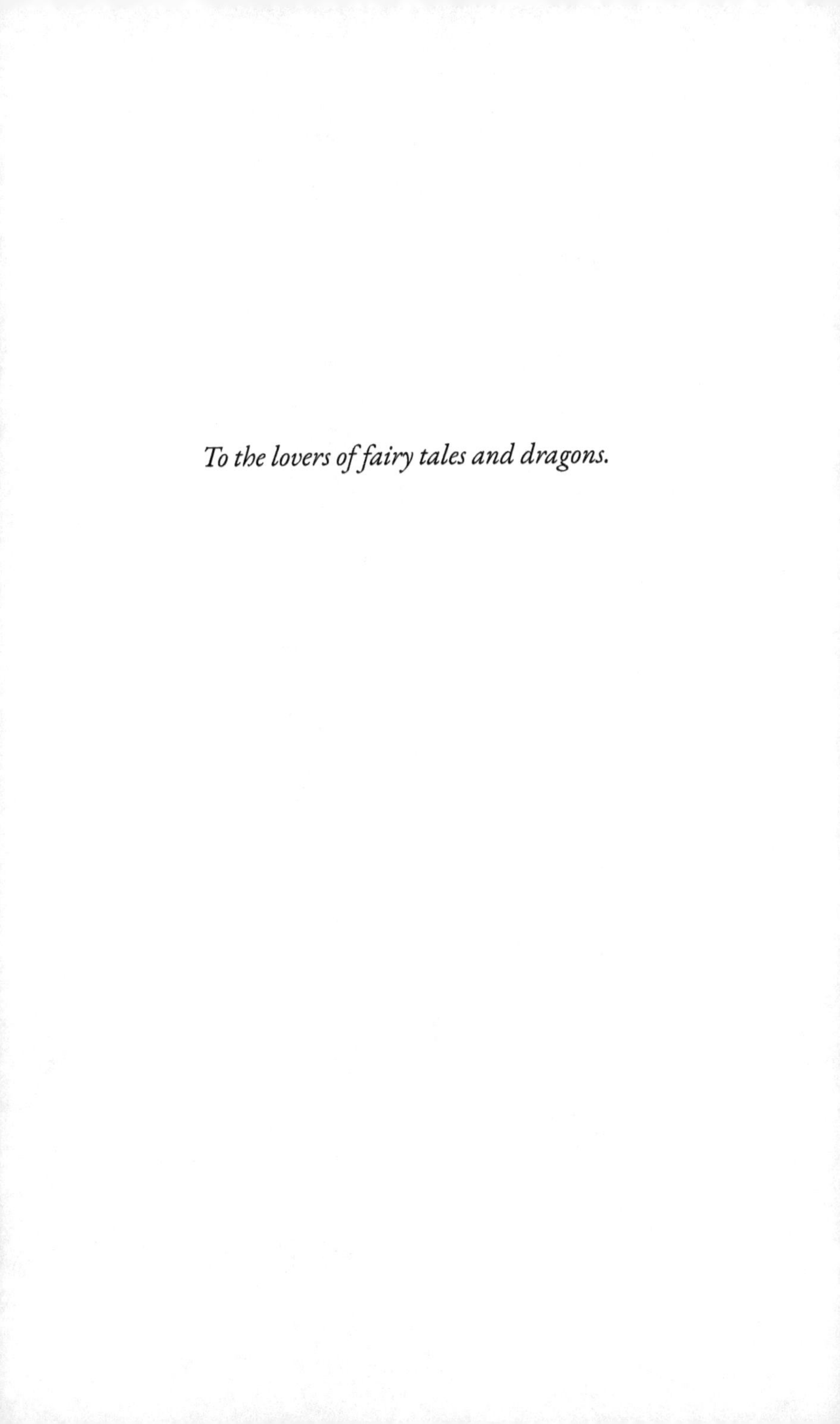

To the lovers of fairy tales and dragons.

Prologue

The crops died first.

It was subtle in the beginning. A bad season or two was normal, nothing to worry over, though it was a hardship for the inhabitants of Rudgarde. But when two seasons turned into three and four, people started to talk. They sought out the religious, begging priests to bless the land, offering sacrifices of lamb and calf.

Rudgarde's people turned to the gods. Ceremonies were held. By day, men tore clothes from their backs as they flailed and beseeched under the fiery heat of the sun god. Skin reddened, burned, and blistered under Irylle's mighty glare. By night, women linked hands and danced beneath the pale moon, offering tears, blood, and song to Keridwen, the goddess of nature and rebirth.

Hope stirred.

The land rebounded, presenting a bountiful yield. But it did not last. Frustrated and angry, the people cursed Keridwen, believing the goddess had forsaken them. Some turned their ire to Irylle, but most feared angering the fire god and remained steadfast in worship, though in their hearts, doubt sowed.

The Wasting sank into the earth, slowly leaching the soil where crops grew. It spread like the vines of a creeper, crawling across the land. It consumed the border towns first, then all of the Kingdom of Mirynn.

And then, like the land, children began to wither.

On the heels of the driest spring in a century, Rudgarde's children started to sicken. By the fall, nearly a quarter crossed the river. By the following spring, more showed the first ominous signs of an illness no medicine or prayer could cure.

Fear set in.

And accusation.

Everyone knew the Shadowlands bordering the town was cursed. Dark creatures roamed the Great Dragon's realm, and only a fool would enter there. But they were desperate. Without Keridwen, they were lost. Irylle and the Dragon, both creatures of fire, became undisputed godlike symbols. Many believed the Great Dragon was the father of man and that the serpent would hear their pleas and save his children.

Offerings were made. First, they were animals and food—each gone shortly after being placed at the edge of the dark forest. But the plague continued—reaping crops and children. They offered more food, more animals, and more prayer.

When the young daughter of Sir Hubert Westin, the local lord, sickened, the wealthy knight offered a king's ransom in jewels he'd collected during his time across the Black Strait. Kneeling at the border of Dwyer Wood, he renounced the old gods and begged the Great Dragon to spare his daughter, placing the sack of precious stones at the base of a gnarled tree.

It was gone the next day. His daughter, Marigold, took her last breath a sennight later.

Keridwen was dead to them. Irylle and the Dragon did not hear their pleas.

So they turned to another deity: Setanta, the god of war.

Setantan priests convinced the people human sacrifice was required to appease the one true god and capture the attention of the Dragon. Serfs were the first to be chained to posts just outside the border. But they were always whole come morning. Unbound and returned to their masters, they told stories of strange noises coming from the depths of the accursed woods. The priests decided someone must enter the Shadowlands and give their flesh and blood to the beasts that roamed there.

Those people prodded at the point of a sword and forced to cross into the forest, disappeared into the trees, their departure followed quickly by bloodcurdling screams. But the Wasting did not abate. The villagers stopped trying to enter Dwyer Wood, and Sir Westin made it a law not to cross into the Shadowlands.

Time continued its relentless march.

Crops struggled. Children died.

And no one crossed into the Dragon's domain.

Decades passed, and the people learned to accept their fate. For every child who crossed the river, three would live and grow to adulthood. For every blight-ridden field, others would yield enough to keep communities from falling into ruin.

It was a world without gods. A world without hope. A world of death and disease and war. Across the kingdom, the once proud temples of Keridwen were razed. What point was there in honoring the goddess of nature and rebirth when she did not listen as they suckled a dying child at their breast?

But even the bravest men lacked the courage to defy Irylle as he hovered, callous and cruel, in the heavens. Like the Dragon, he was a god of fire and might. So they bowed to him even while he made them suffer.

Only Setanta seemed pleased. Only Setanta gifted his followers with plunder and slaves as men marched to war to fight and die for what was left of their world.

Through it all, the Shadowlands remained. Dark and unchanged. Nothing entered and nothing left that place. It became a thing people whispered of beneath the glow of a candle. Stories of Dragon, Dragonborn, and witches grew into legends. But legends are insubstantial things made of words. In time, many believed that, like Keridwen, the Great Dragon was dead. He hadn't flown through the skies for so long that he must have crossed the river like so many others.

But he was not dead. He was trapped, biding his time until an opportunity arose.

And his wait was nearly over.

Chapter One

Gillian Ddraig stood at her brother's bedside, holding a bowl of broth in her hands. Worry creased her youthful face as she watched Rory's chest rise and fall beneath the child's thin blanket.

As before, she'd added tulsi leaves and ginger to the liquid, taking a pinch of salt from their dwindling supplies to enhance the properties of the plants.

Rory's lashes fluttered when she rubbed his chest. Cracking his blue eyes open, a smile wavered on his lips. "Gillian," he whispered, pushing his body against his pillow.

He'd been waking later and later over the last few weeks. Her parents hadn't said the words, but she knew it was the Wasting. They all did.

Ruffling red hair poking out in every direction on his head, Gillian said, "You're sleeping the day away, lazybones. Scoot." She waited for him to shift his body closer to the wattle and daub wall of their small home, then sat on the edge of his raised pallet. "I want you to eat and then come outside and help me in the garden."

He cupped his hands around the bowl and sniffed with a grimace. "It smells bad."

"Then plug your nose."

Rory sighed as only an eight-year-old could, with all the youthful exasperation of a disgruntled sibling.

There was a subtle tremor in his hand as he took the spoon. Gillian watched the utensil wobble, grief threatening to etch its way into the corners of her mouth.

Nobody survived the Wasting. Nobody.

Masking her emotions, she made small talk as he ate, tipping the bowl toward her when Rory claimed it was empty.

"There are at least two spoonfuls left." She pushed it back to him and folded her arms.

"I'm full."

She raised an eyebrow. "Oh? That's too bad. I made a honey cake."

Gillian stood and tugged on the bodice of her drab gown. It was too tight in the chest and arms. In fact, it had been too small last spring, but her parents needed to pinch every penny just to get by. The price of the food they couldn't grow had increased since the blight, and most of the vendors had stopped showing up on market day three years ago when it was clear the townsfolk could afford little more than necessities.

The last thing she needed was to eat cake and strain the seams of her worn clothes, but life had few joys these days, and she was loathe to give up any of them. Making her brother's favorite treat was worth the cost of the flour or another small tear.

"More for me, then." She reached for the bowl.

Rory snatched it away and tipped it to his mouth, making slurping noises. A thin trail of broth ran down his chin, and he wiped it away with a small belch, grinning when he thrust the empty bowl into her hands. His cheeks were flushed, the broth having done its work, but she knew by now the healthy blush would fade, leaving behind a gray pallor.

"May I have cake, now?"

"Hm." She looked at the dregs in the bottom of the bowl and then toward his stomach. "Are you sure those last few drops didn't fill you up? I don't mind eating your slice. Wouldn't want it to go to waste."

"I burped some space," he announced and swung his legs over the edge of the bed.

Her face was pained as she looked at them. They were spindly things. He was withering away before her eyes, and she couldn't stop it. No one could.

Rory had been a gift to her parents after years of miscarriages and stillbirths. Both Naeve and her husband, Lochlan, doted over the boy.

And at ten years older, Gillian was no different, taking special pride in every stage of his growth. But the Wasting cared nothing for status or familial bonds. There wasn't a family in Rudgarde its relentless progression hadn't touched.

Rory shuffled to the peg where a shirt and trousers hung, tugging at his chemise.

Gillian left the room to let him dress, worry furrowing her brow. Setting the bowl in the wash basin in the cramped kitchen, she looked out the window at the garden where she'd planted rows of herbs, each with medicinal qualities, when her brother showed the first sign of illness. She'd read every book on medicine the local bookseller let her borrow. She ventured into every meadow and copse of trees, searching for plants said to cure everything from gout to a chest cold.

But the herbs weren't working. Each day, he grew weaker. Soon, the first black spot would appear on his chest. After that, he'd have a few months at best.

Gillian gripped the side of the basin, fingers digging into the wood hard enough to snap the tip of a fingernail. She winced and popped the digit into her mouth, tugging the ragged edge with her teeth free and spitting it onto the floor.

The sound of voices had her leaning toward the windowsill, where she caught a glimpse of her parents coming in from the small field a stone's throw from their house. They shared the land with three other families, each scraping by on the small slip of earth.

Her stepfather, Lochlan, had one arm around his wife. The other held a bucket of water. It sloshed over the rim with every step.

Gillian hustled to the door and swung it open, standing aside as they entered.

Naeve brushed strands of graying hair from her face and greeted her daughter before craning her neck toward her children's bedroom. "Is he awake?"

"Aye. I made him a bone broth with herbs."

She cupped Gillian's face, her eyes wrinkling at the corners as she smiled. "He's lucky to have you. Your herbs never fail to improve his strength."

Gillian frowned and turned away, busying herself by pouring water into the wash basin and cleaning the dishes from the morning meal. Her mother grasped every speck of hope. It hurt to know that any improvement was fleeting and that each morning he was a little frailer than the last.

She didn't say such things to her parents.

Let them live in a fantasy for a bit longer, she thought, scrubbing a mug with a soaked rag. The sounds of family mixed with the soft splash of water, lulling each of them into a peace that couldn't last as outside, Irylle turned the sky yellow above the horizon.

"I saw it on his back," Naeve cried, her words carrying through the darkness.

Gillian rolled out of bed and pressed her ear to the wall separating their rooms. In the dimness, she picked out her brother, who shared the room, but he was sound asleep. Rory lay sprawled on his stomach, one arm flung out and hanging above the floor.

Putting her palms against the wall, she listened to her stepfather argue.

"It's just a bruise. You know he fell in the garden only days ago." Lochlan paced, his feet pounding dully.

"It's not a bruise," her mother countered, her voice catching on a strangled sob. The meaning of those words penetrated the walls and landed with a thud in Gillian's heart. "I saw it clear as day just below his shoulder. It's just like your nephew Edwin."

With horror-stricken eyes, Gillian drew away from the wall and turned toward her brother. Kneeling at the side of his bed, she gently pulled down his chemise, biting her lip when she saw the unmissable black stain marring his flesh. Sitting back on her heels, she dropped her head and listened to her mother beg.

"I have to go, Lochlan." Rustling followed the statement along with the murmur of her stepfather's low voice. "I can't stay here and watch him die!"

Gillian slipped out of the room and hovered at the cloth strung across her parents' bedroom doorway.

Go?

She couldn't believe her mother would talk of leaving. Not now, when Rory needed her more than ever.

She peeked through a gap in the fabric and watched her mother pull a necklace from her strongbox.

"Put that away." Lochlan strode toward Naeve and tried to grab it. She tucked it behind her back and jutted her chin, defying him with her tears. "Don't even think it," he whispered harshly.

"I have to try." She looped the necklace with a strange medallion over her head. "They have the power to save him. I know it."

"You know nothing!" he said, voice rising.

Naeve shushed him, feet moving closer to Gillian. "You'll wake them," her mother admonished.

Gillian ducked silently into the shadows, straining to listen as their talk grew quiet. Frustrated, she crept closer when Naeve moved away from the curtain.

"The Coven of the Silver Moon has old magic," Naeve said, stuffing clothes into a satchel. "They'll know what to do more than the zealot you want to invite to our son's bedside!"

Lochlan grumbled, his boots scuffing the floor. "It's just

stories, Naeve, like all the other stories of creatures lurking in the Dragon's wood. It's not real."

"And if you're wrong and they could save him?"

He put his hands on his hips. "Alright. Let's pretend they exist. What makes you think they'll speak to you, much less share their power to aid a human child?"

"You know why," Naeve said softly.

"I know no such thing! If they live, they're evil—born of that serpent who'd burn us to ash if we set foot on his land."

"Finn didn't believe that." Her birth father's name had Gillian peeking through the curtain.

Lochlan flinched. "Rory is my son. Not his."

Naeve took her husband's hand. "You're right. Rory is your son. And Gillian, your daughter, though not by birth." She tilted her head, eyes pleading with him. "You need to trust me. Please, Lochlan. Isn't it worth the risk if they could save our son?"

Sighing, Lochlan pulled his wife into his arms and hugged her to his chest. "You don't fight fair, lady." He kissed her brow. "If the medallion works, if the wearer can cross into that accursed place and find the coven, then I should go. Rory needs his mother. Let me do this if it must be done."

Naeve shook her head. "You know they won't speak to a man."

"Aye. I know it." His head dropped to his chest. "But—" He sighed, his words trailing to nothing.

Biting her lip, Gillian went over their argument in her head.

Her mother spoke of witches—of the Coven of the Silver Moon—as if she knew they existed. She'd heard the tales but assumed they were nothing more than fanciful stories. That her father, Finn, had known of them.

It made no sense. In eighteen years, they'd never spoken of such things.

No one crossed into the Shadowlands. Dwyer Wood was a forbidden place—forbidden by law as if they needed such a thing to keep them from entering a realm where the beasts of nightmares lived and breathed.

She glanced toward the room where Rory slept. He couldn't lose his mother. Not now. Not when he may only have a few months left.

"No decision must be made tonight," her stepfather told Naeve.

Gillian peered through the curtain, watched Lochlan take the stuffed satchel, and set it on the floor next to the doorway.

"Sleep on it, Naeve. In the morning, we'll decide what's to be done, and if that decision includes you crossing into that realm, I won't stop you."

Her mother nodded and lifted the medallion into her palm. She studied the stone disc, turning it to catch the candlelight. "Finn would understand, wouldn't he?"

"I don't know. It was meant for Gillian."

Naeve slipped the necklace off and draped it over the satchel. "It can wait until morning."

They doused the lantern. The creak of ropes suspending their mattress told Gillian they were settling in.

She stared at the medallion resting on the satchel through the split in the curtain. Whatever it was, Naeve believed it would grant passage into the Shadowlands and allow an audience with witches. And for some reason, it was meant for her. Should Naeve go, the quest was doomed. She'd never return.

Gillian wouldn't let that happen.

Creeping back into her bedroom, she kissed Rory's forehead, whispering how much she loved him in his ear.

She left a piece of herself in that room when she shut the door, an armful of clothes in her hands. Taking the bag and medallion, she pulled out her mother's things, replaced them with her own, and left the discarded pile on the kitchen table along with a note.

Dawn had yet to break when she strung the medallion over her head, slipped into her red cloak, and fled into the night.

Chapter Two

She was lost.

Darkness had fallen hours ago after a day of fruitless searching, and with the stars came the creatures of the night. Gillian wandered Dwyer Wood, but every tree she passed looked the same. Every incline she climbed only led to a deep ravine she swore she'd already stumbled through.

Panic set in.

Her progress became erratic. She crisscrossed the forest, cursing the Shadowlands, wishing she'd never crossed into them, and hating herself for wanting to give up, knowing what it would mean for her brother's fate.

Why did she think she could enter the Dragon's realm and magically find a group of women who called themselves witches? And if she did find them, why would they listen to her? A human. An enemy if the stories she'd heard were true.

The snap of a branch stopped her, and she swung around, holding her breath. *Damn the clouds for hiding the moon!* she thought, straining to see through the thick canopy of trees.

In the blackness, they were little more than silent soldiers guarding the secrets of that cursed place.

A rustle made her jump, and she clutched the hood of her red cloak, peeling back the edge to peer to her right. The hairs on her neck stood on end as a low growl drifted to her ears. Her eyes widened, her heart beating like a caged bird as something snuffled in the darkness. Gillian clenched her teeth and held still, legs going watery as a beastly grunt carried on the wind.

Like a living nightmare, a dark shape emerged from a dense copse of trees and stopped to sniff the air. It was wolfish but the size of a bear. Hulking and dark, its massive skull pulled its neck down so it hung below hunched shoulders.

Aside from its brutish shape, little more could be discerned in the dimness.

Chuffing, it paced in a tight circle, head bobbing as it caught her scent. The loud snap of a branch had the animal snarling, its massive body spinning around in a defensive posture, the thick hair on its back bristling.

She felt its eyes on her as though it picked her out of the darkness, and she bolted.

The beast gave chase.

Branches grabbed her hood, snatching it from her head and ripping out blonde strands of hair. She zigzagged through the trees. Her lungs sawed with frantic wheezing.

I'm going to die!

She didn't dare look back, only charged forward, leaping over rocks and fallen trees. The lip of a ravine came into view, and she sobbed, pushing her limbs to move faster.

At the edge, a shape lunged from the darkness.

She yelped, feeling her body thrown to the ground. She rolled onto her back, trying to pick out shapes in the darkness.

The beast at her heels roared.

Its growl was met with another, louder and full of violence.

Gillian watched in horror as a man jumped onto the creature's back and plunged a blade into its neck. It gave a throaty gurgle and thrashed, foreclaws digging into the dirt as it crashed onto the forest floor. The man gave his blade a vicious twist. Tendon and bone snapped with a sickening crunch.

Gillian couldn't move. Her legs were leaden things anchored to the earth. She watched with wide eyes as the man swung off the beast, wiping his blade on its shoulder before he sheathed it at his side. She held her breath as he approached her.

Clouds broke, and the moon bathed the scene under her pale glow, revealing who had saved her.

He wore snug, black leather pants and a tunic, the same color, torn and hanging askew from the tussle. Its deep V revealed the pads of muscle covering his chest.

Her eyes flicked to his, and she froze, a rabbit caught in the talons of a hawk.

He moved with a loose-hipped stride. Stopping at her sprawled feet, he raked his eyes over her.

She felt exposed as though he saw through her plain brown dress that had seen better days—through the red cloak that she clutched in her fist against her heart, which beat in a wild rhythm.

Her savior towered over her, the rugged planes of his face shifting in the moonlight. A thin layer of stubble shadowed his tawny features, accentuating the hard angles of his cheeks and jaw, making his striking face dangerous.

But it was his stare that held her fixed. His eyes bore into hers, their buttery color glowing like twin copper flames.

She'd heard of his kind in stories told behind cupped hands in the light of a flickering candle.

Dragonborn.

Gillian scrambled to her feet, dragging her eyes away from his intense gaze, only to find them leveled on his again. He studied her from beneath the dark slashes of his winged brows, his full lips curving into an amused smile when she stumbled on the hem of her cloak.

Scowling to hide her fear, she yanked at her bodice, trying to ease the tightness in her chest.

"Thank you," she said, grimacing at the high pitch of her voice. He tilted his head and said nothing. "I... I'll go now."

He slowly shook his head and crossed his arms, blocking her path of escape.

Pain flashed in her face before she could mask it as she stepped away from him, her back hitting a tree trunk.

Trapped.

Stupid! So stupid, she chided herself. *Why did I think I could do this?*

She knew what would come. It's how every story ended—with the trespasser in pieces. It would hurt when the dragon took over.

She shouldn't have come. It was forbidden.

The medallion she'd taken from her mother's strongbox hung like a noose beneath her woolen gown. Its strange power, the glowing warmth that had allowed her to cross into Dwyer Wood, did not guarantee her safe passage within the Dragon's realm. And now she'd been caught by a predator. A monster whose reputation struck fear in the inhabitants of Rudgarde.

How many stories of his kind had she heard in her eighteen years? Too many to count, and each of them brutal warnings of what would come of those who entered the Shadowlands.

Like a reckless child, she'd ignored the warnings and come to this place, thinking she could accomplish what her mother had sought to do. In her arrogance, she'd robbed Naeve of the chance to save her son.

Awful things she'd heard whispered at night, the stories of evil creatures and people venturing into the woods never to return, came full circle. And she'd invited it. Had entered the very realm villagers feared with good reason.

Would her story be added to the cautionary tales? Would her foolishness and woe be used to deter others from repeating her folly?

By now, her parents had found her note, but they would never know her fate. *Mother will never forgive herself,* she thought. The Wasting would claim Rory as it had taken the lives of so many children.

It would remain. Unstoppable. Merciless.

She'd failed.

Gillian hung her head, tasting defeat. It left a sour residue like bile on her tongue. The hem of her cloak grew cold and heavy, soaked with dirt and moisture after hours of wandering the forest, dragging her shoulders down. Rory's face flared in her mind, momentarily blocking out the fear and anger that coursed through her body.

It wasn't fair.

She'd stolen his chance to live when she'd taken the medallion and come herself. Oh, she'd been willing to trade her life for her brother's.

He needed his mother. Not his sister.

Being slain by one of the Dragonborn was not the trade she'd counted on.

Chapter Three

Calloused fingers lifted Gillian's chin.

She clenched the hilt of the small knife she used to collect herbs and kept her eyes downcast, avoiding those of her captor. The sound of her heart pounding muffled her hearing as she slowly eased the blade from its sheath.

His hand covered hers in a blur of movement, squeezing painfully until she let go of the weapon. It fell to the ground with a soft thump, and she stared at it.

The metal glinted in the moonlight.

Balling her hands into fists, she narrowed her eyes to meet his steely gaze. Gritting her teeth, she fought the urge to strike him.

Let him loose the Dragon and slay me, she thought. *He won't have the pleasure of seeing me on my knees. I'm not begging for mercy. His kind had none.*

"Such loathing in those eyes," he said, his voice curling

around her brain, making it feel fuzzy. "It usually takes longer for someone to look at me that way," he drawled.

Gillian stood rigid. "I know the face of cruelty when I see it."

He rumbled low in his throat. "I see the blind hate of your people has not dimmed."

She glanced at him, seeing his jaw clench, then looked away. "My people have good cause."

He hummed in his throat and rubbed his neck, the silky fabric of his tunic gaping at the neck and exposing more of his muscled chest. "I'm Roman." She stood mutely, and he smirked, asking, "Don't you have a name?"

Her eyes skittered over his features. "Gillian of Rudgarde."

"Ah. Well, welcome to the Shadowlands, young Gillian."

"I've heard stories of your kind," she said caustically.

He raised a brow. "Do tell."

She sniffed and lifted her chin. "They say the Dragon's blood takes over to reveal what you really are. A monster."

"Is that what they say?" He pursed his full lips. "They talk a lot, don't they?"

"Do you claim they're wrong?" He shrugged, and she frowned, her courage sliding back down her throat. "When it happens, I hope... I hope you make it quick."

His lip curled in a grimace. "You speak as if my blood is a duality, something I can turn on and off at will. I can assure you it is not. If I had a mind to kill you, you'd be dead." He flung his arm toward the cooling corpse. "Or I would've let the vauger have you."

She looked at the remains of the beast, mouth twisting in disgust as the musky stench of the dead animal wafted on the breeze. "Is that what it is? I've never seen anything so monstrous."

"There are worse things in Dwyer Wood for a helpless girl like yourself. You should not have come here."

He raked his eyes over her, and she stiffened.

"It is forbidden," he bit out.

His last words seemed half for her and half for himself.

Gillian backed away, clutching the medallion beneath the coarse material of her woolen gown. "I have safe passage."

He cocked an eyebrow. "Do you now?" he asked, clicking his tongue. "Don't you know I can smell a lie on your breath?"

He came toward her and slipped a finger beneath the neckline of her dress.

She wanted to pull away, but his eyes held her in place as though he'd trapped her will. Warm fingers gently tugged on the leather cording, pulling it free of her gown. When he looked down at the disc in his palm, she felt untethered and took a step back, stopping when the slack of the leather cord tightened.

His dark, sharply angled brows creased as he studied the medallion.

Lifting his gaze to her, he said, "These are the markings of the Coven of the Silver Moon." She tried to grab it, but he closed it in his fist. "Where did you get this?"

She gave him a mutinous look, and he clenched his hand. Pain flared in her chest as though she were the medallion and his fist was a vice around her torso.

Gillian gasped. "No! Don't break it!"

He loosened his hold and asked again, "Where did you come by this?"

Staring at his fist, she said, "It was my mother's."

His nostrils flared, and he leaned close, sniffing the air, pupils growing wide and so dark that the coppery color of his irises disappeared. He opened and closed his mouth.

Glancing at the medallion, he turned it over in his hand, tracing his thumb over a collection of lines along the edge that was different from the others. Lips moving in a blur, he mumbled something, eyes fixed on the disc.

Flicking his gaze to hers, he let go of it, letting it thump softly against her chest.

Folding his arms, he said, "She must have stolen it."

Gillian scowled. "My mother is no thief."

"Oh? Then how did she come by such a treasure?"

She clenched her teeth but said nothing.

"Only the Matriarch of the Coven of the Silver Moon could grant such a gift, and I doubt you'd want to cross her path. The witches would sooner slit your throat with an Ashrune dagger and stake your corpse at the mouth of a vauger den than offer you aid."

She cut her eyes at him and lifted her chin. "They would speak with me."

He rolled his eyes. "Arrogance is the predominant trait in your kind."

"I could say the same of yours."

He waved her words away. "That may be, but at least I'm not delusional enough to believe the Silver Moon sisters would let a human near their sacred land, much less speak to one. You should be grateful."

She narrowed her eyes.

"You should. I've saved you from your stupidity. They'd either kill you on sight or take their time, slicing the flesh from your bones and offering it to Keridwen, their impotent goddess."

Gillian looked away from him, eyes roaming the woods before falling on her discarded dagger.

He clicked his tongue. "Such murderous thoughts toward someone who just saved you."

Roman leaned down and picked up the knife, flipping it in his hand with practiced ease. "I'll hold onto it for now. Wouldn't want you to cut yourself accidentally."

Tucking it into his leather belt next to a wickedly sharp, curved blade, he studied her, watching anger and fear at war in her features. "Now, shall I leave you to the beasts of my realm? Or would you rather save your neck and come with me?"

"So you can kill me at your leisure? If I'm doomed already, get it over with!" she spat at him, heart twisting at her brother's fate.

"No."

Glaring, she took a step forward and gave him a shove, grimacing when he didn't move an inch. Lip curling, Gillian lunged again, anger flaring when he chuckled. With a snarl, she whipped her hand through the air; fingers curled to rake her nails across his cheek.

In a motion so fast she hardly saw him move, he snatched her wrist and spun her around, bending her arms painfully behind her back.

"You're as brave as you are foolish. Tempt me all you like, Gillian of Rudgarde. It won't work," he whispered in her ear, his breath hot like the sands of the Red Wastes.

She yanked her arms free, knowing he could've kept her immobilized if he'd wished, and stalked a few paces away.

Muttering, she kicked at the leaf-littered ground, wincing when the soft toe of her shoe met a knobby root jutting from the dirt. Limping, she stormed off, not caring where she went as long as it was away from him.

If Roman followed, he did so in silence.

The forest grew darker, closing in as though the trees bent their branches to block what little moonlight pierced the thick canopy.

Dwyer Wood claimed her.

She felt it and knew the boundary between her world, the Kingdom of Mirynn, and the Shadowlands, where the other-born ruled, was closed.

The medallion resting against her chest was cold—its power leached. She stopped walking and held up the disc in front of her face, feeling the heat of Roman's body as he came up behind her.

The medallion spun slowly. The etchings on each side were dull and bereft of the magic she'd felt thrumming through them when she'd passed into the forbidden forest. Would it flare to life again when she neared the barrier separating her world from this nightmare landscape?

"Don't bother wishing on that useless trinket," Roman told her, stepping to her side. "It will not lead you to them, no matter what your thieving mother may have told you."

He cocked his head, lips twitching when his words hit their mark. "Have you come to your senses yet, or shall I leave you to the creatures who prowl the wood?"

As though to echo his warning, a howl rent the air, making the hair on the back of her neck prickle.

Roman whipped his head around and cursed.

"What is it?"

"The vauger's mate. Run!" he yelled, pushing her toward a steep incline peppered with large boulders.

Hiking up her dress, Gillian bolted.

The rocks were uneven and sharp, abrading her knees and palms as she scrambled up the hill. Below, she heard twin roars as the beast and Roman clashed. The sounds of battle sent her scurrying, heedless of the thorny brambles, tearing flesh and fabric.

A painful shout stopped her mid-lurch.

She craned her neck and looked down the hill, where she saw a tangle of claws, limbs, and bodies rolling on the ground.

It was larger than its mate—an enormous mass of fury on four powerful legs. The vauger's rear feet slashed at Roman, ripping through the leg of his leather pants. He snarled and flipped the animal with a burst of power. The vauger landed on its side and sprang to its feet, unfazed by the surge of energy.

Pure rage fueled its fight as it went for the kill.

Jaws extended, forelegs stretched out, the monster leaped toward Roman's head.

She saw its fangs tear through his throat. Saw the blood spray.

She screamed and thrust out her arms, feeling power bubble up inside of her and burst like a blister.

The Dragonborn staggered back, his neck whole and unscathed. The beast ran into the trees in fits of snarls. Roman watched its retreat, then swung his head toward her, brows deeply furrowed. She dropped her arms, confused and angry that she'd thought to save the very being threatening to trap her in the Shadowlands.

Not waiting to see if he was injured, she spun around and continued her climb. By the time she'd reached the top, sweat made her already tight dress unbearable. Panting, Gillian bunched her satchel to make a pillow and flopped onto her back.

Cool air swept over her face, and she closed her eyes, breathing deeply, centering herself.

The sound of Roman climbing pulled her mouth into a frown. Heaving her body into a sitting position, she crossed her legs under the skirts of her dress and waited.

Roman's hand grasped the top of a boulder, his grim face rising behind it.

She turned away, tucking her arms against her chest. He finished the climb with a mutter and stalked off a short distance from her. She couldn't help but notice the way he favored his right leg.

Serves him right, she thought sourly.

He stood close by, head cocked to the side, sharp eyes peering into the darkness as though he could see through the gloom. Shifting toward her, he announced, "It's time to go."

"Unless you're going to lead me to the coven, I'm not going anywhere with you."

Letting out a long sigh, he limped toward her, stopping at her feet. "You're like a dog with a bone."

She glared up at him. "Fine. Take me home then, and I promise never to cross into your land again."

"Oh," he purred. His breath was hot against her cheek as he leaned down and whispered, "It's much too late for that."

Chapter Four

Gillian balked and leaned away, eyes darting across a landscape whose shadows tried to swallow her. "You can't keep me here."

Roman's full lips curved in the corners. "Who's going to stop me? You?"

She hopped up and shoved him, throwing him off guard.

Hiking up her skirts, she ran, cutting through the undergrowth as she fled down the other side of the summit. The canopy of the forest closed in, shutting out the moonlight as she careened through the trees, struggling to recall the direction she'd come.

The sound of heavy feet followed her, and she picked up her pace. The medallion flopped against her breasts, a cruel reminder of her recklessness.

As the minutes passed and the terrain steepened again, her legs grew weary, and she found herself clutching her side, trying to ease a stitch. Breath sawing in and out of her lungs, Gillian halted and turned in a slow circle.

Nothing and everything looked familiar.

Had she passed that cluster of bushes? Was that tree the same one she'd leaned against earlier in the day?

Fear clogged her throat as Roman's loping tread grew louder.

Above the trees, she heard a loud screeching and shrank, stumbling toward the trunk of a massive oak. Gillian strained her eyes, seeing little more than patches of the starry sky through the thick branches. But she could hear, and the sounds filling her ears were unearthly wails that sent tremors down her spine.

"Unless you'd like to end up in the talons of that myrax, I'd suggest you stop running from me," Roman said, emerging from the darkness.

Gillian started and whipped her head around. "Help me find the coven, or let me go home."

"Why do you persist in wanting to find the witches when I've told you what they'll do to you?" His face looked strained, and in the moonlight cutting through the branches, she saw blood drying through the ripped leather on his leg.

She ignored the healer within her who wanted to patch and mend his torn flesh. Instead, she glared at him and fisted her hands. "I have to try. My brother..." she paused, jaw ticking. "He's sick with the Wasting. I came here to save him."

"You thought you'd find a cure *here*? Is that the lie your mother told you?"

She glared at him. "The witches can save him. They have old magic."

Roman gave her an amused expression. "Old magic? Aye, I suppose you could call it that. Let's pretend they allowed you to enter their land. Why would they agree to save a human child?"

Lips pressed together, Gillian lifted her chin. "Perhaps they have some humanity. Unlike you."

"Humanity?" He chuckled. "If it's humanity you're after, you've come to the wrong place."

She shrugged. "The least you could do is allow me to try. If they refuse, what is it to you?"

"I suppose I could." He raked his eyes over her body. "But, as I've told you before. I won't be handing you over to them."

Gillian made a frustrated sound. "Fine. If you won't allow me to seek them out for the sake of my brother, then lead me to the border and let me go home."

"This is your home now."

Her eyes narrowed. "No. It's not."

His eyes crinkled in the corners. "I do enjoy your spirit. That quality will either make what's to come easier or harder."

She frowned.

"Forget your plans to return to your family. Your brother will die, and you won't be there to see his passing. That is the way of it."

Gillian flinched at his words. In her mind, she saw Rory's pale face grow still. Saw his last breath slipping from blue lips.

Shaking her head to rid herself of the vision, she looked at Roman through the slits of her eyes. "You're cruel."

He pursed his lips. "I'm a realist."

"No," she said, shaking her head. "You're a monster."

His jaw ticked. "It matters little what you think of me. You're not going to the coven's lands, and you're not returning to the world of men. If your mother was truly given that medallion, she should've warned you of the risks of entering the Shad-owlands."

"She didn't know."

"That is often the way with humans."

He walked slowly toward her, the pace masking his injury. He was a predator stalking its prey.

Gillian clenched her hands. He didn't care about Rory's fate. On some level, she understood that. They were enemies. Not by deed but by ancient history.

Refusing to give up, she changed tactics."I could help you."

He stopped and lifted a brow.

She pointed to his leg. "If it's not treated, it'll fester. I could pack it with herbs."

She dug around in her satchel for the bundles of herbs tucked into linen bags she'd brought from home. Their familiar scent made her eyes sting.

Closing one of the bundles in her fist, she said, "Let me help."

Roman eyed her warily. "Why?"

"As repayment for killing the vauger before I became its dinner."

He tapped at her mind, reading the ploy in her thoughts. She sought to curry his favor. To heal him and win him over so he'd do her bidding. But she was no master. And he was no puppet.

Still, he was curious about her skill. He'd heal on his own. Already the wounds were closing. But there was something about her that he wanted to delve into. It could lead nowhere, of course. Still, he gave a mental shrug. Why not allow her to think she could ply him?

"Very well. Shall I remove my pants?"

Her face flamed. Pig. "That's... that's not necessary. Just sit over there, and I'll tend the wounds through the rip."

He smirked and perched on a rock. Roman stretched out his leg, frowning at a flare of pain the movement caused, and watched her. She sifted through her herbs, avoiding his eyes.

He made her uncomfortable. Or was that anger? They were equally alluring. She was a fighter. It was a quality he recognized and begrudgingly respected.

Gillian took pinches from three of the bags and rubbed them in her palm. It had become a habit to talk to herself as she mixed her remedies. Her mother said she whispered to the herbs.

Acutely aware of Roman's heavy gaze, she clamped her lips and spoke only in her mind, mixing and pressing until she had a damp mass in her hands.

Seeing her kneel at his feet, head bowed in concentration, made his gut clench with need. He looked away, balling his hands into fists.

She tugged the torn leather aside, expecting to see stripes of torn flesh. Instead, there was a lone claw mark, deep but shallow enough to make her wonder how he'd come away relatively unscathed. She pinched off pieces of the mixture and rubbed them into the wound until it was covered in a film of herbs.

Sitting back on her heels, she looked up at him. "That should keep it from souring."

He kept his attention on her, slowly bending his leg so his knee brushed the side of her breast.

Her eyes narrowed, and she scooted away.

Roman chuckled and stood up, offering a hand that she

sniffed at and ignored. He shrugged and flexed his leg muscle, surprised to feel the concoction working already. Strange.

"Will you take me to the coven?" Gillian stood at his back.

She was relentless. "No."

"Please. I'll do anything."

"Aye," he said, his voice pitched low. "You will."

Brows knitting, she brushed off the warning in his words. "If you won't lead me to the witches, then let me go home. I don't belong here, as you've made clear."

"It's too late for that."

She made a frustrated sound and put her hands on her hips. "You're mad if you think I'm just going to let you drag me across your foul kingdom like a mindless slave."

His mouth twitched.

It made him look devilishly handsome, which only served to irritate her and make her next comment barbed. "Or is this how you find a mate? By stealing them because no one can stand your miserable company."

His eyes flared. "You will never be my mate."

Gillian lifted her chin. "Good. I'd hate to think of a life bound to someone I loathe."

"You don't loathe me," he gave her a lascivious grin, "though I find it amusing to watch you try."

"You swine."

He oinked like a pig, and she kicked him, her foot landing on his wound.

"Enough," he shouted, pain drawing his mouth down.

Roman moved in so close she felt the heat of his body. She made to dodge around him when he rested his hands on her shoulders, but he pinned her with his stare, and she froze, locked inside it.

His eyes glowed, the copper color bleeding into crimson. Cupping Gillian's face, he leaned down and released a slow breath. Pheromones clinging to every particle of air and moisture on his breath slipped into her nostrils and sank into her brain, each acting as a tiny barb that latched onto her mind.

Drawing away, he gazed down at her. It would drain him to keep her under his control, but if she continued to fight, he'd— Roman shook his head. This was the only way.

He released his power, holding back enough so he wouldn't hurt her.

Gillian's mouth parted, eyes wide and unblinking.

He traced a finger along her jaw to her rosy lips. So precious. He'd felt the moment she'd crossed the border. His mind was in tune with the energy living within the Shadowlands, and she was a brilliant flame entering the darkness.

Roman had never thought to feel such a thing. Like all of his kind, he'd given up hope when that cursed barrier was born. But when she'd passed into Dwyer Wood, he'd stopped cold.

It hadn't taken much to find her bumbling through the forest, lost and unprepared for the dangers of his world. When he saved her from the vauger, he sensed her exhaustion and fear. But it wasn't until he caught her scent and saw proof of it in the medallion that he realized what she really was.

His father would be pleased.

He almost felt pity for her. For her fate. But she'd crossed into the Shadowlands of her own free will.

And now she would never leave.

Gillian stared through eyes that felt as though they belonged to someone else. She wanted to fight it. To fight *him*, but she couldn't.

Whatever he'd done when he'd leaned in close had trapped her as surely as a spider with its web.

Moments of clarity cut through the haze of blind obedience. Springing to life when he picked her up and slung her over his back.

She came roaring to life then, smacking at him until he growled and set her down.

Glaring, he doused her with more of his power, only to find it useless when he attempted to carry her again. Touching her somehow broke the spell.

Grumbling, he relented, resigning himself to moving at her pace. It would take days to reach his home, but her strong will was already taking its toll, and he couldn't risk relaxing his guard.

They trekked through heavy undergrowth, pausing now and then when creatures she heard but couldn't see prowled too close. Roman didn't touch her. In fact, he rarely looked back to see that she followed, somehow knowing she did.

Feeling her presence trudging along at his back.

Hours passed, and her eyes grew heavy. She wanted to sleep, but her body was not her own.

She was a marionette. Her limbs moved, propelling her to follow as though she were tethered to her brooding captor.

Only when her foot snagged on an exposed root, and she fell face-first on the leaf-covered ground, did he stop.

Roman sighed and hauled her up, letting her lean against his body for a moment before scowling and stepping away. She wobbled and watched him warily.

Roman muttered under his breath and released his mental hold on her. His shoulders slumped with relief. Jerking his chin toward an outcropping of rock, he said, "We'll sleep there tonight."

Gillian eyed the dark crevice and stumbled toward it.

Falling to her knees at the mouth of the opening, she crawled toward the back and curled into a ball on her side, legs pressed against the rock.

The son of the Great Dragon stood outside the shelter, staring at her.

She looked so small, huddled there in the dark. He wondered what she'd think of his ancestral lands. What she'd do when she learned of the truth of her captivity. Not that it mattered.

She would submit. Eventually.

Crouching at the edge of the shelter, he gathered sticks and dead leaves, his long, nimble fingers arranging them into a small pyre. Holding a hand above the pile, he whispered a word.

The dead material smoldered, then caught fire, flames licking at the wood. Roman watched the fire, absently adding small sticks. A soft whimper had him turning on his heel, eyes boring into the darkness where she slept.

Nightmares had her. The blackest thoughts and beings came to vivid life in his world. Closing his eyes, he sent a mental dart and slipped into her mind.

Images flashed behind his lids. A woman, middle-aged with graying red hair—not the girl's birth mother, though he imagined she didn't know it. And a man about the same age, time's stamp in the wrinkles along his eyes and mouth.

Roman focused on his face, searching for similar traits to the woman he'd captured. But the man had nothing in common with her. Where she was fair with delicate features and eyes the color of the sky before a storm, he was brown-eyed, his face squared and brutish.

Hm. Interesting.

Roman allowed her dream to guide him to the small form lying on a thin pallet.

Her brother. He gazed at the boy-child. His painfully thin body and wan face. His chest did not rise and fall.

She was dreaming that he was dead.

Roman felt the weight of grief in her mind. It made him uncomfortable to feel it.

Gritting his teeth, he smothered the emotion and let the scene play out. When her mind shifted to another dream, he cut off their connection.

The small fire had burned out, twigs smoldering.

Roman glared at it, jaw ticking.

She could get under his skin if he weren't careful, and he couldn't let that happen.

The girl belonged to his father. She had since the moment she crossed into the Shadowlands. He would do well to keep that fact at the forefront of his mind.

Chapter Five

Gillian's back throbbed painfully when she awoke the following day. Groaning, she rolled over on the hard rock of the cave, the muscles at the base of her spine spasming. She winced and rubbed the area, trying to ease the ache.

Glancing around, she sat up and looked for her captor, head hanging in relief when he was nowhere in sight. Coming to her feet, she hobbled out from under the overhanging rock, her hand pressed to her lower back like an old woman.

Early morning light broke through the trees, revealing the remnants of a small fire she had no recollection of. Kicking the smoldering embers, Gillian muttered and took in her surroundings. She frowned as her eyes skipped from place to place, nothing sparking a memory. The Dragonborn scum had led her deep into the forest, probably hoping she'd abandon any thought of escape.

But she had no intention of kowtowing to his whims.

Glancing at the angle of the sun, she got her bearings and

looked east toward Rudgarde Village. Not knowing how long Roman would be gone, she readied herself for what would likely be a full-day trek home.

Rubbing her hands together to rid them of the chill, she shook out her dark red cloak and pulled out her small knife. Much to her surprise, Roman had let her keep it, along with a snide comment about her inability to use it to do anything more than wound herbs.

Lifting her soiled hem, she sliced off six inches of fabric, ruining the gown. Leaving the ragged fabric on the ground, she surveyed her work, happy with the ease of movement, and left the site.

Gillian had just cleared a copse of pine trees when she heard Roman's drawl. "Going somewhere?"

Her shoulders slumped. She craned to look at him, noting the two dead hares he held in his fist. "Home."

He sighed and set the rabbits on a flat rock. "I thought we'd covered this."

Roman's lanky stride ate up the distance between them, copper eyes flashing beneath winged brows.

He was entirely too good-looking, sensual with his full mouth and dark stubble, which irritated Gillian as much as it appealed to her.

"And I thought I told you I had no intention of remaining captive."

She darted a glance at a rough path through the trees, perhaps the way they'd come the night before, though she had no recollection of it. Or it could be a game trail. One she'd be better off avoiding unless she wanted to come across another vauger.

Roman towered over her, the bronzed skin of his muscular chest visible beneath his tunic. He leaned down, and she took a step back, but not before he released a long breath.

He smelled of spice and heat. The scent filled her nose and shot straight to her brain. Her eyes went wide, pupils dilating, and her mouth parted slightly.

He studied her face, the gentle curve of her jaw, the pale lines of her eyebrows. Being forced to stun her with the pheromones racing through his body and using their power to enslave her mind was an annoyance. She'd be nothing but a puppet on a string until he released her. And holding her within his power was draining.

Unlike his father, he had limits, and she was intent on pushing them.

Gillian frustrated him. Her disdain and refusal to bend to his will both irritated and interested him.

He told himself she was just stubborn and arrogant like any human, but part of his mind that grew increasingly louder each day in her company admired her spirit. Seeing her blank expression was like looking at a walking corpse.

In all honesty, he'd take her biting tongue over the blind obedience he'd induced, but they needed to move on, and he couldn't be bothered trying to chase her down should she flee again.

Turning away, he grabbed the rabbits and stalked to the remains of the fire.

She followed, unable to fight the hold he had on her.

Pointing to a smooth boulder, he watched her sit, shaking his head and muttering. Coaxing the smoldering embers, he fed the weak flames, adding more tinder until heat radiated outward. Roman gutted the hares, tossing the innards into the fire rather than into the brush where a vauger or rusk could sniff them out, the latter with reptilian coldness and ruthless fervor.

Making a spit with sticks, he hung the carcasses above the flames and crouched, eyes flicking from the cooking meat to the mute girl. He flipped through the years in his mind and stared at her. She'd be eighteen if she were who he believed her to be.

Eighteen years.

A blink in the lifespan of his kind if the Wasting hadn't plagued Dragonborn since his father took witches from the Coven of the Silver Moon to wife.

Eighteen years during which the cursed plague's virulence within the Shadowlands had hastened, siphoning Dragonborn life and power.

It was the same ailment Gillian's brother was afflicted with. Only it wasn't always the young among his people who suffered.

Some of the afflicted were those who'd walked the earth long before he was born.

His brother, Draven, was the last child of the Great Dragon. The sounds of a babe hadn't rung through the halls of Valon since Maud, the last witch-wife, slit her throat and then leaped from a parapet, killing herself and the child she carried.

The grief and rage her foul act elicited in his father had been awful to behold.

The land itself had darkened, spawning ever more monstrous creatures under the weight of his anguish. It had not only been the loss of the unborn child she'd carried but the loss of the witch herself that had driven his father into darkness.

From that point on, there were parts of the Dragon he

could no longer touch. Parts that would never again see the light.

Gillian would change that.

Irylle—god of the sun, god of fire—would bless his father with young. His people would live on. They had to.

Roman released his hold on her when the meat finished roasting, tugging on the thread connecting them until it snapped.

Her body jerked as the tie severed. Blinking, she looked around, her head clearing in moments.

With a scowl, she pinned him with narrow eyes. "I wish you wouldn't do that."

He took the stick on which both rabbits were skewered and said innocently, "Do what? Feed you?"

She huffed, muttering about arrogant other-born males.

He smirked and tore off a hunk of meat, handing it to her. The smell wafted into her nose, tickling her throat.

Gillian's mouth watered as she debated rebuffing his offer. But the snarl of her empty stomach, loud in the quiet space, made her decision for her. Snatching the meat, she winced and blew on her fingers, tossing the cooked flesh from hand to hand to cool it.

Roman's brows creased. "Sorry. I should've warned you it was hot."

Gillian made a face and popped the cooled piece of wild rabbit in her mouth. It was delicious. Her tummy growled, demanding more. "The heat doesn't bother your hands?"

He shook his head and pointed to the flames, then himself. "Fire. Dragonborn."

She considered that and watched him blow softly on a hunk

of meat before handing it to her. She took the rest of his offerings without complaint.

Pulling a waterskin from his belt, he held it out to Gillian, watching her throat work as she took a long pull. Wiping her mouth with the back of her hand, she leaned back, satiated.

Roman kicked dirt onto the remnants of the fire and motioned for her to rise. She tucked her legs to her chest and glared at him.

"Must I subdue you again?"

She glared. "No."

"Then I suggest you get off that rock and follow me."

Gillian rose and brushed the dirt off her cloak and gown, but made no move to follow.

He sighed and stretched his neck with a series of little pops.

"Let me go," she said softly, watching him pause and look at her. "By holding me captive, you're sentencing my brother to death. Does that mean nothing to you?"

"I grow weary of this discussion."

He held out his hand, letting it fall to his side when she refused it. Roman closed the distance between them, his slow strides making her heart hammer.

When they stood toe-to-toe, he bent his head, snagging her attention. "I need only release a breath laced with my power, and you will obey my every whim."

He reached out to trace a finger along her cheek.

Gillian slapped his hand away. "Don't touch me."

He clenched his fingers and dipped his head. "As you wish. But know this. Your life in Rudgarde is over. There's no sense in thinking of it anymore."

Her mouth pulled down, eyes welling, though she stubbornly reined in her emotions. "Why are you doing this to me?"

"Because you entered my world."

"Pretend you didn't see me," she pleaded.

He lifted his chin. "I can't do that. He already knows you're here."

"Who?"

"The Great Dragon." His eyes glowed. Twin copper flames. "My father and your future mate. Marius."

His words reverberated in her mind as Roman led her farther from the border. Farther from her brother, whose life was slowly being eaten away.

She rubbed her spine, sore from the hard ground and relentless travel, glaring at his back as his strides ate up the miles. Slowing her pace, she fell behind, smiling smugly when he spun around and scolded her.

Gillian shrugged, blamed human frailty, and planted her backside on a fallen tree.

Roman lowered his head and stormed toward her like an angry bull. "Get up."

"Make me."

She'd noticed how it drained him to use his power to control her. If she drained him enough, she could get away. Setting her satchel on the ground at her feet, she met his glare and didn't budge.

"You'll be the death of me."

"One can hope."

His mouth pulled down, and he yanked her to her feet, releasing a long breath in her face. She swayed, eyes going glassy, but a sliver of her mind remained aware. He was growing weak.

It must have been only a couple of hours by the time he released his hold on her. She got her bearings and watched him covertly.

His usually tawny features were pale and strained. There was no time to be pleased. Exploiting his weakness, she pretended to use the bushes while he gathered wood and sprinted.

A roar of rage silenced the animals of the forest when he realized her ploy and took after her.

Though her legs were screaming at her, she pushed herself to go faster, noting how he was unable to catch up with her with his preternatural speed as he'd done before. But nevertheless, she could hear him tearing through the forest.

Sliding down a short embankment, she dodged to the right and ran for a small stream. Splashing through the water, she slipped and stumbled over slick rocks, dragging her sodden cloak behind her as she clambered to the other side.

Roman was yelling, and she blocked him out.

But his shouts grew louder and more frantic.

She paused, bending over to take huge gulps of breath, and that's when she heard it—the deep growl of a vauger.

Gillian spun around wildly, trying to determine where the animal was coming from. She heard a guttural yowl and raced back across the stream, heading toward Roman's shouts of warning.

A blur of movement in her peripheral vision revealed the mate of the slain vauger, back from wherever it had run off to. It roared, flecks of foaming drool spraying into the air as it glared at her with rage-filled eyes.

She lunged to the side, cutting through underbrush just as Roman burst through the trees.

The two predators collided, but this time, the Dragonborn male visibly struggled, falling under the weight of the beast.

Claws slashed as it scrambled onto its feet and charged at Roman, throwing him to the ground. He rolled and sprang to his feet, flinging out his arms to release power that wasn't there.

A pang of guilt lit her mind, and she smothered it, taking advantage of the fight to race for freedom.

She didn't get far. Roman's yelp of pain stopped her.

Scanning the ground, she grabbed a large rock and ran toward the scuffle.

The vauger was even more nightmarish in the light of day. Huge with a dark bristling pelt and massive paws tipped with long, sharp claws. It snapped jaws filled with blackened needle-like teeth at Roman, who strained to dodge the attack.

Not stopping to think, Gillian threw the rock at the creature, striking its shoulder.

The vauger snarled and swung around to face the new attacker.

Her mouth dropped open at the feral rage pouring from its sunken eyes. A dribble of liquid ran down her leg as her bladder lost control when it lunged toward her.

Hot, rancid breath struck her face, spittle landing on her cheeks as the vauger opened its mouth to snap her head from her neck.

Roman's hands were slick with blood as he watched the animal charge Gillian.

Fear gave him the strength his body lacked, and he sprang into the air. His blade slashed, ripping through flesh and bone as it slid across the beast's neck, nearly severing its head.

Gillian's legs gave out, and she crumpled to the ground.

Roman doubled over, panting next to the dying animal.

"Don't. Ever. Do. That. Again." He dropped his short sword and fell to his knees, head hanging to his chest.

She nodded, eyes fixed on the bloody mass. The ground was wet where she sat, soaked with urine. She couldn't stir herself to care.

That thing had nearly killed her because she'd tried to save him. *Him! The evil spawn of the Dragon!*

Gillian wanted to hate her actions, to chastise herself for not letting the vauger tear Roman to pieces while she escaped, but she couldn't. He was taking her away from everything she knew and loved, and she'd *saved him!*

Gillian's hands shook as she levered herself off the ground and moved away from the mutilated animal.

Roman glared at her and rose to his full height.

She ignored the anger that was turning his face ruddy and motioned to his chest, where fresh wounds bled in a steady flow. "There's a stream where you can wash away the blood so I can tend you."

He was too drained to enslave her with his mind and too tired to chase after her if she chose to run again. Taking her wrist in a firm grip, he looked down at her and said, "Lead the way."

His hand was as good as a manacle. Not that she needed it.

The adrenaline racing through her body only minutes

before was gone, leaving behind exhaustion so profound she wanted to curl up and sleep.

Roman stripped off his tunic and tossed it on the ground, warning her with his eyes as he knelt at the water's edge.

She stared at his naked back as he cupped the water and splashed it onto his chest, washing away blood, sweat, and dirt. His muscles rippled with every movement, pulling at her in a purely instinctual way.

Disgusted with herself, she turned away and moved to another part of the stream.

Dragging her satchel off and tossing it on the ground, she got to her knees and dipped her hands in the current. She scrubbed her face and neck, then grimaced. Her legs felt sticky, and she knew in a few hours, she'd stink of dried piss.

Removing her cloak, she surreptitiously splashed water on the insides of her thighs where trails of pee had cut through grime she hadn't realized was there.

Yuck. A bath sounded absolutely decadent.

Finished, Gillian dug into her bag and pulled out a change of clothes. Ignoring Roman and his warning mutters, she ducked behind a thick cluster of bushes and stripped off her smelly clothes.

At home, Rory complained about the time it took for her to dress when he was locked out of the room. She smiled sadly at the memories, thinking he'd be shocked to see how fast she threw her clothes on now.

Leaving the bushes moments later, she busied herself washing her underclothes, slapping them against the rocks to scrub the dirt off. They wouldn't dry before she had to put them into her satchel, but at least they'd be cleaner.

She sensed Roman rise and waited for the sound of his foot-steps. When she heard nothing, Gillian craned her neck and found him staring at her, an inscrutable expression on his face.

Wiping her hands on her skirts, she sat on her heels. "What?"

"Thank you."

Gillian nodded. "You're welcome."

Roman held out his hand, and she took it, feeling his heat radiating through his skin.

"Truce?" he asked, a smile tugging at the corner of his mouth.

Damn him for being so handsome!

Gillian cleared her throat. "I suppose."

She pulled her hand away and bent to pluck bags of healing herbs from her satchel, motioning for him to sit.

He nodded and watched her with unnerving intensity.

The wounds on his chest were superficial for the most part. Only a couple needed more attention and really should've been sewn had she a needle and thread.

His skin was hot beneath her palms as she smoothed the mixture onto the claw marks. Muscles twitched with each pass of her fingers, and she flashed her eyes at him.

What she saw made her stomach flip.

Her hand trembled before she brought her thoughts under control. It rankled to know he saw it.

He missed nothing with those hawkish eyes.

Finished, she rinsed her hands in the stream and told him he ought to treat the deeper gash daily until it healed over.

"Won't you be doing that?" he asked in a voice that was more like a purr.

"I... no. I'm going home."

Roman sighed. "Is everyone from Rudgarde as thick-headed as you?"

"But I saved your life!" she shouted. Her body throbbed with something powerful, anger bubbling like water set to boil. It erupted from her when she spat, "Let. Me. Go."

He flinched, eyes becoming glassy. As though he were thrown off balance, his body swayed. In moments, he regained control, face hardening. "Stay out of my head."

Gillian looked confused. "I don't know what you're talking about."

"Do that again, and I'll throw you across my back like a sack of grain."

She fumed. "I saved you. You owe me."

"Do I now?" He put his hands on his lean hips. "I remember that differently. In fact, I recall saving your life twice before. So, I believe it is *you* who owes *me*."

He leaned down, his mouth mere inches from hers, breath puffing against her lips. "Perhaps I should collect my due."

Gillian's hand whipped out, striking his cheek with a loud slap. "Touch me, and I swear to Setanta you'll lose more than your hand."

He leaned back and lifted his chin, a red stain from her hand blossoming on his cheek for a moment before it disappeared.

"I acknowledge no god but Irylle."

As if shaking off something more than her slap, his face shifted, becoming his typical arrogant mask.

"Gods and their powers aside, I've not changed my mind

and taken pity on you. No actions you take will alter what is inevitable."

Chapter Six

Valon, the stronghold of the Dragonborn, sat on a bluff overlooking a silver lake. Springing from a mountain range, the castle was a thing of rugged beauty rising up like a Goliath.

Gillian didn't want it to be beautiful.

She wanted Roman's home to be as cold and ugly as his callous nature.

But it was breathtaking.

A sprawling castle with outbuildings and grazing land dotted with creatures that looked like shaggy cows, aside from their hulking shoulders and long tails. The structure was built of black rock with veins of gold, so it sparkled in the sunlight.

As if the keep was a conjoined twin, a massive peak stood behind it—a silent sentinel overlooking the landscape.

Gillian stood rooted to the ground. She'd dreaded this moment, the finality of it.

They'd traveled for three days, saying little to each other. Days Roman had groused over.

She'd discovered he could run at dizzying speeds, a talent he'd used when he'd sensed her crossing into the Shadowlands. He'd also used it each time she'd tried to run.

She never got far.

Maybe a few hundred feet and there he'd be, blocking her path and glowering.

After her last escape attempt, he'd tried to convince her to let him carry her. But Gillian had crossed her arms and refused, in no hurry to drift farther from her home and freedom.

He'd grumbled and stomped away, prowling the forest as the sun set, snatching wood for a fire and tossing it into a sloppy pile.

It had been a tense evening, ending with her back toward him following a small meal. Even in the dark, she felt his eyes on her, making her skin crawl with awareness.

Despite the slowness of their travel, miles passed, and she was no closer to convincing him to let her go. He was immune to every plea—hardened and implacable.

As she stared at the magnificent fortress, Gillian accepted that he was a lost cause. She'd need to convince his father if she had any hope of returning to her family. The thought made her queasy.

Roman nudged her shoulder. "Keep moving. I'd like to arrive in my father's hall before sunset."

She glared at him. It was just after midday. "Do you honestly think I care what you want?"

"That goes both ways," he said, jaw ticking.

Looking away from his cold stare and the majestic fortress in the foreground, she craned her neck, staring wistfully to the east. "Your cruelty confirms everything I've been told about your kind," she whispered.

"It's not cruelty. It's indifference."

Her shoulders stiffened. Roman had no mercy.

Gillian glared at him. She was exhausted and dirty. Everything hurt, even the roots of her hair.

The thought of trekking back across his cursed realm made her head pound.

She was so far from home. Even if she could escape his power and flee, he'd catch her long before she crossed the border between their worlds. Or something else would hunt her down.

But to capitulate. To become a slave to his father.

Gillian shook her head and swung her gaze toward the castle.

There were people milling on the grounds among the outbuildings. From her perspective, it almost looked normal.

Almost.

Nothing could blot out the enormous stronghold emerging from the earth like a foreboding monolith.

Roman sighed and put his hands on his hips.

She ignored him. Straightening her shoulders, Gillian readied herself.

This is not surrender, she told herself. *You'll find a way to escape.*

Roman watched her. Her rigid body. The stony look in her eyes.

He'd have to warn his father not to trust her.

He saw her chin lift. Her hands clenched as though she fought her body's urge to flee. He raised a brow and stood aside to let her take the lead.

If her legs trembled, she hid it well, taking slow strides until something unlocked and she shifted into a normal gait. Emotions flashed across Roman's face.

Surprise. Respect. And something else he felt and snuffed as soon as it surfaced.

He fell into step at her side, his hand brushing hers until she whipped her appendage away.

Roman rolled his eyes and tucked his hands behind his back, keeping pace with her.

The rolling pastures were dotted with wattle and daub structures—homes for the serfs who worked the land—each adjacent to a small garden or carefully tilled field. If she didn't know she was in the Shadowlands, the idyllic place could be somewhere in Mirynn.

But she wasn't in her homeland. And this was anything but normal.

Gillian's gaze swept the landscape, her eyes falling on one of the hoofed creatures that grazed contentedly.

She paused and studied its shaggy, bovine form. It was nothing like what she'd grown up seeing in the fields of Rudgarde. The huge beast had horns like a ram tucked against its massive head and powerful shoulders that rose up above its thick neck. It lowed to a member of its herd, the sound deep and familiar despite its otherworldly appearance.

"Cragga."

Gillian glanced up at him questioningly, and he jerked his head to the animal.

"They're docile enough when grazing, but have been known to balk at milking if forced. As a boy, I saw a riled cow stomp a man to death, coming back when he lay still on the ground to smash his innards to a pulp."

"Is that meant to frighten me?"

"Only warn you."

She backed away from the animal, putting more distance between herself and the cow-like creature.

Roman chuckled, the sound grating on her nerves.

Cutting her eyes at him, she sniffed and stalked off, giving a wide berth to the other cragga they passed.

Roman followed, watching her toss her head and march as though she were about to do battle. In truth, she had no idea the depth of the battles that lay ahead.

They traversed the sprawling pastureland, avoiding the herds, and crossed into the small village beyond the keep's gates.

Men, women, and children looked their way, some pausing to stare while others glanced at Roman and scurried on.

Everywhere she looked, there were people. Her people. Her kind.

Shock made Gillian stop and swing around to pin Roman with a hard stare. "Humans? You have human slaves?"

She indicated the many people going about their business. "Have you no people of your own that you must take captives?"

He cocked his head. A lock of dark hair fell across his forehead, distracting her and making him look boyishly handsome.

She clenched her teeth and put her hands on her hips, waiting for a reply.

"You don't have serfs and tradesmen in Mirynn?"

She swept her eyes from person to person, mouth pulling down. "Aye, we do. But we're not in my kingdom. How did you get these people? Did you steal them from their families?"

Roman smirked. "You have such a low opinion of my kind and such a high opinion of yours. I wonder how you'd feel if you knew how your king and his vassals treat those who share their land?"

"I'm sure they treat them better than Dragonborn."

But as she looked around, seeing health and plenty, she began to wonder. Not that she'd tell him as much.

He shrugged. "There's no sense in telling you the truth. Gentle lies have always gotten further with your kind than hard truths." With that, he strode toward the castle, motioning for her to follow.

Gillian avoided the looks she passed, keeping her head down until Roman led her to the gates of the castle.

They yawned open like a passageway to the underworld.

Guards in black armor traversed the wall-walk while others lingered just inside the keep's outer walls, watching her. It was impossible to tell if they were human or Dragonborn with the helmets they wore.

But one thing was certain: escape would be nigh unto impossible.

Roman paused and looked back, his face a mask of challenge.

Envisioning being slung over his shoulder like a sack of potatoes and hauled into the castle forced her limbs to start moving again. She gritted her teeth and strode to his side, trying to ignore the sense of foreboding each step evoked.

Human guards dipped their heads to her captor, giving them a wide berth as they came through the inner bailey.

Gillian stopped at the base of the stairs leading into the castle and craned her neck, trying to take it all in—black stone with rivers of gold that winked and shimmered in the sunlight. Spires pointed to the sky with windows and arrow slits letting in light.

And behind it, as though the structure was flowing from the earth itself, stood that mountain whose peak dwarfed the majesty of the fortress.

Despite being a captive. Despite having been dragged across the Shadowlands like chattel. Gillian felt self-conscious.

Until now, she'd never traveled beyond the borders of her home in Rudgarde. She had never seen the seat of her kingdom in Warrington. Nor met a great lord, though she'd seen a few passing through her village over the years. Noted their pompous demeanor as they sat upon steeds so fancy even those animals looked down on folks like her.

Never mind the scores of men-at-arms and knights who'd shoved the likes of her aside.

Now she would meet with the king of a race her people likened to demons.

And she was dirty, smelly, and travel-worn.

Her red cloak felt heavy, the edge coated with layers of grime. She picked at her dress, thankful for its dark brown shade, cringing at what the color likely hid. Gillian wanted to ask if she could at least tidy herself, wash her face, which probably sported smears of dirt, and brush her hair, relieving it of the twigs and leaves snagged within its snarls.

But when she glanced at Roman and saw his sardonic

expression, as though he'd read her mind, she decided his father wasn't worth the effort.

Gillian took the steps two at a time, breezing past him as the doors to the keep swung open.

The steward stood gaping when she stormed past and did a double-take before rushing to Roman, who waved his concerns aside.

"Would the young lady like a bath and fresh clothing?" the man asked.

Roman knew she heard the steward and replied, "No. She stays as she is."

She ground her teeth but said nothing, only followed the stone as it curved around to a large room.

The great hall opened before her, and she came to a halt, her feet anchored to the floor as she took in the splendor. Ebony tables filled half the hall, with one wall dominated by a massive fireplace. Freshly laid rushes covered the floor, mixed with lilac and sage that wafted to her nose.

On the walls hung tapestries of Dragons, some flying through forests and vales, others holding dominion from the peaks of mountains.

Roman appeared at her side, tracking her eyes to a large tapestry above the fireplace.

The figure dominating the artwork had dark red scales that covered his body except for the swath of gold stretching along his neck and underbelly. Powerful wings fanned out at his sides, the same rich color as his scales, their width greater than the length of his body, including the tail. Coppery eyes, set with golden thread, seemed to follow them. Unnerving in their clarity and detail.

Beneath his black talons were mounds of skeletal corpses still wearing armor.

"Impressive, isn't he?" Roman asked, folding his arms across his chest.

"For a murderer."

He snorted. "If the Great Dragon wished to make war on your people, they'd be nothing but ash. But I don't recall any such events. Do you?"

She glowered, accepting a mug of watered wine from a maidservant and returning her attention to the tapestry. "Is that a relative of yours?"

"You could say that."

She looked at him.

"He's my father."

Her stomach dropped, eyes whipping back to the image. His father? Goddess, help her. *That* was who he'd meant when he spoke of her future mate.

That thing would spit fire and devour her.

Roman sensed her fear. "Calm yourself. My father has no designs on consuming your flesh. You will be his mate, not his meal."

Her eyes flicked to him, then back to the artwork.

"Be easy. You won't see his true form unless he wishes it."

She took a step away, her heart beating in her chest like the wings of a trapped bird.

I can't do this, she thought. *I can't be here.*

Her eyes swept the hall where guards lingered among the servants. They were human, but she knew they wouldn't aid her.

She was trapped. Alone.

Just then, the slow tread of heavy feet echoed through the hall.

She spun around to find the source, breath catching as a powerful figure melted from the dimness of the stairs.

He wore a robe of pure black that swirled around his body, giving the impression of wings. Long, black hair framed swarthy, angular features that were brutally handsome, with the shadow of stubble lining his jaw and upper lip, accenting the fullness of his mouth and planes of his face.

He scanned the room—a predator in the midst of prey.

Roman stiffened as the figure took the last few steps, his copper gaze falling on the Dragonborn male who waited at her side before his attention shifted to her.

Gillian's body locked, nostrils flaring. Her mind went blank.

The Great Dragon had arrived.

Chapter Seven

Marius studied Gillian, his penetrating eyes boring into hers while his mind slipped into her brain like a needle.

He read every thought. Tasted every fear and longing. She was so young, innocent of the world. Ignorant of who and what she was. He flipped through her memories, learning of her brother's illness and her bid to save him.

He saw her steal the medallion and cross into the Shadow-lands, searching for the elusive witches she believed could halt the Wasting that had taken root in her sibling.

The Great Dragon saw her memories of wandering the woods, unwitting prey to the beasts that dwelled there.

He raised his brow and glanced at Roman while his mind's eye watched the vauger scent her on the wind, feeling her fear as his son's hand clamped over her mouth, immobilizing her.

Marius was amused by her defiance when it was made clear she would never return to her home and his son's exasperation in the face of it. He did not find the other emotions stirring beneath the surface of her mind amusing at all.

When he'd seen enough, he let Gillian go, watching her body twitch and eyes focus.

In a voice that rumbled through her as if it came from the earth itself, Marius said, "Welcome, young Gillian."

She blinked.

"I am Marius, ruler of the Shadowlands and father to Roman."

He bowed, robe billowing out to reveal the deep purple of his silken tunic and form-fitting black leather pants.

Again, there was an impression of wings. Of great size and ancient knowledge.

She stared at him, sensing his power, feeling his heat. Her lips parted, a reply on the tip of her tongue, but all that came out was a breathy rasp.

He smiled down at her, the action crinkling his eyes at the corners of his otherwise unlined, angular face.

She gawked. Mind a jumble of words and images as she watched him watching her.

It seemed his features shifted for a moment, muscles rippling, eyes appearing cold and reptilian, his entire being becoming something dangerous and primeval.

It was gone as soon as it came, leaving the form of a man whose face and form made her want to cover herself.

Gillian forced her eyes to break contact, turning her head against the desire to remain fixated, and looked at Roman, who stood stiffly at her side.

She took half a step behind him, but he ignored her, keeping his attention on his father.

She glanced from one to the other.

Marius was brutally, almost painfully handsome, and yet there was no hint of softness, no trace of empathy or understanding in his expression.

He was like some glorious, callous god. His son, too, had an almost otherworldly beauty, but there was something more in him, wasn't there? Some hint of softness? She swept her eyes to Roman. No. As soon as their gazes met, what she thought she saw was gone.

Gillian shouldn't keep looking at him. She shouldn't silently beg him to turn back to her, sweep her up in his arms, and run from the Great Dragon.

Roman felt nothing for her beyond duty to ferret her away to this place, far from everything she knew and loved, into the arms of a creature who was surely spawned from some wizard's demented nightmare.

It made no sense to look at him, but she did.

He was her only link, foul though he might be, and her only path to freedom.

Roman looked at her with a dead stare, making her shrink. He watched her shoulders cave inward as hope guttered.

Her eyes dimmed. Wounded. Lost.

He clenched his jaw, curled his hands into fists, and dipped his head to his father before stalking away.

She followed him with her gaze, her body swaying toward his despite his eyes' clear message.

The Great Dragon watched and waited, missing nothing.

She felt Marius prowling in her mind. She wanted to shut him out, scream at him, and claw his perfect face.

He sensed her anger, clasped his arms behind his back, and waited her out.

A servant strode to his side and spoke softly. He nodded, his eyes never leaving her.

From the kitchen came the scent of roasted meat and simmering spices. Her stomach growled loudly, and she flushed, darting a glance at Marius.

He smiled and motioned to the largest table, where a bevy of servants laid out platters of bread, fruit, cheese, and roasted meats and vegetables. Gillian thought about refusing, but realized she'd only be punishing herself.

Looking up at the powerful lord, she asked, "May I wash before we eat?"

"Of course. I'm embarrassed my son did not give you a chance. Forgive me for the oversight," he said, motioning for the steward, who directed a maidservant to bring a bowl of warm water and a cloth.

The young woman, maybe two years older than her, placed the bowl on a table by the fireplace and gave Gillian a small smile. She tried to return the gesture, but it came out as a grimace.

Taking the cloth, she dipped it in the water and scrubbed her face and hands until they were pink.

It took an effort to drop the used cloth in the bowl and turn toward Marius, where he stood waiting.

Even a couple of feet away, she felt warmth radiating from his body as though he was fire itself. But her mother didn't raise a coward. Lifting her chin, she went to him.

The air shimmered around his form like heat coming off the

ground on a hot summer's day. Or perhaps it was an illusion conjured by her weary mind. There one moment and gone the next.

She allowed the Great Dragon to lead her to a chair he pulled out, sitting gracefully at her side.

They would share a trencher.

Gillian watched as he ladled meat and vegetables stewed in a thick sauce onto the bread. Her mouth watered at the sight of such an assortment of food.

Much to her surprise, Marius selected the best piece of meat and offered it to her before taking anything for himself. She tried to chew slowly, to savor the spices and tenderness, but her stomach wouldn't hear of it and demanded more. Snatching a wedge of cheese, she stuffed it into her mouth and followed it up with a handful of figs.

His lips twitched. "It appears my son did a poor job of feeding you."

She swallowed and grabbed a goblet, downing the watered wine in three gulps. "He's a brute."

"I apologize for that. Roman has always been the more serious of my brood."

He held out another piece of meat, and she accepted it, keeping her eyes on his face though his attention remained on the fork slipping between her lips. He flashed her a heated look and shifted his attention to the food.

They ate silently for a while, and she began to relax enough to notice that no one had joined them. Not even Roman, though she didn't want to see him. At least, that's what she told herself.

"Is no one else joining us?"

He leaned back in the chair. "I thought you'd be more comfortable without my children present."

"You have more children?"

"Aye. Dozens, though most live beyond the castle walls with families of their own."

Gillian thought about that and wondered if the human mates of the Dragonborn had been willing or if they'd been captured—forced to live and raise young with monsters. She eyed him from under the fan of her pale lashes.

He looked younger than her mother, Naeve, and she was five and thirty years. How old *was* he?

Marius read her thoughts as easily as if she'd spoken them aloud. "I have walked this earth since before the dawn of man. My mate and I brought life to this world."

"Your mate?"

"Ashael." Grief flashed across his face, raw and human. "She was beautiful. There," he pointed to a tapestry of a blue Dragon flying through the sky at sunset.

Below her serpentine body was an expanse of water extending into the horizon. "I lost her in the great upheaval."

Gillian didn't want to feel sadness, but his lingering heartache was palpable. "I'm sorry."

Marius looked at her. "Are you?"

"Why shouldn't I be? Unlike your kind, I'm not devoid of empathy."

He shook his head. "If Roman led you to believe we are cold and emotionless, he did you a great disservice. We feel deeply."

Marius looked at her. "We love deeply and without limit."

"Love? Is that why you had me stolen from my home?" Her face grew cold. "I could never love something like you."

Marius' nostrils flared, and his copper eyes glowed, something flickering in them she couldn't discern. "It is my understanding that you crossed into the Shadowlands of your own free will. Is that not correct?"

She frowned. "I didn't come here for *you*."

"Yet here you are."

"I came for my brother, and now, thanks to you and your son, he'll die of the Wasting!"

His eyes blazed, copper bleeding into scarlet.

Again, the sense of a massive winged body and ancient power filled her mind—blinking out in a moment.

"Everything that enters my realm is under my dominion. Even you. You should've known that before crossing the barrier."

Gillian shook her head. How had it come to this? She sat in a foreign land with a Dragonborn king at whose hand she was fed as though she were precious to him. While across the border, her brother weakened, the Wasting slowly degrading his body until it finally took him.

How much longer did he have? Four months? Three?

Her hands curled into fists, nails digging into her palms until they pierced the skin in perfect half-moon shapes.

Marius' eyes flicked to her lap, watching her knuckles turn white. He smelled the blood. It stirred something possessive in him. The scent of her lineage hung in the air, and he closed his eyes, breathing it in.

So much untapped power.

She would turn to him, open her arms and heart. He would

plant his seed in her belly, and she would ripen, bringing forth a new generation of young.

Like the others of her kind that he'd mated over countless years, she could never birth a Dragon. Not a true Dragon.

His rookery would remain cold and empty. Locked away in darkness and coated in neglect.

He was the last Dragon in this world. The last to reign the skies.

The death of his mate, Ashael, had ensured that cruel truth. But the half-bloods he'd sired since her passing were a balm to his grief-stricken soul. In their veins ran echoes of his power. Fragments of what it meant to be Dragon.

But he took solace in his half-breed offspring born without wings. Without the ability to birth new worlds.

But they had voices and songs of their own.

He studied Gillian. That she had come to his realm after so many years of fruitless searching and wasted efforts to tear through the veil shielding her world from him was a gift. One he would not squander.

She had no idea who she was. She was ignorant of her power and her bloodline. And he would keep her in that ignorance, shielding knowledge of her existence from those who might sense it and try to steal her away from him.

She was strong, much stronger than his son, Roman, could've guessed.

Marius tasted the will she pitted against him. Knowing it would shatter if she refused to bend.

She would give herself willingly.

And, if not, he would overwhelm her senses until all she knew was love for him. In the end, she would usher in a new generation of progeny. And when her time came to an end, he'd use her blood to sunder the barrier between worlds and reclaim his rightful rule.

When that was done, he'd find those who'd gone into hiding and gather them to himself, bringing forth a new era where Dragonborn ruled.

Chapter Eight

Gillian had no memory of leaving the great hall. No recollection of disrobing and tucking herself into bed.

Her mind was foggy, thoughts muffled and jumbled with fragments of images and words. Marius' voice bounced off her skull as though he were in the room with her. But she was quite alone—in so many ways.

Beyond a narrow, stained-glass window, she heard voices, a mix of men and women going about the morning. It sounded so normal.

A fire danced in the grate, taking the chill out of the room but not out of her body. While opulent compared to her home in Rudgarde, where she shared a small room with her brother, the luxury felt more like a prison than a comfort.

Gillian rubbed her temple, trying to dispel her mental fog.

Again, Marius' voice and face lit up her mind. His long dark hair. The shadowy stubble lining his jaw and wrapping around his sensual lips—so like Roman's. The coppery eyes that saw more than she offered.

He'd acted like a gentleman. At least how she imagined gentlemen would act, serving her the choicest cuts from their shared trencher, attempting to engage her in conversation.

But beneath that civil veneer was something distinctly predatory. He had undressed her with his eyes and ravaged her with his thoughts. Neither had spoken of it, neither had even hinted of it, yet both had known it.

A soft knock sounded at the door.

When it swung open, there was a young woman poking her face in. Seeing that Gillian was awake, the maidservant stepped into the room, a bundle of clothing stacked in her arms.

"Good morning, miss," she said with a curtsy.

Gillian frowned at the title. She wasn't a lady. Not by society's standards.

Of course, here... She shook her head and scooted her body into a sitting position, wincing when pain flared in her head. The feeling was similar to when she'd snuck into the larder and consumed a bottle of homemade mead when she was ten. Running her hand over her face, she swung her legs out and let them hang on the edge of the mattress.

"Good morning." Her voice sounded raspy, and she cleared her throat, giving the woman an apologetic look.

The servant bustled about the room, picking up the discarded gown and cloak. Gillian cringed when she saw the red hem caked in layers of dirt from her travels, and though the dark brown of her dress hid the worst stains, she was certain it was covered in grime. She took a tentative sniff of her body, nose wrinkling.

I stink, she thought, wondering how Marius had tolerated sitting next to her the night before.

"What's your name?" Gillian asked.

The young woman's face split into a surprised smile. "I'm called Mary."

She ducked into the hallway and returned with a deep blue gown and a set of underclothes. "Lord Marius chose these for you, milady. I'll have these rags put on the fire."

"No!"

The maid was startled. "Milady?"

"Please, don't burn them. Not the cloak. My mother made it for me. It's all I have left of her."

"Of course," she patted Gillian's hand. "I'll wash it myself and mend any tears in the fabric."

"Thank you, Mary."

"You're welcome, milady."

It felt strange to be addressed as if she were nobility. She didn't like it. This assumption that she belonged here. Waited on and catered to.

"Please call me Gillian."

Mary's face brightened, green eyes sparkling against her freckled face. "Is there anything I can get you?"

"A bath?"

The servant grinned. "Aye. I can see you've been traveling. I'll have it brought in."

Clutching the soiled clothing, Mary headed toward the door.

"Mary," Gillian called out. The servant paused and looked at her. "Are you... are you a slave here?"

The woman looked offended. "A slave? No, miss. Lord Marius has no slaves. We're free folk."

Mary took a few steps toward her. "Is anything amiss?"

Gillian didn't know how to answer that. She wanted to grip the woman's hands and beg for help to escape. But what if she went straight to Marius or Roman? She couldn't recall the hours after her meal and assumed the Great Dragon stupefied her, as his son had done on their travels, and taken her to this bedchamber.

She looked around, plucking at the nightgown she wore. Had he undressed her himself? Her face flamed.

"Milady? Gillian?" Mary went to her side. "Are you all right?"

Mary's face was so open, trusting. Gillian wanted to confide in her, but the words sat on the tip of her tongue and then crawled back down her throat.

She nodded. "I'm well. Just... tired. And dirty."

The servant tilted her head, hands bunching the clothing in her arms. "I'll have a bath brought right in. If there's anything more you'd like..." The words hung in the air.

Gillian shook her head. "A bath would be perfect."

Mary dipped her head, flashing Gillian a look before closing the door behind her.

The silence after her departure was palpable. The woman had extended an offer of confidence and been rebuffed. She couldn't know how much Gillian longed to accept it, to grab her hands and spill her heart. The aftermath of such a confession made Gillian pause and bite her tongue.

If Marius heard from servants that she was begging for aid,

would he punish them? Would he confine her to her room and allow only the deaf and mute to serve her?

Better to swallow her words and feign acceptance. She would play Marius' game and win his trust. He'd allow her freedom to roam the halls and grounds in time.

When that day came, and it needed to arrive soon, she'd plot her escape, and, this time, neither Roman nor the Great Dragon would find her.

Of course, the logistics of such a move were a mystery and dependent on many unknowns. But she had to hold the possibility in her heart. She must have hope. Without it, she may as well capitulate entirely. Consign Rory to death and become a mate to the monster of the Shadowlands.

Gillian rose and went to the window.

She looked out the warped, stained glass. The figures below were distorted. Shapeless blobs moving about the inner bailey. She watched them, thinking how their misshapen images reflected her life.

An uncomfortable bathing experience finished the morning, during which Mary took charge while servants waited with buckets of hot water, exotic oils, and soaps.

One woman scrubbed her skin with a brush until it was pink while she sat with her knees pressed to her chest, where her medallion hung between her breasts after she'd refused to remove it. Another dumped water over her head, making her sputter, before washing and finger-combing the tangles from her blond locks.

They primped and fussed, trying to coax her from the water until she finally shooed them out.

Leaving her room after a midday meal took more courage than Gillian wanted to admit.

She stood at the door, hand hovering above the latch as though it were a venomous snake, girding herself up to grab it quickly and avoid being bitten. Lowering her arm, she muttered, fighting an inner battle.

Beyond the door were the guards of her prison. Capable of snuffing out her will, so she was a puppet on a string.

Gillian fingered the fine fabric of her gown, the deep blue material slick and shiny beneath her hand. The bodice, embroidered with tiny red dragons, dipped lower than anything she'd worn back home and hugged her form, accentuating her small waist and the curves of her hips.

She felt feminine in a way she'd never felt before. It made her feel out of place, like she was pretending to be someone else.

Footsteps sounded in the hall.

She'd seen guards and servants through the open door when the brass tub had been brought in and later removed. This time, the heavy tread stopped just beyond the threshold instead of passing by as they'd done before.

She cocked her head, straining to listen. The latch on the door shifted, slowly lifting, only to stop before it slipped from its lock. It fell back into place. She frowned, wondering who was on the other side.

Snatching at it, she yanked it open and found Roman staring at her.

He tried to look nonchalant, but she'd seen his eyes widen

and his face flush as he noticed the swell of her breasts above the low neckline.

"What do you want?" Gillian asked, planting her hands on her hips.

He raked his eyes over her. "I came to offer you a tour of the keep. Of course, you're welcome to keep hiding in your room if you'd prefer."

She balled her hands into fists to keep from slapping the smirk off his face.

He was taunting her, daring her to take the bait. Gillian thought about refusing, but knew she'd see a look of triumph on his face. In all likelihood, she'd see that look regardless, but touring the castle would provide an opportunity to find escape routes.

Gillian sniffed and lifted her chin. "While I'd prefer a different guide, I suppose you'll do."

She stepped into the hall and clasped her hands loosely at her waist.

Roman nodded and gestured. "This way to the solar."

They didn't speak as they walked through the dim halls illuminated by torches in evenly spaced intervals. Keeping pace with him lest he thought she believed herself inferior meant their arms often brushed.

She flinched at the first contact but didn't pull away, determined to pretend the close contact didn't bother her. But it did. It grated her nerves and elicited other feelings, which only increased her ire.

He paused when they reached a room marked by an ornate doorframe of etchings of tiny Dragons perched among flowering vines and said, "The solar where we spend many evenings."

"We?"

"My brothers and I."

Brothers. She wondered how many siblings he had and why he mentioned no sisters. Marius had told her he had dozens of children. Dozens.

She darted a look inside and frowned when she saw two figures seated in chairs next to a crackling fire. They appeared to be reading.

She backed away and whispered, "Have you no sisters?"

His eyes shifted from copper to muddy red, then back, while shadows danced in their depths. After centuries, Marius had yet to father a living daughter. "No."

There was more to his reply than a simple no, but something told her not to delve deeper. She let it go for now, part of her cruelly pleased to see he'd suffered.

The feeling didn't last, though. Replaced by shame.

"Would you like to go inside?"

Gillian hesitated for a moment. Was she ready to face more of his kind?

Girding herself, she nodded curtly and stepped into the room. Two heads lifted in unison, eyes swinging toward her and nostrils flaring as they caught her scent.

The taller one rose slowly, dropping his book on the cushioned seat of his chair.

Like Roman, he was strikingly handsome, with bronzed skin and cropped hair so dark it was black. Fingerlike lines of red scales bloomed from the neckline of his tunic, crawling up the thick cords of his throat and spreading out like the roots of a tree up the left side of his face to his hairline. He looked younger than Roman, not in his face but in his eyes that retained innocent echoes of youth.

"Draven, meet Gillian," Roman said, gesturing to her. The young male bowed at the waist. "Gillian, this is my youngest brother, Draven."

Draven strode toward them in a loose-hipped gait, his crimson tunic hugging his chest beneath a high-necked vest.

Reaching out, he took Gillian's hand and pressed his lips to her knuckles.

His touch went through her skin like a glowing ember. Within it, she felt heat and longing. He glanced up at her from beneath his brows, still bent at the waist, and winked.

"Don't let his boyish charm fool you," Roman drawled. "He's a rake."

Draven's mouth dropped open in exaggerated shock as he pressed his other hand to his chest. "I?"

Roman rolled his eyes, and his brother said with a sultry wink, "Welcome to our home, Gillian."

He went to his brother's side, rested his arm on Roman's shoulder, and looked at her, asking, "So, am I to call you mother after the nuptials?"

Roman jabbed him with his elbow, and Gillian sputtered. He felt her emotions flare and threatened to beat his younger sibling senseless. Draven held up his hands and backed away with a chuckle.

"I apologize for that. He's not fit for company." Roman drew her attention away from Draven and motioned to the other sibling. "This intimidating cur is Ansel."

Where Draven and Roman were alluring, Ansel was hostile.

Broad-shouldered and hardened, his demeanor matched his face, riddled with patches of blood-red scales so dark they were the color of blood after it sat in the air too long. One large patch grew across his cheek and wrapped around the side of his skull, preventing hair growth and leaving his ear like that of a snake, an open hole.

Ansel tilted his chin but made no move to touch her. "Welcome," he said, but his voice held no real greeting.

She mumbled hello and fidgeted, wanting to get away from the cold stare Ansel threw at her.

Roman hissed at his brother, who did nothing more than raise a brow and sit back down, pulling out his book.

Draven rolled his eyes and sauntered to Gillian. "No doubt Roman has been boring you with his brooding silences and sullen glares."

He pushed his brother aside and offered his arm. "Perhaps you would prefer fairer company?" His eyes roamed over her body. "I'm sure we could find much to see and explore."

"Careful, little brother," Roman warned. "This one bites."

The young male lifted a brow. "Oh? I'd like to see that." He leaned close to her ear. "And feel it."

Ansel laughed, earning a glare from Gillian.

He met it with an ugly smile on his ruined face.

She turned her back on all of them and wrenched open the door. At the threshold, she looked at Roman and said, "Let's get this tour over with so I can go back to looking out my window and watching the grass grow, as that's more pleasant than your company."

Draven snorted and slapped Roman on the back. "I like her."

Roman said something to his brothers too quietly for her to make out and joined her in the hall to resume a tour she wished would end.

How many more Dragonborn males would she have to meet? If they were all as intolerable as those two, she didn't think she could bear it without losing her temper.

According to Marius, most of his sons found mates among the people living within Valon. Each child born of those unions was a ghostly shadow of the Dragon, the blood thinning as it mixed with that of a human.

Gillian couldn't imagine such a life. Bound to a Dragonborn mate. How did the women do it? Their lives were short compared to the children of the Dragon. She eyed Roman. What would it be like? To watch him take newer, younger, prettier mates every few years as she grew older and frailer. Until, eventually, she was forgotten and abandoned, plucking at her needlework in some distant corner of the palace.

It would be awful.

Oblivious to her thoughts, Roman led her through a maze of halls and along a series of rooms whose purpose he rattled off. She forgot them as soon as he spoke, her brain too scattered to pay attention.

That changed when he swung open the library door on the keep's third floor.

Chapter Nine

She'd heard of libraries but had never seen one.

Warrington, the seat of Mirynn, held the largest one on the continent, said to house thousands of titles across its many floors. Most people of her station could barely read, much less find themselves at the doors to such rooms of knowledge. Only lords and ladies entered those hallowed halls, and only the wealthy could afford to purchase written works.

Naeve had instilled her love of books, painstakingly teaching Gillian her letters at the kitchen table.

Between the pages, she discovered everything from philosophy to fantasy. She grew to love the written word. To cherish it as a portal to another place and time. They owned one book. Passed down from her grandmother, it was a tome filled with fables, its spine so worn the binding was coming loose, pages often falling out when she picked it up to reread stories that had become old friends.

In her village, there was a permanent bookseller's stall. The vendor, an elderly man, often lent her titles, knowing she hadn't the coin to buy them. She treated those borrowed works with a reverence Rory found amusing. More than once, he waggled jam-coated fingers and threatened to thumb through the pages or suggested she tear out some paper when the kindling ran low.

Roman held out his arm, inviting her into the room, pleasure temporarily lighting his face when he felt her joy as she stepped inside. He'd ruthlessly stolen memories during their travels, tucking them away should he need them.

Reading had been a surprising passion of hers, and he'd assumed she'd enjoy the library, but this exceeded his expectations.

It was like entering a church, hushed and worshipful.

She paused halfway into the room and turned in a slow circle, the skirts of her blue gown swishing in the quiet.

The Dragon did horde treasure. It just wasn't gold.

The room smelled of parchment, ink, and candle wax. Lined with highly polished wooden shelves that spanned the walls from floor to ceiling, it called to her, beckoning her to come inside, pick a tome, and settle in.

A large fireplace sat at one end, offering light from the dancing flames, while interspersed throughout the room were torches and wall sconces. A pair of overstuffed chairs sat in front of the fireplace, the perfect spot to curl up on a cold winter night.

Her fingers twitched as she entered the room and spun in a slow circle.

Gillian's eyes locked on an ornate case that held an open text. It pulled her like a lodestone past a set of cushioned chairs.

She didn't dare touch the glass as she leaned over to inspect the precious tome.

Pinpricks of awareness buzzed through her head as the heavy weight of a stare crawled across her body. Spinning around, she found Marius seated on one of the chairs she'd passed, a discarded manuscript on his lap, watching her.

Her eyes swept the room, looking for Roman, her mouth turning down when she watched him duck out, shutting the heavy wooden door behind him.

Anger flared. He'd lured her here and trapped her with the Great Dragon.

The pang of betrayal pricked her eyes.

She swallowed the emotion and turned away from Marius, ignoring his presence and studying the book encased in glass.

It was an ancient text, laid open to pages filled with ornate writing in gold-leaf ink. Intricate drawings lined the inner border of the parchment.

Dragons, their scales reflecting every color in a rainbow, twined their tails around each other in knotwork with no end or beginning. She leaned forward, her breath clouding the glass as she tried to see the details. The metallic ink for the eyes and needle-fine lines carving out faces.

Shifting her attention to the text, she admired the swoops and whorls of the lettering but could make nothing out of the words themselves. It was a language she'd never seen before.

Marius' body unfurled from the chair, his ever-present robe rustling softly as it flared out at his sides.

Gillian felt the heat of him as he stood next to her and tried to ignore how her stomach flipped when he breathed out.

"It is the story of Dragons. Our origin and birthright." His voice penetrated her mind like smoke, making her thoughts hazy. "Would you like to hear it?"

She nodded, keeping her attention on the text as she listened.

"The story tells us we were born from Ystri, the southern star. Long had she desired to drift in the cosmos with other stars, but she was still. Fixed. Unable to wander the skies and look down upon other worlds. Millennia passed, and she remained, as did her longing. When she knew she was dying, that her inner light was fading, she gathered weaker stars to her, taking in their energy. Ystri's celestial body exploded in her death, releasing the energy she'd harnessed, birthing gods and goddesses whose unions brought forth the first Dragons— beings who could travel the cosmos as Ystri had dreamed of."

He paused, then added, "Though your people are ignorant of the history, you may be interested to know it was the union of Irylle and Keridwen that birthed Ashael."

Her brows lifted, and she glanced at him.

He spoke of the old gods. Only Irylle was worshiped now, and his followers were dwindling with the rise of Setanta.

"Your kind has a penchant for violence," he said quietly, reading her thoughts. "Unsurprisingly, they honor the god of war and turned their backs on the one who brought them life."

"I could say the same of you. Wasn't it Dragons who scorched the earth, leaving nothing but ash during the battle of the Iron Lords? Even now, a thousand years later, nothing grows there. The Red Wastes are a barren land because of your violence."

"There is much about that battle your histories leave blank. But that is another story for another time."

He lifted his hand so that his palm hovered above the glass. The case trembled, stilling in moments as whatever power he wielded pierced the glass to touch the book. With a gentle wave of his fingers, the page turned.

Too stunned to say anything, Gillian stared at the text, the words and images blurring as his voice again took hold of her mind.

"We are the bringers of worlds, able to cross the vastness of space and time. Life thrives where we establish our rule, growing from the primordial sludge, and we are part of it. Tied to it in a way that anchors us to every living thing, like threads in a tapestry. Remove Dragons from the world they shaped, and it falls to ruin."

Gillian kept her attention on the page, ignoring the longing he exuded, and made a noncommittal sound.

Marius traced a finger along the glass above the shape of a blue Dragon with iridescent scales.

"When we grow to maturity, we leave our parents. Traveling galaxies and singing songs through the heavens, we search for a mate. There is but one mate for every Dragon, and some may never find it. The lucky ones unite in a way only our kind experiences. We claim a world as our own, knowing we can never leave it. We are connected to it as surely as a body cannot live without its heart. I am tied to this world. And I am alone."

His deep voice drifted to silence, the last words hanging in the air like a hook.

And, fool that she was, she longed to grab it. To ease the ache they'd sprung from.

Like the book itself, it was a beautiful myth. Within the telling was Marius' grief.

His Dragon mate was gone, and he was stuck here. Alone.

Gillian glanced at him from the corner of her eye and

caught him watching her. She wanted to look away, to resist the pull she felt as he drank her in. But she couldn't.

Whatever power he wielded was too strong.

She wanted to hate him. To see him repaid for stealing her away. For wanting to lock her away in his castle. For choosing her fate for her while she stood helpless.

Gillian understood the star in Marius' story. She was Ystri. Trapped.

Chapter Ten

Marius held out his hand.

Gillian looked at it, the long fingers that were slightly curled. The supple skin and the gentle curve of his black fingernails. It looked like an innocent gesture. But she dared not touch him, fearing the sway he'd have over her should their skin touch and amplify his intoxicating presence.

Tucking her arms behind her back, she tilted her head and raised a brow.

The corners of his mouth curved, and he flicked his wrist, indicating the doorway. "Would you like to see the rest of the castle?"

"I believe Roman showed me all there is."

"Not all."

He turned and strode to the door, his cloak fanning out behind him. "I would take you to my true home. The mountain."

The mountain? She recalled viewing the keep from a

distance and observing how the structure grew from the face of the mountain as though it were part of it.

Hearing that she could go inside was too intriguing to pass up. Something she was sure Marius was well aware of. He knew which lures to cast, and she was curious enough to take a bite.

"Very well." Gillian strode to his side, ignoring the hand he continued to extend and the amused expression when she again refused it.

He led her through a series of hallways, past rooms and a garderobe, then down a steep set of stairs. At the base was a large wooden door with an etching of a Dragon's face carved into it.

There was something familiar etched into its reptilian features. Something undeniably Marius. Like the tapestry in the main hall, its eyes watched her, seeming to follow her movements as she tried to shift away from their stare.

Marius pulled a heavy key from his pocket and unlocked it, swinging it open for her.

Gillian glanced at him and stepped toward the dimness. An unused torch hung suspended on the wall of a narrow passageway. She shifted to the side as Marius moved by her, the heat of his body whispering over her flesh and stirring the chill air.

He grabbed the torch and waved a hand over it, lighting it with a word before saying softly, "The mountain is the heart of Valon. It is where Ashael and I spent our happiest years. The castle was built after her death."

It bothered Gillian to hear him talk about his dead mate. It made her pity him. It made her heart pang with shared grief and longing to offer comfort. She recognized the danger of allowing those feelings to blossom and ruthlessly smothered them.

Marius was no better than a jailer, and she was his prisoner. How many others came before her? How many had taken his hand and given all, only to be forgotten and discarded? There were no tapestries or carvings of women like her.

Hardening herself, she nodded curtly and waited for him to continue.

They walked in silence for many minutes. Behind them, the passageway grew so dark she could make out nothing of the door they'd passed through.

She ran her fingers along the cool stone, feeling the dips and bulges on the rough surface. It had been carved by hand. She wondered how long it had taken and who'd done the work. Had it been Marius? She thought not. Imagining him wielding a hammer and chisel like a common mason was difficult to picture. It was so at odds with the refined persona he projected.

Although she had no doubt he had the muscles to do it. Despite his lean appearance, he exuded physical strength. And beyond that was a deeper, darker power.

Gillian squinted as the passage slowly opened into a large chamber. She craned her neck, trying to see beyond the soft glow of the torch.

Marius told her to wait and loped ahead, lighting torches anchored into walls.

As the light penetrated the darkness, she could make out a vast circular room with multiple tunnel offshoots, like the hub of a wheel. Each spoke was a passageway easily three men wide and tall. It was impossible to discern how deep into the mountain the tunnels went, nor where each might lead.

Looking up, she saw nothing but darkness beyond the

flames. The vastness of the cavern was astounding. Made for the height and breadth of a Dragon.

Her eyes skipped from offshoot to offshoot, each wide enough to allow such a creature to travel like a worm through the earth.

Marius strode slowly toward her under the glow of the torch he held. His body moved in the same loose-hipped manner that Roman's did, his copper eyes glowing with an inner light beneath the dark wings of his eyebrows. He stopped when he was a foot away.

She wanted to take a step back and put some distance between their bodies, but she forced herself to remain still, refusing to appear cowardly.

He whispered an unfamiliar word, and the light grew, illuminating the walls of the chamber.

Her eyes were drawn to evenly spaced cuts in the stone, each covered in what looked like golden plaques. Her brows knitted.

"The tombs of my mates."

Gillian stared at them, her attention fixed on one that was brighter than the rest. Newer.

These were not the tombs of Dragons.

These were the tombs of women—human mates—and if she did not escape, she would be among them one day.

He let out a long breath, his spicy scent and power filling the air in front of her face.

She blinked, the tombs momentarily forgotten.

"Come." He waved his arm, indicating a dimly lit tunnel to her right.

Gillian followed, listening to the soothing murmur of his voice as he told her of his arrival with his mate, Ashael. How they'd crashed into the earth like twin comets, igniting the horizon with their passion.

They'd found the primitive world and lit the skies with their fires, breathing life into it until it flourished, feeding off the flames and ashes.

During the day, Irylle bathed the new world with heat and light while Keridwen glowed in the darkness against the stars at night, bringing forth all manner of living things.

Eventually, others came—those whose magic was able to forge roads between worlds, peopling them as they went. The Dragons allowed it for a time until a wizard arrived.

The mage had brought human slaves, molding the land at his whim over decades as he dug into the power within the earth like a tick, feeding off of it and growing stronger. In time, his slaves revolted, their numbers having grown too great for him to control. He began killing them, destroying entire lineages with wizard's fire.

If Marius and Ashael hadn't intervened, humans would've been wiped from the earth.

The Great Dragon killed the mage after a lengthy battle that nearly took his life, and the roads the wizard had created were broken so that no others could follow.

Marius and Ashael established themselves as the rightful rulers, overseeing humankind as it thrived and spread, keeping a close eye on the witches spawned from the wizard's seed—half-breeds born from the human women the mage had bred.

Within a few decades, the blood of those who'd once had the magic to forge roads grew thin, and people forgot that knowledge until their descendants were completely bereft of it.

But the witches remembered—not how to forge roads but

how to bend the world to their will. They kept their magic alive, shaping it over time, connecting it to the elements.

Marius and Ashael could've destroyed them, but they let them live. The Coven of the Silver Moon remained in the Shadowlands, only leaving their place of power when the urge to reproduce came upon them.

People spread beyond the borders of Valon, the heart of the Dragon's domain. Beyond the boundaries of the Shadowlands, living off the earth and thereby binding themselves to the Dragon lords who'd shaped it.

In time, they established their own rule, forgetting where they came from, until a new history was written and Dragons became legends. Marius and Ashael allowed it, content to pour their energy into the making of young.

They were peaceful times during which he and his mate brought their first hatchlings into the world.

Marius paused at the entrance to a large cavern at the end of one of the passages they'd traveled.

"Our rookery," he said softly.

Gillian walked forward slowly. She felt him behind her, felt his profound sorrow.

Throughout the room were a dozen raised mounds, their stone centers carved out to create shallow bowls large enough for her to stretch out. Each was lined with thick layers of fur, now tattered with age, to cradle the precious treasure within it —a Dragon egg. Only small shards of shells remained, fragments of the new life they'd carried. Crushed and discarded and covered in layers of neglect.

She crouched at the edge of a nest and touched its fur-lined center. Within it lay the broken piece of a shell. She glanced up at Marius as he stood above her, watching her movements.

He nodded, face tight.

Reaching forward, she picked up the remnant and cupped it in her hand. It filled her palm to overflowing. Reverently, she turned it this way and that, fingers running over the marbled surface. Hues of blue and red flowed together in swirls of color.

"Symira, my daughter. The last of our young." His eyes shifted from copper to deep red, then back. "Ashael died shortly after our daughter sang her song of leaving and left this world to find a mate."

Gillian stared at the shell, leaning over to gently place it on the bed of fur. She sat on her heels and stared at the sad remnants of his old life.

How had it come to this?

She recalled him telling her that his mate had died during an upheaval, but she'd never heard of such a thing. Had people rebelled against his rule?

Reading her thoughts as clearly as though they were spoken, he said, "Allowing mankind to establish their rule and forget they were beholden to us is my biggest regret. I should've reminded them. If I had, Ashael would be at my side."

His eyes shuttered. "And you would not be."

Rising, Gillian faced him. "You can't bring her back by keeping me here."

He shook his head. "I do not seek to bring her back."

Inside, his thoughts roiled, anger and blame laid at Keridwen's celestial feet. Men had shot his mate from the sky, but it was the goddess who'd allowed Ashael to cross the river.

"Then, why keep me here? I can never replace her."

She reached inside and poured every ounce of persuasion into words when she swung an arm to encompass the space and said, "I will never fill this room with Dragonlings."

"Don't test your power on me, Gillian. You're grossly unprepared for the challenge. And do not speak to me as if I do not know what your frail body cannot provide."

His eyes flared. "My mate is *dead*. There will never be another Dragon of my making to birth new worlds. Never again will I hear the song of a hatchling echo in this chamber."

"Is this what your mate would've wanted? To take me from my family and keep me in a beautiful prison?" She glared at him. "Ashael's heart must have been as ugly as yours."

Fury spread across his face, steam pouring from his nostrils like white clouds.

She took a step back, her heel bumping the edge of the nest.

Marius' body grew and expanded, his face shifting from human to serpent. The pupils of his copper eyes turned to narrow vertical slits. His cloak, the swaying folds that gave the impression of wings, fanned out behind him, becoming the thing her mind had glimpsed countless times.

Gillian stumbled back as his skin swelled and split.

His neck grew to an impossible length, topped with a serpentine head where twin horns tore through the illusion of human flesh as they spiraled toward the ceiling. A massive chest lined with scaly armor breathed deeply, the sound causing the ground to shudder. Huge, taloned feet slammed into the rock, sending shards in every direction.

She covered her face, feeling the sting as a sharp piece sliced the back of her hand. Heat blasted from his body, slamming into her like a fist.

She landed hard in the bowl of the nest, her backside smashing the shell she'd held moments before.

The Great Dragon towered over her.

He spread his wings, filling the room from edge to edge, the skin covering each wing stretching tight over the bones, tendons, and veins rippling within them. His long neck, layered in red and gold scales, curved as he bent low so that his reptilian face hovered above her, flames licking his snout.

She felt the red-hot huff of his breath wash over her, singeing her skin. She shrieked and curled into a ball.

"Submit," his voice boomed, teeth snapping.

"Keridwen betrayed me a millennia ago, leaving me mateless. But the cruel goddess shall not take everything from me. I will have young. My bloodline will remain in this world until the heart of it burns out, and every living thing turns to dust!"

Gillian whimpered and clamped her hands over her head, sure the entire chamber was going to come crashing down with the force of his anger.

The beast eyed her dispassionately, nostrils flaring as he stretched his wings to their full length. Wickedly sharp black talons gripped the rock, gouging it as he struggled to rein in his anger.

"You will yield," he hissed, his forked tongue lashing the air. "When the earth's shadow eclipses the pale goddess, you will be mine. You will breed a new generation of Dragonborn, or I will tear you to pieces, then cross the border to slaughter your family and all of Rudgarde."

Her chest tightened, and she clutched it, feeling her heart hammering. She curled tighter around herself, wrapping her arms around her legs and keeping her eyes clenched shut.

Gillian heard the scrape of claws against stone and flinched, imagining them piercing her skin. She bit her lips, trapping the sob crawling up her throat.

Marius breathed heavily, puffs of smoke pouring from his nostrils.

He narrowed his eyes and tasted the air. Fear and hatred coated his tongue.

He'd hoped it would be different with this one. The scar Maud, his last witch-wife, left when she took her life, remained in him like a living thing, feeding his anger and determination.

He didn't want to stand over Gillian's broken body as he'd stood over Maud's. Seeing her lifeblood spilled on the unforgiving stone. Hearing the final, faint beat of her unborn's tiny heart.

So he'd tried to coax Gillian with kindness and tales of his past, each word laced with persuasive power. But she was too strong, too stubborn, to be swayed by such subtleties.

Her will was too powerful to allow surrender.

So be it, he thought.

Let her pit herself against him for now. In the end, she'd be no match for the strength of his true power.

<h1 style="text-align:center">Chapter Eleven</h1>

Gillian burrowed deeper under the covers of her bed, face pressed to the pillow she'd spent the last five days punching or raging into. She hadn't left her room since the Great Dragon terrorized her in his mountain.

She tried not to think about what occurred within its depths, but she had no control over her dreams. What she'd seen and felt as he'd burst into his true form.

Her memories of running through the halls to escape the anger radiating from Marius became a web of nightmares that visited her even in the light of day.

Roman had tried to stop her when she fled, grabbing her arm as she streaked past him.

All she remembered was how he'd flinched when she screamed at him to release her. The look on his face before he'd turned to stone and opened his hand with an impatient flick.

She'd finally come across the maidservant, Mary, who'd looked at her with pity before leading her to the bedchamber.

A light tapping sounded at the door, and she groaned

and ground her teeth. As with every knock, her heart stopped for a couple of beats as she imagined Marius on the other side of the wood, eyes glowing red and body covered in scales.

But he hadn't set foot in her room.

Instead, he'd entered her dreams every night since she ran from him. Whatever images and scenes that played out as she slept were gone by morning, but the residue of their longing and lust remained.

No, it wasn't Marius who kept knocking.

He wouldn't knock anyway. It was likely Roman. Again.

He was her tormentor, refusing to coddle her like Draven did when he swaggered into the room, voice booming with levity as he tried to draw her out each day.

He waggled his eyebrows or thrust out his lip in a pout. "Come now, Gillian. I know you fantasize about walking the grounds with me or visiting the village baker so I can buy you a crumpet."

"Go away, Draven," she told him, knowing he'd only plop down on a stool and fill the room with inane chatter.

"You'd miss me if I left. I'll save you the grief."

She pulled a pillow over her head. "Leave me alone."

"What was that? I couldn't hear you with the pillow over your mouth."

Gillian's hands curled into fists, squeezing the down-filled fabric. She threw it at him when he started singing, but he only caught it and tossed it back.

To him, it didn't matter if she were a stiff board in his arms as he dragged her out of the chair and paraded around the room to a waltz only he could hear. Or played a one-sided game of chess during which he crowed with delight when he beat himself.

Truthfully, she spent most of his visits trying not to smile and laugh. It only encouraged him.

After a couple of days, she gave up expending energy on pushing Draven out the door and switched tactics, making innocent inquiries about the castle and its workings. Every detail was filed away and added to the information she wheedled from her maidservant.

It would be useful when she escaped her beautiful prison. That is, if the Dragon's sons would leave her alone long enough to duck out unseen.

Roman was worse than his younger sibling.

He, too, visited, but his visits were marked by frequent intrusions into her room, three or four times a day, to provoke her.

"Gillian! The cockerel crowed three hours ago," he announced, ripping back the curtain on her window. "Want to watch me butcher him?"

"No."

"Yes, you do."

He dragged the covers off, smirking when she tried to snatch them back. "Get dressed. You can sit in the shade, watch me stalk the beast, and ring its neck. Then, I'll have cook make you rooster pie."

"I'd rather watch you choke on the pie."

He shook his head, undeterred, and tossed her freshly cleaned cloak on the bed. "Put on a gown or not. It matters little to me. Though my men may find the sheerness of your nightclothes distracting."

Gillian gasped and clutched her chemise, bunching the fabric to hide her breasts. "You're a pig."

"You've called me that several times. I suggest you find another insult to make these little spats more interesting."

"Get out!" she screeched, jumping out of the bed.

He obliged, raising a brow as he met her furious face at the threshold. "Look at that. You're out of bed."

She slammed the door, shouting a curse when he chuckled.

He was infuriating.

How many times over the last few days had Roman poked her back as she huddled under the covers or leaned into her face as she sat by the fire, averting her eyes?

He was like a mother hen pecking at her each time he came by. *Are you planning on spending the rest of your life in this room? Are you still wishing on that useless medallion you insist on wearing to magic you home? Aren't you tired of staring at the same four walls?*

Or bursting into her room and wrinkling his nose. *It stinks in here. You should get some fresh air.*

No. It didn't matter what she said or did to dissuade Roman. He was just as irritating as he'd been dragging her through Dwyer Wood.

More so. Glaring and trying to shove him out of her room did nothing.

He was like the sun, immune to pesky human intervention.

Irylle save her from Dragonborn males.

She grumbled when a tap sounded on the door again and rolled her head on the pillow, expecting to see Roman standing there, hellbent on annoying her. She told herself she'd prefer bubbly Draven if it had to be one of the Dragon's children.

But it wasn't him who came to life in her dreams. It was his brother. And that rankled.

Mary poked her head in when she remained silent. "Milady?" The shuffle of her feet on the stone filled the room. She went to the side of the bed. "Good morning, milady."

She sat up. "Mary, I told you to call me Gillian."

"Yes, mi—Gillian." Her face glowed with pleasure. "May I get you anything? Perhaps a small meal?"

Gillian shoved back a wild tangle of pale blonde hair and swung her legs over the side of the bed. "Where are the Dragon's children?"

The fact that Roman hadn't woken her at the crack of dawn as he'd done the morning before surprised her.

"They're in the lists with the men."

She glanced toward the window when Mary pulled back the curtain and considered what the maid had said.

"Why do they train? Have you had trouble here before?"

"In my grandfather's time, there were quite a few skirmishes between the far-flung settlements."

"There are more towns outside of Valon?"

"Oh, aye. A dozen or so. The lord visits quite often, ensuring no further uprisings, though the men train regardless. Master Roman likes to send patrols out to remind the town mayors who rules the land."

Gillian pictured the Dragon sailing through the sky above small towns like Valon—a winged demon roaring fiery warnings to any who thought to challenge his rule.

Mary shook out the bedding and said slyly, "Besides, training with the lordlings keeps the men fit and pleasing to the eye."

Gillian laughed and poured water into a bowl to wash her face.

"I'll bring up a tray from the kitchen." The maid picked up the empty bowl from the night before. "You might consider taking your midday meal in the great hall."

She wrinkled her nose at the suggestion. "I prefer to eat in peace."

"Very well." She went to the door and turned to add, "You ought to leave this room and walk the grounds. It's a lovely bit of land. I'll bring you a bowl of porridge to fill your belly, and then you can be on your way."

With that, she bustled out of the room.

Gillian knew the maid was right. She needed to walk the grounds and find the best escape route. Already, she had a rudimentary idea of where she might go.

Of course, if Roman or Draven were dogging her heels, she'd never have a chance.

And what if Marius was below, waiting for her?

She clutched the medallion she refused to take off as though it gave her strength, even though its power seemed to have bled out when she'd crossed into the Shadowlands. It offered no comfort other than the familiar weight in her hand.

The prospect of facing the Dragon made her question the wisdom of her decision to leave the safety of her room.

She poked the fire and circled the room a few times, mumbling to herself as she waged an internal battle. By the time she dressed and combed out her long hair, her mind was made up.

Mary returned with a tray laden with porridge, a crust of bread slathered in butter, and a mug of watered wine.

Thanking her, Gillian set the tray on a small table by the hearth. She ate slowly, each swallow renewing her strength and fortifying her against the wrath she knew would come when she faced Marius.

Swinging her red cloak around her shoulders, she laced it at her throat and unlatched the door.

Darting her head into the hallway to look around, Gillian breathed a sigh of relief and slunk down the passageway, ducking into the shadows when she heard footsteps.

Nearing the solar, she paused and listened.

Male voices argued in low tones.

She thought she heard Roman among them, but couldn't be sure and had no desire to find out. She'd rather be well away when they left the solar if they were arguing about her. Servants bustled about the great hall when she crept down the stairwell.

Picking up her pace, she lifted the hem of her gown and sped across the rushes, choosing a side door rather than leaving through the front, where she was bound to run into either Marius or one of his brood.

No one stopped her or asked where she was going as she left the castle grounds through the garden. The sun was out, casting afternoon shadows across the pastures and outbuildings.

Skirting hives of activity, she headed toward the base of the mountain that abutted the castle, hoping to reach a better vantage point and find an escape route. Climbing a craggy hill, she got winded and clutched her side.

Wishing she'd thought to grab a waterskin, Gillian sat on the grass and tried to ignore her parched throat.

Mary was right. The landscape was lovely. Picturesque with its rolling hills, imposing mountain, and quaint village life. She wandered the hilltop a while longer, letting her feet take her where they willed.

Eventually, she came upon the ruins of a stone structure tucked at the edge of a forested strip of land. Vines climbed up the sides, and saplings sprouted through gaping holes in the roof where the thatching had rotted and fallen away. The door hung askew, sagging on one hinge.

She hiked up her dress higher and squeezed through the opening. Her leg brushed against a sharp splinter of wood, and she yelped, stumbling the rest of the way and landing with a thump inside the ruins. Gillian frowned and looked at the blood welling from a large gash on her leg.

Tearing a strip of linen from the hem of her underdress, she tied it around her limb to stem the flow and got to her feet.

Wooden pews, most sagging and broken, lined the floor, each facing an altar on a raised platform. It was a rectangular slab of stone on which a bowl lined with dirt and debris sat.

She picked at the muck covering its base, revealing gold beneath it. Glancing up, her eyes fell on a mural obscured by stains from rainwater drippings and layers of dust. Stepping around the altar, she rubbed away some of the grime, revealing a male form.

The figure had fiery wings that extended well beyond his outstretched arms. Behind his body was a glowing orb, the sun.

Gillian realized she was looking at an image of Irylle, the fire god.

At his side was Keridwen, goddess of the moon. She wore a gossamer gown of blue so pale it was nearly white. One hand reached for her mate. Irylle's fingers intertwined with hers, sealing their union.

Gillian's gaze traveled down, noting the goddess's rounded belly.

Their unions birthed the first Dragons, Marius had shared when telling the story of Ystri.

But there were things he didn't say. Things his expression alluded to before he drew a mental curtain over his mind.

Gillian spun in a slow circle. The building must have been a temple. By its size, it was a place of worship for the people of Valon. Maybe even Marius himself, when in his human form. It was also evident that worshiping the god and goddess in that space had ended years ago.

It reminded her of the Dragon's rookery. Neglected. Forgotten.

She turned back to the mural and slowly walked around the altar. The toe of her boot hit something, and she paused. Bending down, Gillian brushed away leaves and moss, revealing the torso of a statue.

She picked it up and ran her finger over the stone. It was a female representation. From the slight bulge below the figure's breasts, broken off by a violent hand, she realized what it was.

Keridwen—Moon Goddess—destroyed and discarded.

She placed the sad remains on the altar.

What prompted such a defilement? Like the rest of mankind, they still worshiped Irylle.

Her curiosity quickly turned to ire. What did she care about their history or worship? If they, too, had turned their back on the goddess, so be it. Perhaps Keridwen had punished them for some transgression.

They deserve it, she thought sourly.

Birdsong drifted through the ruins, and Gillian paused to listen. It sounded like home.

Sinking to the floor, she rested her back against the stone altar and hung her head. Tears welled, and she brushed them away angrily. Crying wouldn't help her escape. She needed to plan, gather some provisions, and squirrel them away. Not sit here feeling sorry for herself.

However, this could be a good place to hide out if she needed to. From the state of disrepair, no one had set foot in it for a decade or more.

Her leg throbbed, and she stretched it out, tugging up her gown to look at it. Blood had seeped through the cloth, but it wasn't too bad. She'd ask Mary for a poultice when she returned to the keep.

The thought of going back made her angry and scared. When Marius had exploded out of his skin, becoming the stuff of nightmares, he'd told her she had until the lunar eclipse.

How soon was that? What if her time had nearly run out?

Gillian couldn't face that possibility. Her life couldn't be over.

Rory's life couldn't be over.

She had to escape. She had to find the Coven of the Silver Moon. Roman wanted her to believe they were evil women who would sacrifice her to their goddess. But beneath his dire warnings, she'd sensed fear.

Not fear for her safety, but fear that she'd see through him as though his warnings were nothing more than lies.

Naeve believed the witches could save her brother. She'd been willing to come to the Shadowlands herself, so great was her belief. That was good enough for her. She'd find them, beg for aid, and return home to Rory. She had to.

But the thought of all the journey entailed was terrifying and overwhelming. How was she supposed to trek through a forest full of monsters blindly? Did she think she'd magically stumble upon them?

It was crazy. It was a death sentence.

She pulled her cloak around her body to keep out the chill that consumed her, tucking her head into the hood until all one could see were strands of pale hair and the tip of her nose. With a sigh, she bent her knees, laid her arms on them, and rested her head.

She'd close her eyes for a moment, nothing more. Just enough to ease the anxiety squeezing her chest.

The moment turned into hours. It was Draven who found her.

Chapter Twelve

Draven scented the fresh blood from her wound as he searched the grounds well away from the castle. Easing into the ruined temple, his copper eyes picked her out of the darkness.

She was nothing but a small lump curled up at the base of the altar.

He stared at her for a few moments, sniffing the air. The smell of her filled his lungs and stirred his loins.

Had she any idea the uproar she'd caused on her arrival? He doubted it.

Roman had let him know she was ignorant of her heritage. If that were true, she'd be unaware of the lure of her blood. His father had yet to claim her. When he did, the allure would fade, but he wondered if some of it would always linger. If she'd unknowingly torture him and his brothers until her death.

Stepping over scraps of roofing, vines, and other debris, he made his way to her sleeping form. She looked so small and helpless. One of her legs was exposed. The hem of her cloak and gown bunched up to reveal the supple limb. He saw a strip of linen tied around it, stained with blood.

He inhaled deeply, throat burning with desire. The bleeding had stopped, but she needed the wound cleaned, stitched, and dressed properly to avoid infection.

Draven crouched at her side. He could take her now, run off with her into the woods, and pray to Irylle that the medallion she stubbornly wore had magic enough to let them pass into her homeland.

His father's wrath halted his thoughts. All would suffer if he took her.

Part of Draven screamed at him to steal her anyway. To have one of her kind as his own, as no other child of Marius had done. To love her and sire young, raising a family beyond the Dragon's reach.

He hung his head and balled his fists. He couldn't do it.

He may yearn for what she could give him, but he was devoted to his family. Pity that.

Sighing, he gently nudged her shoulder.

She moaned and rolled toward him, her head lolling, face exposed beneath the hood of her cloak. He stared at her parted lips. The white tips of her teeth were barely visible.

He traced a finger along her mouth. His heart thundered, loins aching. He shifted uncomfortably and clenched his jaw.

She wasn't his. He had no right to her.

"Gillian," he said, voice pitched low. "Gillian, wake up."

She mumbled and tucked her chin into the folds of her hood.

Shaking her shoulder, he said more forcefully, "Gillian."

Her lashes fluttered, eyes going wide as she focused on his

face. She gasped and jerked away from him, her head hitting the stone of the base of the altar.

"Ouch," she muttered, rubbing the back of her skull.

He leaned back on his heels, hands hanging loosely. "Hiding?"

She sat up and looked around, reorienting herself. "Not very well, it appears."

Draven chuckled and rose, holding out his hand. "While I'd love to find a dark corner in this decrepit place and discover your secrets, we should return. The whole castle is looking for you."

"I don't want to go back," she mumbled, turning away from his hand.

"I'm a failure with the fairer sex." He dropped his arm. "Sadly, you don't have a choice."

"Why is this happening to me?"

He looked away for a moment. "Why did you cross into the Shadowlands?"

She huffed and crossed her arms.

"Did you willfully ignore the risks? Or did you simply not believe they applied to you?"

She tucked her legs under her and got to her feet, using the altar for support, when her leg flared with pain and the gash split open.

Gillian made a face and shook out her skirt. "I didn't know."

His eyes flicked to her injured limb. He couldn't see it beneath her gown, but smelled the fresh blood.

"You're a terrible liar. Your people have been telling stories of the dangers of Dwyer Forest for hundreds of years."

"Fine. You win. I knew. But—" She made a frustrated sound. "My brother is dying of the Wasting. When I discovered the Coven of the Silver Moon had magic that could cure him, I had to try. If one of your brothers were dying and you could save him, wouldn't you risk everything to do it?"

Draven's considered. "Well, maybe not Ansel. He's a sullen bastard."

"Ugh. Can't you ever stop being a clown and just be... I don't know, serious?"

"I can, but where's the fun in that?"

"You're infuriating."

"Gillian, my brothers *are* dying. We're all that's left."

It wasn't the response she wanted to hear. She didn't like seeing them in human terms, seeing their grief and hardship. But these Dragonborn males had a way of getting under her skin.

"That's why you're here. It's why you'll become my father's... mate." His eyes flared red when he said mate, then dimmed. "When you crossed the boundary between our worlds, you sealed your fate. Without you, my kind will die out."

"That's ridiculous." She rubbed her eyes. "Your father could find someone else. The world is full of women. It doesn't have to be me."

"There is no one else. Not like you."

"I don't believe that. I'm just the one who fell into his trap!"

Draven took a step toward her, his chest mere inches from hers. Warmth and something dangerously potent radiated from him.

Gillian gripped the edges of her cloak to keep from reaching for him and looked at the ground, avoiding the desire she knew would be stamped on his face.

He lifted her chin with his finger, forcing her to look at him.

"I can't let you leave, Gillian."

Run away with her, his mind screamed. He battled the inner voice, eyes shifting to crimson as his wants went to war with his reason.

"You can. You're just too scared to do what you know is right."

Take her! A voice boomed in his head.

Gillian took a step away, the echo of his voice striking her mind. She furrowed her brow, looked beyond the struggle stamped on his face, and unintentionally slipped into his thoughts.

It was seamless, like dipping her toe in the water. Only the pool of thought she entered was dark and swirling.

It sucked her down into a black abyss, and she rocked back on her heels, mentally shouting, *Stop!*

Draven's eyes were glassy when she dragged herself out of his mind.

What the hell? She shook her head, keeping an eye on him as he stood with a blank expression. Gillian waved a hand in front of his face.

He snatched her hand, emptiness turning to shocked anger in a heartbeat. "What did you just do?"

She wrenched her hand away. "Nothing."

Narrowing his eyes, he leaned down until his face hovered above hers. "That's a lie, isn't it?"

She shook her head and clamped her lips.

"Roman warned me you had some latent power."

Draven shielded his mind, erecting a mental barrier to keep her out. He should've heeded his brother's warning.

She was strong. Her power was raw and untrained. Dangerous.

Roman was better at mentalism than he was. He'd always been more powerful in every way, and lately, Draven felt the inherited strength he had waning. In truth, it had weakened for years, though he'd said nothing to his father or siblings.

Gillian watched him study her, seeing emotions flicker across his face before he masked them.

What did he mean by power? She had no power. If she did, she would've used it the moment Roman captured her.

Forehead wrinkling, she thought about what Draven could mean, flipping through memories. And there they were—two instances with Roman and Marius. They'd both felt... something. Each had warned her to stop. But stop what?

She'd always had a talent for winning people over, her family members in particular. But that was just part of her personality. Wasn't it?

What if he was right? What if whatever Marius and Roman sensed about her was real?

Maybe things were different here. Maybe the Dragon's realm allowed her to become more than what she was on the other side of the border between their worlds. Roman was able to drown out her will with a power-laced breath. Perhaps she could convince Draven to abscond with her.

"I don't know what you're talking about." Gillian kept her eyes fixed on his, exuding the pretense of honesty. Inside, she focused on the features of his face, thinking about what they meant, imagining the thoughts behind them.

He frowned. "My brother would call me a fool, but I believe you. Not that it makes any difference. We need to return. Now." Draven held out his hand.

She looked at it and slowly reached for his fingers, continuing to keep her attention on his face. Their hands touched. His warmth radiated through the contact, and she thought she heard a whisper of his thoughts within that heat.

His fingers curled around hers.

Again, that voice inside of him rasped, *Take her. Take her now.*

Draven's arm trembled as he fought the urge to sweep her into his arms.

Gillian saw it, felt it, and grabbed hold of his slip in control. "Take me to the coven."

Into each word, she poured her longing, grief, determination, and will.

His face twitched as he fought her.

"I can't do that," he said, but his voice was stilted, as though he was reciting something that held no weight.

"Take me to the coven. Help me save Rory."

She pulled memories of her brother and flooded her mind with them, wanting Draven to see and feel them. Rory's voice. His smile and touch. His wasted body.

"Help me."

His nostrils flared, the scales along the side of his face and neck shifting subtly. "I... I... can't."

She reached for his silky tunic, curling her fingers in the fine material along the V of its neck. "Draven."

His name on her lips had a palpable effect.

She saw his face shift, eyes going black, red, then golden. The scales along his cheek and neck lifted and settled in a rolling motion.

Sensing he was on the cusp of capitulation, she leaned into him, eyes fixed on his face. "Draven, please help me."

"All right."

Chapter Thirteen

They sped into the night, Gillian clinging to Draven's back, her head tucked between his shoulder blades. His strength rarely wavered, though he often slowed as though climbing through a mental fog and realizing he wasn't where he should be.

When she felt those moments, she pressed her lips to his ear and whispered to him, using his name each time. It was a heady feeling to sense his response.

She had power in this place.

It was as though the Dragon's presence in his realm tapped into something that had always been there, hidden in her world. Gillian didn't understand it, but she used it, determined to fight her way to the coven, to her brother.

Draven took her deep into the Shadowlands—up and down steep inclines.

Hours passed, and she grew weary. Gillian stopped trying to sway him.

And yet, he kept going. Somehow, during the long hours of

the night, he'd decided on his own to help her. Too tired to think about why, she begged him to stop well past midnight.

Her head ached from the constant bouncing.

Gillian slid from his back, landing on the leaf-littered ground in a tangle of limbs. Her leg ached dully where she'd cut it. Scooting to a tree trunk, she rested her back and tugged up her dress, angling her limb to catch the moonlight filtering through the trees. The gash oozed fresh blood, the skin around it caked in blackened smears and flakes.

"It needs to be sealed," Draven said, crouching at her feet.

"I know. But unless you have a needle and thread, it will have to heal on its own."

"Fire would work." He wagged his fingers.

"Are you thinking of burning me?" she asked with a startled laugh.

"It would serve you right for convincing me to defy my father. Besides, it will keep splitting open if you leave it untended." He put one knee on the ground and reached for her leg. "May I?"

She nodded and watched his movements with a cautious eye.

He whispered so low she couldn't make out the words. Scales, the same fingerlike projections visible on his neck and face, also extended from his left wrist around the side of his hand to his palm before disappearing under the fabric of his sleeve.

Like the feathers of a bird, they shifted and rippled, glowing subtly with his words. Holding his hand above the wound, he flicked his copper eyes at her from beneath his dark lashes.

"This will hurt."

Fiery heat bloomed across her skin, and her eyes went wide. She tried to scramble away from the pain, but his other hand held her leg in an immovable grip.

The gash on her leg sizzled. *It sizzled!*

She yelped and twisted her body, clawing at the tree trunk behind her. Her face twisted in pain, sweat beading on her forehead despite the chill of the night air. The agony was over in moments that felt like hours.

A soft breeze washed over her skin, and she craned her head to see Draven bent over her leg, full lips curved as he blew gently. Panting, Gillian watched him, slowly pulling her leg away when he let go.

The wound was an angry red and puckered. But the bleeding had stopped. It would leave a nasty scar, not that she cared. If things went wrong, she'd end up a slave to Marius and didn't care how he felt about her appearance. The thought of being tied to him indefinitely made her shudder.

Draven saw her tremble and offered to build a fire. She nodded mutely, not wishing to explain how the shaking had nothing to do with the cold.

He gathered wood and coaxed flames as she'd seen Roman do. Thinking of the Dragonborn male made the corners of her mouth pull down in an unhappy frown. If he hadn't come upon her, she'd be home now with a cure for Rory.

No, you wouldn't, an inner voice said. *You'd be dead because the vauger would've killed you.*

She sniffed and tried to quiet her thoughts. She was mostly successful.

Draven soon had a small fire lighting up their surroundings, the flames warming her body. However, they couldn't reach the icy places in her heart. The places where dread lived and breathed.

He tried to engage her in conversation, but she pleaded exhaustion, pulled the hood of her cloak over her head, and curled onto her side. She watched the flames dance in the darkness as she peered through the narrow gap in the folds.

"Why are you helping me?"

He crouched, leaning back on a heel with one leg forward to rest his arm. His eyes flicked to the ground before looking at her from beneath his thick, dark lashes.

"Maud, my father's last mate, was my mother. She killed herself. Whether it was to escape my father or for some other reason, I'll never know. But I—" He looked away and picked up a stick to poke the fire. "I don't wish the same fate for you."

She had no trouble imagining why Maud resorted to suicide. Being tied to Marius seemed like no life at all. It was surprising she'd had a son before taking the ultimate escape.

"I'm sorry about your mother." Gillian sat up. "It must have been awful."

Draven nodded and sighed. "Aye." He poked at the fire.

"Thank you for helping me."

He chuckled. "You're very convincing."

Gillian picked up a dead leaf and tore it apart, considering what he meant. "I've never had any power other than my stubbornness. Roman can attest to that."

"He'd say it was more than obstinance."

She shrugged. "I don't know what it is, and honestly, it doesn't matter to me as long as I get to where I need to go. My brother is the only reason I'm here, Draven. The only reason I left my homeland."

"I know."

The fire crackled and popped, sending sparks into the air. Gillian's eyes grew heavy, her body lulled by the warmth of the flames.

Draven's voice pulled her back before she slipped into an exhausted sleep. "I understand my father."

She blinked and covered her mouth in a yawn, forcing herself to sit up. Her body shook with tremors of pure exhaustion. Pulling her cloak tighter around her body, she looked at him.

"You'd have to be made of stone not to sense his loneliness. I feel it. I've always felt it, even when Maud was alive. Nothing can fill the hole Ashael left." He shook his head. "He keeps trying, though. But there has to be another way."

A shriek ripped through the sky, followed by the beating of wings. Gillian lurched to her knees, ready to bolt.

Draven's head was tilted up, eyes scanning the breaks in the trees.

"What is that?" Gillian asked, scooting closer to him.

"A myrax. She must have caught your scent. They usually don't come near fire."

Gillian followed his stare, eyes going wide, when a black shape hurtled across the sky above their heads, screeching in its wake.

It was easily the size of two men. Large enough to carry her off.

"Will it attack?" she asked, pitching her voice low.

He glanced at her. "No. They fear my kind."

She tucked her head into her hood and shifted closer to him, ignoring the quirk of his lips when their hips touched. If she had to, she'd sleep at his side rather than risk being dragged away and devoured by that creature.

After a few more passes, each punctuated by shrieks and wails that raced down her spine, the myrax left in search of easier prey.

Gillian tried to relax, forcing her hands to loosen their grip on her cloak. "How much farther is it?" she asked, nudging Draven out of his silent reverie.

"If we travel quickly, we should reach the Gealach Forest before nightfall tomorrow."

Traveling quickly would mean he'd carry her again. The idea irked her. She felt like a helpless babe hugging his back like that. But if they walked, as she'd done with Roman to delay their arrival in Valon or try to escape, they could be found by whoever was tracking them. And she didn't need to ask if someone was.

She'd felt it in the tenseness of Draven's muscles as he carried her. Had sensed his internal war and felt him wavering.

When his pace slowed, she'd whispered in his ear, pleading with him to continue. And he had.

But for how long? If his father tracked them and demanded her return, would he rebel?

They needed to reach the coven before any Dragonborn found them. If they didn't, Rory would die, and she would likely never see the light of day again.

Draven shook her awake just before dawn. Gillian groaned and burrowed into the folds of her cloak.

He squatted at her side, peeling back the edge of her hood. "Wake up. We need to go." She tugged on the fabric, trying to cover her exposed face, but he'd have none of that. "Gillian, get up! Roman is coming."

Even in her semi-consciousness, the mention of his name was better than a bucket of water. She jolted upright, whacking her head against his. "Ouch." She massaged the sore spot and looked around bleak-eyed.

He'd let the fire go out during the night, leaving their tiny corner of the woods cold and damp. Rubbing her arms, she stomped around in a tight circle to get the blood flowing and clear her head. He stood to the side, a smile on his face that even the predawn light couldn't hide.

"What?" Gillian asked sourly. She was not a morning person.

"Just enjoying watching you circle the grounds like a chicken."

She shook her head and muttered. As if to punctuate her misery, her stomach gurgled with a particularly loud snarl. She'd eaten nothing since the bowl of soup Mary had brought the day before.

Glancing at Draven, she asked, "Do you have anything to eat?"

He fetched a stick that was leaning against the side of a rock and handed it to her. Skewered on one end were the roasted remains of an unrecognizable animal.

She tilted the stick to see it better. It looked like some type of rodent. A large rodent.

It's a rat, an inner voice said in disgust. *It's not a rat,* she argued, holding it closer to her face. But she admitted that it had the appearance of one.

"It's a rockhopper."

Gillian made a face and poked at it. "Is that like a... rodent... or something?"

He shrugged. "It's a type of hare."

A rabbit. She'd eaten rabbit stew since she was a babe.

Nodding, Gillian peeled off a piece of the meat and popped it in her mouth. It had a smoky flavor from the fire and was cold, having sat in the chill air, but it was good.

She offered some to Draven, but he declined, telling her he'd eaten when she'd slept. Gillian finished her meal and tossed the stick into the ashes of the fire. Wiping her greasy hands on her cloak, she thanked him and asked for a few minutes of privacy.

She took care of her needs and wove her way through the underbrush, stopping when she caught his expression as he looked west toward Valon.

"Are they close?" she asked, moving to his side. Gillian looked up, expecting to see Marius flying across the sky in search of her.

"Aye. It's just Roman. He'll reach us soon if we don't make good time."

Gillian followed his stare but saw nothing aside from thick clusters of trees. "What about your father?"

He got a faraway look. "He's not coming."

Draven's mouth pulled down, but he didn't add anything else. He reached for the tenor of his father's thoughts, but they were strangely dark, as though he was blocking Draven. There was no time to consider why.

Watching her escort, Gillian wondered why Marius wasn't

going after her and was on the cusp of asking before deciding it was a distinct advantage. If the Dragon wasn't going to hunt them down himself, she wasn't about to complain. They'd never outrun him. Roman, on the other hand...

"I'm ready to go."

He glanced at her and went to one knee.

She hesitated for a moment, uncomfortable with how intimate her position would be again, and clambered onto his back, curling her arms around his neck. With a last look toward Valon, Draven rose, wheeled around, and started running. The food she'd eaten jostled in her stomach as she bounced along, the queasiness amplifying her anxiety. Determined not to be sick all over Draven's back, she clenched her teeth and breathed deeply.

They were less than a mile from the Gealach Forest when Roman caught up to them. He appeared from the shadows of a dark copse of trees when they stopped for Gillian to stretch a painful kink in her back.

One moment, Draven was waiting impatiently; the next, he and Roman circled each other like feral dogs.

The scales along Draven's left side glowed an angry red. He looked dangerous, his lean body slightly hunched.

But it was Roman who was downright sinister. He needed no scales to warn others of the danger he posed. It was stamped on his face and in the way he slunk toward Draven, hands curled into claws.

Watching them face off against each other gave Gillian an

opportunity to flee. She gauged their attention, waiting for one of them to make the first move.

As expected, it was Roman. He launched himself at his brother, grabbing Draven's upper body and knocking him onto his back. The younger sibling snarled and swept his legs out, throwing Roman off balance. He sprang up and charged.

Two iron wills clashed. Bodies wrestled to the ground in a blur of movement and dust.

Gillian didn't wait to see the outcome. Ignoring the pang of guilt she felt abandoning Draven, she ran, ducking around trees and praying to the goddess she was headed the right way. Draven had indicated the general direction to the grove, but he'd been suspicious and deliberately vague.

The terrain changed subtly, rocks sprouting up amongst the pine-needle-littered slopes, catching her feet. She stumbled, falling hard and rolling into a narrow ravine. Her cloak snagged on a thorny bush, stopping her downward motion while tightening around her neck enough to choke.

Gasping, Gillian grabbed roots and rocks, pushing herself up and tugging at the laces of her cloak. Yanking, she tore the cloth free of the thorns and assessed the damage with angry mutters, pressing her hand to a tender bump on her head.

Rolling onto her knees, she used the blunt point of a sunken boulder to rise, her leg giving out when she put weight on it. She sat and hitched up her soiled dress to look at her ankle. Gingerly slipping off her leather shoe, she poked around the joint, wincing at the pain.

Great.

Her leg already sported an ugly burn from the gash Draven had sealed, and now she had to deal with a bad sprain. Grumbling, she yanked her dress down, whipping her head around at the sound of running feet.

She caught a flash of movement far above along the ridge of the ravine and flattened her body against the hill, holding her breath and pulling her hood tightly around her head to mask her scent.

It was impossible to tell whether it was Draven or Roman. Her ankle was swelling painfully, and if it were the latter, she'd be caught in moments, unable to run, much less walk. The footsteps receded, and she breathed a sigh of relief.

It was short-lived.

In minutes, she heard the sound of someone approaching again. Although this time, they were trying to muffle their steps and were coming from a different direction.

Gillian brushed pale strands of hair off her face and leaned out to see along the ridge when a twig snapped. Swinging her head around, she peered into the base of the ravine.

While not far from her resting place, it was shadowy, the ground hidden from view by juts of rock and thick clusters of trees. A prickle of fear raced down her spine as whoever or whatever it was drew closer.

She glanced around and grabbed a shard of rock. The tip was pointed and blunt, but she could wound and maybe disable using enough force.

Her heart raced as the memory of the vauger popped into her mind. And hadn't Roman mentioned some reptile called a rusk? Her hand tightened around the rock, and she started to wish it were Roman or Draven. At least they were a risk she knew and could face.

If it were a predator stalking her... She shook her head, refusing to entertain the dark images her mind conjured.

The sounds grew louder, though whatever was making them took pains to keep them quiet. She strained, eyes darting from shadow to shadow, heart thundering so loudly that blood swam in her ears, and she could no longer hear anything but the panic flooding her body.

The low branch of a pine shifted, and she zeroed in on the point, fingers gripping the shard of rock so hard it cut her skin. Expecting a monstrous creature to launch itself at her, she couldn't contain her yelp of surprise when a woman in layers of coarse, flowing skirts the color of wet leaves stepped from beneath the boughs and fixed her eyes on her.

Chapter Fourteen

The woman's hair was long and white with age, bound in a thick braid to her waist. Her face was lined with time, the shadows of her youth stamped into each crease and wrinkle.

Gray eyes penetrated Gillian, who sat frozen, a thin trail of blood running down her hand where it hung limply at her side, the rock in her fist forgotten.

Morrigan, the Coven of the Silver Moon's matriarch, watched her, a soft smile playing at the corners of her thin lips.

"Rowena," she whispered, the sound carrying on a breeze that began where she stood and traveled the distance between the two before dissipating.

Gillian's brow wrinkled. "I... I'm Gillian."

The high witch nodded and lifted her chin. "Aye, daughter, I know who you are."

"Are you a—" She paused, Roman's warning of a slit throat ringing in her head, and not knowing if calling the woman a witch was an insult.

The woman smiled knowingly. "Aye. I'm Morrigan, high witch of the Coven of the Silver Moon."

Morrigan scanned the top of the ravine before striding toward Gillian, who scooted back and raised her bloodied fist, ready to bludgeon.

"Fear not, child. The trees told us you'd come. I felt you in the wind and tracked you here to aid your escape from the Dragon."

Flicking her eyes to the rock in Gillian's fist, she muttered under her breath.

Gillian's hand grew warm, the broken skin knitting together. She looked down, dropping the rock smeared with blood, and turned her wrist to stare at the flesh of her palm where a small cut was little more than a pink line of healthy skin.

Her mouth dropped open, and she flexed her fingers, eyes going wide as she looked from her palm to the woman standing at her feet. "How did you—"

"I will answer all of your questions once we are safe within the embrace of the Gealach Forest. Come," Morrigan held out her arm.

"I can't walk." Gillian tugged the hem of her dress to reveal her swollen ankle.

Frowning, the high witch crouched and held her hands above the joint. "'Tis broken."

"Could you fix it like you did with my hand?"

"Aye, but bones take more time, and the Dragon's son is coming. We must leave now."

Reaching for Gillian's arm, she slung it over her thin shoulders and hauled her to her feet. Morrigan led them into the depths of the ravine, taking Gillian's weight with surprising ease. Once on level ground, the high witch picked up her pace, Gillian half-hopping to keep up.

Gillian watched as ancient trees shifted as they approached, their branches bending toward Morrigan as though they longed to embrace her. They creaked, leaves rustling. The low groan of branches and trunks moving of their own will met her ears as they ducked under the thick boughs.

"Are they alive?"

"Of course they're alive."

"No, I mean. Do they... think?"

It felt silly to suggest such a thing, but she couldn't ignore what she saw as oak, ash, and pine stroked the high witch when she passed with gentle touches of twig and branch or the strange language they appeared to speak in creaks and groans.

"What do you believe?" she asked with a sly smile.

Gillian took a hop-stumble, gripping the thick dark fabric of Morrigan's waist-length cloak. "I—I don't know."

"Dark is the wood, child. The Shadowlands hold many secrets."

She turned to the right, angling the pair toward a massive wall of ivy and moss-covered granite easily the height of ten men.

"To answer your question, yes. While different from us, they live and think. They sorrow and rage. The trees have long memories."

Gillian thought about that, her eyes jumping from tree to tree as they neared what appeared to be a dead end. She'd never thought of the forest as sentient. Not the way Morrigan described it.

Living, yes. Sentient? That was something at odds with what she knew.

The forest on the outskirts of Rudgarde had never been more than living and nonliving things. Ordinary things. But maybe she'd never looked at them the right way.

Morrigan stopped at the base of the giant slab of rock and lifted Gillian's arm from her shoulders.

Hopping to a fallen trunk, Gillian plunked herself down and watched the coven leader. The wind stirred, shifting the heavy folds of her skirts as the matriarch's arms extended outward, palms facing the granite face.

Tangles of ivy hanging like a leafy waterfall over the rock twitched. The woody stems writhed, twining around one another to pull to the right and left, revealing an opening roughly Morrigan's height but narrow and dark.

Hefting Gillian from her resting place, the high witch pushed her into the crevice, sealing the opening with a curtain of greenery as soon as she tucked her body between the slabs of rock at Gillian's side. Darkness fell over them, broken by pinpricks of light from sporadic openings along the top of the crevice.

Gillian gritted her teeth and moved sideways along the rock, hands trailing the damp, gritty surface coated in tiny rivulets of water. Her ankle throbbed with each step, but she kept going, Morrigan nudging her.

Aside from their breathing, it was silent. Even birdsong was shut out within the confines of the rock.

There came a point when Gillian could go no further. The passageway narrowed to mere inches in width, room enough for her arm to slip into but nothing more.

She stopped and turned toward Morrigan, whose eyes glowed like those of a cat at night. "I can't go any farther."

Morrigan gave a sly smile. "Oh?"

Gillian looked from the crevice to the high witch, wondering at the laughing expression on her face.

"Place your palms on the rock."

Forehead wrinkling, she did as she was told, then craned her neck when nothing happened.

The matriarch had her eyes closed, lips moving rapidly. Gillian tried to catch the words she muttered, but they were said too quickly and in a tongue she didn't recognize.

Her attention swung back to either side of the crevice where her palms lay pressed to the rock. Subtle vibrations radiated through the granite, growing stronger until the rock shook so forcefully that her arms buckled. She twisted her body and locked her elbows, keeping her hands fixed on the gritty surface, jaw falling open as the two slabs of granite shuddered and drew apart.

Her arms dropped to her sides, and she stood dumbfounded as light poured in from the opening. She squinted and leaned into the newly widened gap, seeing a meadow of tall grasses touched by the midday sun.

As though pulled like a puppet on a string, Gillian stumbled forward, her eyes never leaving the scene unfolding before her as the roar of a Dragonborn male echoed beyond the border of the coven's land. She paused for a moment, thoughts of Draven pulling at her, then fell to her knees as she scrambled out of the gap in the rock, hands digging into a thick layer of grass sprinkled with meadow flowers. Her leg throbbed, but she shut out the pain.

She'd made it. She was safe.

As soon as the thought took shape, eleven women of varying ages appeared along the perimeter, creating a loose circle.

Morrigan entered the tiny glade, the last piece of the circle.

Gillian looked at every face, seeing welcome in smiles and misty eyes. The women linked hands, and as their fingers interlocked, palpable energy surged through the glade. Tiny hairs on Gillian's arms stood on end as prickles of awareness raced up her spine to wrap around her skull.

She'd found the Coven of the Silver Moon. Or, rather, they had found her.

Every pair of eyes, in faces that ranged from her mother's age to the ripeness of the coven's matriarch, fixed on Gillian. As one, their voices rose in the gentle cadence of a chant that was as familiar as it was foreign.

It reminded her of a cradle song. One she knew at once yet had never heard. It made no sense.

Yet, within every syllable was power. A power she felt tickling at her senses and crawling around her mind. Gillian sat and stretched out her injured leg, too overwhelmed to do anything but watch and listen. Feel and absorb.

It felt like home.

Chapter Fifteen

The witches of the Coven of the Silver Moon surrounded Gillian. Weathered hands lifted her, taking her weight while others touched her face and stroked her hair, exchanging happy whispers of welcome.

They didn't draw an Ashrune dagger and slit her throat as Roman had assured her they would. There was no vauger den.

She was led to where they staked her body for the animal to feed on.

Instead, they greeted her as though she were a lost sister who'd finally come home. She didn't know what to make of it.

They introduced themselves, jostling each other to grasp a hand or pat a shoulder. Gillian tried to focus on names and faces, but they blurred together.

Morrigan shooed the women aside and took Gillian's face in her hands. "You have your mother's eyes."

Gillian blinked.

The high witch's mouth quirked. "You think me confused."

"I—" she scanned the faces watching her. "I don't know

what to think. She never spoke of you except to say you had magic that could help us. When did Naeve come here?"

Morrigan shook her head. "She didn't."

Gillian waited a few moments for her to say more, but the high witch just studied her in silence. "Rory, my brother, is gravely ill," she blurted. "It's the Wasting."

Expressions ranging from pity to resignation danced upon the faces of the coven.

Morrigan nodded slowly. "Aye, it's touched us all. Even those born of the Great Dragon."

One of the witches hissed and folded her arms over her chest. Gillian tried to recall her name. "His kind deserves no better," the woman bit out.

"Olwyn." Morrigan gave her a pointed look. "That is not for us to decide."

The witch harrumphed, her pinched face pulling into a frown beneath a riotous cap of hair the color of carrots. "What did he think would happen when he turned his back on Keridwen?"

"Even the best of us may choose wrongly," Morrigan said, waving a hand when Olwyn opened her mouth to say more. "The Great Dragon had his reasons, though he was too blinded by grief to see the error of them. But enough of this. Come."

She motioned to one of the coven, a burly middle-aged woman with a soft face who whispered her name in Gillian's ear when she took the girl's weight.

The high witch noted the fatigue pulling down the corners of Gillian's mouth. "You are weary and full of questions best asked with a full belly and a comfortable resting place."

Morrigan led the way out of the grove, the rest of the coven falling behind Gillian and her escort, Edith.

As before, the trees stretched their woody branches toward the matriarch. She smiled and stroked their leaves, speaking softly as though they were old friends. Birds and small animals ceased their chatter and scurried to watch with beady eyes as the coven passed.

Within a ring of oak trees sat a smattering of structures.

Overgrown with moss and time, they looked like they'd grown from the forest floor. A long oval hut with a thatched roof sprouting flowers and tall grasses dominated the miniature hamlet. It looked like it had grown up out of the ground, its walls covered with lichen and leafy vines. Gillian's eyes fixed on it for a moment, then moved to the smaller huts and lean-tos, a chicken coop, a central fire, and a large garden overflowing with ripening fruits and vegetables.

Edith indicated the oval shelter and helped Gillian inside. It was dim and smelled of sage and smoke from the hearth at one end. Neatly arranged along the walls were rows of raised pallets, some in disarray and others neatly tended with blankets draping over the edges.

There were thirteen beds and twelve witches, including the matriarch of the coven, though it was impossible to pick out her bed amongst the others.

Gillian was taken to a pallet near the hearth. There was a sprig of dried poppy flowers, their petals deep red and brittle.

Remembrance.

Mother had told her that, meaning when she'd buried her sixth stillborn child at the foot of a birch tree—the same tree whose roots intertwined with each of the babes who'd never drawn breath.

Gillian leaned forward as Edith unhooked her arm and traced her fingers along the edge of one of the petals, frowning when it crumbled.

Olwyn knelt at Gillian's feet, gently probing her ankle, and slipped off her shoe. Pushing the woolen fabric of her dress farther up her leg, the witch paused and glanced at Gillian. "What's this?"

Leaning forward, she followed Olwyn's eyes and saw the ugly burn. Sighing, she said, "I cut it on a jagged piece of wood, and Draven sealed it with a burn."

The witch frowned and shook her head. "Dragonborn know nothing of healing."

Waving her hand over the puckered flesh, she whispered, her brow wrinkling in concentration. The wound tingled and grew warm. Sensations like worms burrowing under her skin grew in intensity, and Gillian clutched her knee, ready to whip her limb away.

Olwyn placed a firm hand on her leg and continued, her other hand hovering an inch above her skin.

Eyes wide, Gillian watched her skin stretch and constrict, knitting itself together. In moments, the wound was a patch of new skin, pink and healthy.

Olwyn winked at Gillian's gasp of surprise and wonder. "That was the easy one. There's a small break in your foot that needs mending. The tears in the ankle caused the swelling."

"Do what you can, Olwyn," Morrigan said, handing her a cup of tea. It was pungent, and Gillian wrinkled her nose. "Drink. It will ease the swelling."

She made a face and took a sip, tasting licorice root and black pepper. Morrigan watched her down the awful brew and took the clay mug when she refused to chew on the dregs.

Leaning back onto the pallet, Gillian let Olwyn swing her legs over and watched through slitted eyes as the witch rubbed an ointment on her ankle and foot, rough fingers kneading her flesh to the point of pain.

The witch flashed her eyes at Gillian every so often as though watching for something before fixing her attention on the rhythmic movements of her hands.

Gillian's eyes drooped, and she shifted her elbows to prop herself up. But they slid out from under her in moments. Her eyelids fluttered and closed, refusing to open no matter how hard she tried.

A last thought drifted through her mind. *What was in that tea?*

The crackle of fire woke her.

It was dark, save for the light of the flames dancing across the wooden beams of the ceiling. Her ankle ached dully, and she pushed aside a heavy quilt to peer down at it. Strips of linen tied in a small knot bound the joint. She flexed her foot, grimacing at the stab of pain the movement caused. Scooting into a sitting position, she scanned the room.

Every pallet held a small mound buried under blankets and sheets. Soft snores filled the room, mixing with the gentle crackling of the fire in the hearth.

"Unable to sleep?" Morrigan asked from the raised pallet across from hers.

Gillian started and gripped the bedding. She shook her head, wondering how long the woman had been watching her.

The high witch peeled back her covers and shuffled to the hearth, her bare feet scuffing the ground. She poked the fire and tossed another log onto the flames. Fire reached upward as she coaxed it with whispers. Grabbing a knitted shawl from a peg, Morrigan wrapped it around her shoulders and sat on the bed next to Gillian.

"You have questions," she said quietly.

"Many."

Morrigan folded her hands in her lap. "Let us start with your arrival. The forest told me of your coming. I heard it in the trees, from the voles and rabbits. In a hawk's wings beating against the air. Your arrival was celebrated even as it brought fear to those of us who knew the risks."

"Risks?"

"Aye. You have only just escaped the most pressing one."

The Great Dragon.

Gillian glanced at the fire and watched the flames licking the wood. Roman told her he'd felt her presence when she'd crossed the border. If the coven knew the dangers he posed, why hadn't they intercepted her before she was captured?

"Ah. A good question."

Gillian's eyes narrowed.

Morrigan gave a sly smile. "I can see your thoughts plain enough. No need for dark spells to pluck them from you."

Licking her lips, Gillian asked quietly. "Why didn't you stop him?"

Morrigan breathed deeply. "We couldn't risk venturing so far from our sanctuary. You see, we, too, are hunted by the Dragon. But he cannot pass into our realm. Our wards were forged by the goddess."

"I don't understand any of this." She picked at a loose thread in the quilt. "And I don't know that any of it matters."

Gillian looked at Morrigan. "I need to save my brother, Rory. That's why I crossed into the Shadowlands. The Wasting is taking him, and I don't know how much longer he has. The other children—" She swallowed through a blur of tears. "They didn't last more than six months. I can't stay here. I told Roman, but... he didn't care."

Her throat bobbed. "I've been here too long already. I need to get back to Rory with something that'll stop the disease before it kills him."

Morrigan looked at her. There was pity in her eyes, but no offer to aid her sibling.

"Will you help me?"

"Help you how?"

"With a cure. You have magic. Can't you use it to... to stop it before it kills him?"

Her brow arched. "Keridwen, the goddess of the moon and keeper of the cauldron, blessed us with power. Magic runs in our blood, but even that gift has limits."

Gillian's heart sank. She'd come all this way. Been through so much.

She shook her head. "No. You can help him. Mother believed you could."

"Your mother?" Morrigan shook her head. "Ah, child, the

woman who raised you is not your blood." Gillian's brow wrinkled. "Your mother was Rowena—a powerful witch."

"You have me confused with someone else," Gillian told her.

"Believe that if you will. It changes nothing."

Morrigan rose and went to a small chest in the corner of the room. She rifled through it and returned moments later with a small painting the size of her palm.

"This is your mother. Your father painted it when they were courting."

Gillian cradled the image in her hands, tilting it to catch the firelight. It was her face—hair so blond it was nearly white and stormy gray eyes. She glanced at the high witch. Morrigan had the same eyes.

"Are you...?"

She looked back at the portrait and then at the matriarch again.

"The blood of the first witch runs in my veins as it does through each of us." Her eyes swept the room. "Your mother's mother left us many years before your birth."

She handed back the portrait. "I admit the likeness is striking, but I would know if Naeve wasn't my mother. She would've told me."

"Would she?" Morrigan set the image on her lap. Her face tilted to study it. "Perhaps Naeve sought to protect you by shielding you from the truth of your parentage."

"She wouldn't lie to me." Gillian crossed her arms, trapping the emotions raging through her inside her body before they spilled out.

Hardening her face, she said quietly, "I need your help. That's what I came to ask for. Either you will or you won't."

The high witch took a deep breath, letting it out slowly. "I would help your brother if my skill allowed."

"What do you mean by that?"

Gillian's hands twisted, and her heart thundered at the meaning within her words.

"The Wasting is not a disease. It was not born of a sickness that travels from man to man."

Crackles and pops from the fire punctuated each word, the jarring sounds in the quiet room like death knells.

"The origins of the Wasting are tied to the goddess. And the Great Dragon."

Chapter Sixteen

Morrigan faced Gillian, tucking her leg onto the bed while the other dangled, toes brushing the floor.

"Dragons are the bringers of life. They forged the first roads between worlds that others followed. Long before the Great Upheaval, Marius ruled our world alongside his mate, Ashael. Many traveled their roads. Others built roads of their own. Life flourished. But not all who found their way here sought peace. One yearned for power."

Gillian leaned back, bunching the thin pillow behind her. She would hear what Morrigan had to say, and maybe within the tale, she'd find a way to help her brother.

If not, she'd return to Rudgarde and stay at Rory's side until he breathed his last.

"His name was burned from memory. But what we know is that he was a powerful mage who sought to usurp Dragon rule. He bred with women, and from those unions came the first witches—though he shunned his progeny.

"Their magic did not reflect the darkness of his own. We looked to the moon. To Keridwen, who bathed us in the light of her pale face. Who gifted us with earth magic."

She opened her hand and stared at her palm, at the crescent line in her skin. "It was then that the mage turned away from us fully. But his power still runs in our veins." Curling her fingers, she rested her hand in her lap.

"Marius and Ashael were blind to the mage's lust for power. The wizard infiltrated Valon, destroying a clutch of unhatched Dragonlings, thinking to end the age of Dragons. Marius' vengeance was swift and brutal. There was nothing left of the mage when his wrath was spent.

"The Dragon sought to kill our kind then. To rid his world of every trace of the mage. But he spared the coven at the behest of his mate, who saw that we did not embody our creator's malignant nature.

"For many years, there was peace. The world of men grew and spread while the Dragon's lands remained untouched by time.

"Some witches ventured into the greater world when it suited them, most returning here to our ancestral land. Dragonlings were born and raised, leaving this world when they reached maturity to find mates of their own. Mankind bred.

"They forgot the old ways. Soon, they outnumbered every creature within the Dragon's realm a hundredfold."

She paused and stared at the fire. Its light flickered across her face, smoothing her wrinkles and making Morrigan look young.

Her mouth turned down as she continued. "Men are a

fickle species. Susceptible to corruption. Marius should have foreseen what would come, but he was blind to it.

"They strayed from the old ways. They waged war against settlements within his realm, sending armies and slaughtering everyone. Marius and Ashael unleashed their fire on them, but they kept coming.

"A never-ending wave with war machines, no creature of the wild had ever dreamt of. And they had iron. Iron spears and iron tubes that spit fire from great distances. During the last days of the battle, Ashael was shot from the sky."

Morrigan's voice trailed off, the image she conjured playing in Gillian's mind. She could see it. The blue-winged Dragon battling an army stretching hundreds of miles. Her wings beating against the sky, scarlet with blood, as she plummeted to the earth.

"When Ashael lay dying, her body broken on the rocks, Cyrena, the high witch, found her. She tried to heal her, but the damage was too great. Ashael heard the ferryman calling her. The river is not wide, and she would travel across it.

"Before she passed into the other world, she bade Cyrena drink her blood. To take in her power and fight alongside her mate.

"She did. Then cut her flesh and bade her sisters drink from her body—her blood mixed with Dragon. The Dragon's power enhanced ours. The witches wielded their strength, harnessing the elements with deadly force to fight the armies of men along-side Marius. And they won.

"But the cost was great. Ashael's blood now ran through our veins, dooming us."

Olwyn stirred and rolled over, her face barely visible

beneath her covers. "Ashael should've known what grief her gift would bring."

Morrigan craned her neck to look at the witch. "How could she? Even if she had known, would she have made a different choice?"

Another voice piped up in the darkness. "Dragon blood or no, Marius chose to do what he did."

Nodding, Morrigan said, "Would you have chosen differently?"

Flipping onto her back with a huff, Olwyn muttered, "You defend him when it's our sisters who've suffered."

"I do not defend his actions. But I understand them." Gillian's forehead wrinkled, and Morrigan patted her hand. "Our power springs from the earth. From all living things. We are tied to it, just as the Great Dragon is.

"Ashael knew this when she gifted Cyrena her blood. What she didn't know was that her gift would mean our downfall. Without a mate, there would be no more Dragon young. Marius faced eternity alone. No mate. No Dragonlings. Nothing but the world he'd created. One that became his prison. I understand his grief... and the awful choice he made in the face of it."

Morrigan rose and tossed another log on the fire.

She held her hands toward the flames and spoke in a low voice. "Memories are passed down from high witch to high witch. I am the bearer of our history, just as my successor will be when I am gone.

"To understand Marius' actions and your place in this, you must know what happened. Irylle and Keridwen gave Marius and his mate unmatched strength and power. In battle, their

Dragon fire, a gift from the fire god, slew thousands. Even after Ashael's death, Irylle's hand turned the tide of the uprising."

The high witch was silent for a few moments, watching the fire crackle and pop.

"When Ashael was wounded, Marius begged Keridwen to use her healing power and save his mate. But the goddess did not stop her death. Her power didn't bring Ashael back. No power could've saved her.

"In Marius's mind, the goddess turned her back on Ashael and left his mate to die.

"The Great Dragon blamed the goddess for her death and took terrible vengeance—renouncing Keridwen, shunning her light while he nursed his resentment and anger.

"His betrayal wounded our goddess in ways no one could've foreseen. From that weakness was born a plague. The Wasting took hold, slowly spreading across the world, fed by the anger and blame mankind laid at the goddess's feet. Keridwen, abandoned by the Dragon and mankind, grew resentful and allowed the festering disease to grow until it became a monster no one and nothing could contain."

"So, you're saying—" Gillian hunched forward, "Keridwen created the Wasting that's killing my brother?"

Morrigan's lips thinned. "That is what I believe, but I don't know if it was born of her or the Dragon. I do know the Great Mother did nothing to stop it."

Her eyes hardened as she thought about what the witch said.

Morrigan lifted her thoughts from her mind. "Do not judge the goddess too harshly. Like the rest of us, she is fallible. Besides, one does not anger the gods and escape retribution."

Gillian muttered and crossed her arms. "I thought they were here to protect us. Not kill us off."

"Whatever made you believe that, child?"

She shrugged.

"That is human thinking. And perhaps that is why she took such vengeance when mankind turned its back on her."

The high witch sighed. "The Wasting took hold, and, all the while, Marius' anguish stained this realm. Touching every corner of it. And, so, the Shadowlands were born.

"Darkness warped creatures living within its boundaries, giving rise to nightmarish beings like myrax, rusk, and vauger. The trees grew thick, blocking out the light. It became a forbidden realm. Dark. Dangerous. A land men feared. Thus, they did not venture here. Stories fell from their tongues of the dangers of the dark wood.

"It was those tales that separated the two worlds like a barrier. Intangible. Crossed only by those who wished for death. Fear created it and holds it still.

"In lonely desperation, Marius took on the form of a human, crossed the border, and went among them. He was determined to continue his line, to once again fill his empty halls with young, though they'd be half-breeds. He used his gifts of persuasion and coaxed women to his bed.

"But humans cannot quicken with Dragon seed. Those with whom he tried remained motherless. Many chose to remain in Valon, and he allowed it.

"Eventually, he brought men among them, and as years passed, they raised families of their own while tending the land, spreading out and forming other settlements in the Shadowlands. You've seen some of their descendants in Valon.

"In time, he built a castle in the fashion of those of your homeland and became its lord. But the life that surrounded him was not enough, and Marius fixed his gaze on the Coven of the Silver Moon."

She shuffled back to Gillian's pallet.

Olwyn sat up with a grumble and draped her quilt over her shoulders. "We were cursed," she spat, eyes flashing. "That's what Ashael did when Cyrena drank from her, when the witch then shared her tainted blood with her sisters, dooming us all."

The high witch emitted a long breath. "It was a blessing and a curse. We birth but one daughter in our lifetimes. And that comes of a union with a man. It is how our line lives on. When we hear the song in our blood and the fever comes upon us, we venture to the realms of men and find a mate. The daughter of that union ensures our survival. That is how it's always been.

"But when we drew Marius' eye, our fate was sealed. What became of us was unnatural. The first witch, Sorya, who succumbed to Marius, loved him in his human form. Nothing could come of such a union without love. Her womb quickened, and she birthed a son. Dragonborn. Half-breed. Aberration.

"We were both human and mage before we drank Ashael's blood. Now, we are also Dragon. Together, it is a potent mix. And while we can never bear a true Dragon, with his seed, we can ensure his line.

"Word spread among the coven and, with it, fear. Sorya lived at his side for many years. During that time, she gave birth to two Dragonborn offspring—both male.

"Though my sisters would disagree, I believe Marius loved her in his way. But our lives are short to an immortal, and with him, she lived beyond the touch of Keridwen, beyond the goddess's ability to sustain her to a full life. She eventually died.

"When Marius approached the coven for another wife, the high witch refused. His anger was swift."

Gillian knew an ugly history was coming. She shifted her gaze and stared at the flames as Morrigan continued.

"Witches fell under his eye. Suffused with the Dragon's power until they fell in love with him—unnatural though it was.

"They became mates, breeding stock until the magic in their blood grew cold. Some witches escaped into Mirynn and went into hiding. Their descendants live there still. The magic within our blood is thinning over the years.

"Others remained in the Shadowlands. They prayed to Keridwen, begging the goddess to protect them. She looked on them with fondness. They became her chosen, and she answered their prayers, gifting them with magic to fortify Gealach Forest with powerful wards the Great Dragon wouldn't breach, though it weakened her to do it.

"From that point on, leaving the safety of our sacred realm meant risking surrender to the Dragon's power. But his allure is strong.

"You know this, having heard of Draven's mother, Maud. The young witch left the safety of our realm of her own accord and never returned."

Morrigan looked away, lost in memories. "Marius was not always callous, seeing witches as vessels. Something changed in him over the years. Turning away from Keridwen made him cold and calculating."

"What of Rowena?" Gillian asked.

She couldn't call the witch Mother. Naeve was her mother. She was the woman who'd raised her like a child of her own flesh and blood.

The high witch dipped her head. "With Keridwen's blessings, we live many lifetimes when counted by mankind. Not immortal but long-lived.

"Your mother, Rowena, was the youngest of our coven, brought to Gealach Forest by your grandmother to live with Keridwen's chosen. She left her daughter with us and chose to return to the man she loved.

"We kept Rowena hidden as she grew to womanhood and masked her scent when the Dragon flew near. She was safe. But the fever came upon her, as I knew it would.

"She defied my warning and crossed into your homeland, where she eventually met your father, Finn Ddraig."

Morrigan looked away as though she could see into the past. "I believe he loved her. He must have.

"We heard nothing of her for two summers. Then, she returned to the safety of Gealach Forest after she quickened to bathe under a full moon in Keridwen's in the sacred Darach Grove, praying to the goddess to bless her unborn daughter.

"I begged her to remain with us. To raise her child within the safety of our realm. But she loved her man and would not be parted from him. Sometime after returning to Rudgarde, she had a vision."

The matriarch turned to Gillian and pinned her to the pallet with her stare. "For those of us with sight, visions are a blessing and a curse. My gift allowed me to see the choice she made and understand why.

"Rowena had a vision of you, as you are now, enslaved by the Great Dragon. Out of love, she left you with your father.

"When she crossed back into the Shadowlands, she prayed to Keridwen—begging the goddess to protect her daughter. To protect her true disciples by preventing the Dragon who'd forsaken Keridwen from crossing into the kingdom of men.

"But the goddess was not as powerful as she once was. Marius reviled her, cursing her when Maud took her life, killing the child in her womb, and his people followed his example.

"Beyond the Shadowlands, mankind had turned its back on a goddess who stood aside and let the Wasting eat away at the people of the kingdom."

Morrigan's voice grew husky. "Keridwen was weak and bitter. In desperation, your mother sacrificed herself."

Gillian gasped.

Flicking her eyes at her, the high witch patted her hand. "She loved you."

Her eyes welled as she imagined the woman who'd brought her into the world facing such a terrible choice. Only a mother's love could've wrought such a desperate act.

"Using old magic, she returned the power Keridwen had blessed her with. The goddess accepted the offering, seeing it as a way of punishing Marius for abandoning her, and forged a barrier the Dragon could never breach. Rowena gave her lifeblood to keep you safe.

"And for eighteen years, the Dragon has remained absent from mankind's realm. His shadow hasn't passed over a town or city. Perhaps they think he is dead."

She shook her head and stood up, walking slowly to the fire. Morrigan stared at the flames for a few moments.

"There is no mate of childbearing age within this realm. Those who could usher in a new generation are beyond the barrier separating our worlds."

Turning toward Gillian, she said quietly, "That is why you were safe from him. Rowena died to keep you from Marius.

"And now you've come. He will not let you go. As long as you remain in the Shadowlands, he will hunt you."

Chapter Seventeen

Roman prowled the border of Gealach Forest beneath the light of a full moon.

It was heavily warded with old magic, and he couldn't cross it, though he'd spent the last light of the day looking for areas of weakness.

A short distance away, Draven followed, the hairline fractures in his ribs from their brawl knitting together, though he still favored one side and traveled slowly.

Touching the slash marks on his face, little more than strips of pink flesh, Roman frowned. He and Draven had never fought before. Not like that. Not as though they meant to kill.

And he could have. He'd had his brother pinned on the ground, the deadly tips of his claws inches from his throat.

Instead, he'd bludgeoned him into unconsciousness only to find Gillian missing. His roar echoed through the forest, silencing birds and mammals.

Even the Myrax had ceased its braying.

By the time he caught her scent, it was too late. The Coven had her.

It took hours for the flames in his eyes to cool. For the black claws protruding from his fingers to slip back under his skin.

Tilting his head back, Roman curled his hands into fists and called to his father, feeling the Dragon's ancient mind tap at him with sickening power. He felt the moment Marius burst from his human shell and shifted into his true form.

The Shadowlands shuddered as the Great Dragon erupted from the mountain, red wings beating like thunder.

Dark clouds eclipsed the stars and moon, blanketing the landscape in total blackness. Everything went still.

The Great Dragon passed over land that shrank from him, trees bending, their limbs twining together in terror. Leathery, blood-red wings stirred the air as he passed. Their wind snapped brittle branches.

It flattened grasses and sent every living thing scurrying from his path.

Marius dove toward the earth, releasing the clouds that had swallowed the paleness of the night. The tip of his tail sliced through the tops of trees as he fixed his blazing copper eyes on his son.

Roman stood rigid and watched his father come.

Oak and ash bent as he angled his wings and body, rear legs extended toward the earth. The ground shook when he landed on the bare peak of the hill above where Roman waited.

The black claws protruding from the Great Dragon's forelegs gouged the earth, scoring the rock in deep gashes as he swung his massive head toward his son.

Roman felt the heat of his father's breath wash over his

body and imagined Marius spitting fire and burning him to ash where he stood.

"You failed me," the Great Dragon hissed, eyes smoldering like the hot coals of a fire.

"Forgive me, Father."

Roman went to one knee and bowed his head. The tap of a claw on rock sent vibrations racing down the hill, where they traveled into his body as he knelt in deference.

Marius huffed, smoke curling in the air around his snout. "Where is your brother?"

Roman clenched his hands into fists. He would not give up Draven if it meant his brother's death. "I left him unconscious."

A low rumble met the lie, but Marius didn't challenge him.

Lifting his head, the Dragon scanned the landscape, picking out his wayward son where he hid beneath an outcropping of rock. Eyes narrowing to slits, he lowered his scaled neck and stabbed at Draven's mind.

His awful power sent his son sprawling, hands clutching his skull to keep it from splitting open as the Great Dragon let him taste his rage.

Just a sip.

Should he let him feel all of it, it would kill him. And that would be no less than the boy deserved for his treason, but he was a merciful lord.

"Father!" Draven screamed, the sound slicing through the forest.

Fire played along the edges of his snout. "Feel the cost of betrayal."

Roman gritted his teeth as Draven's screams drifted on the wind.

But he didn't rise. He didn't come to his brother's aid. He knew his place.

Moments that felt like hours passed until Marius finally released his hold. Draven collapsed.

"Forgive," he whispered, face tight with pain.

"Do not return to Valon until you can prove your worth."

The command was laced with power that made Draven cringe.

With a dull growl, Marius turned away from Draven, ignoring the whimper that escaped his son's lips when he flopped onto his back, mind blank and eyes staring blindly.

He swung his head toward Roman.

He was not the eldest of his offspring. But he was the strongest. Though his body didn't bear the overt stamp of his parentage like many of his siblings, it was Roman whose blood was most like his, though he had yet to understand the depth of that power.

For this son to be thwarted by the young witch was... disappointing.

The Dragon was not powerless, even when his quarry was beyond his reach. He'd known there was a possibility Gillian could find her way to the coven before he claimed her and had taken precautions.

"You will return her to me," Marius commanded, the words coiling in Roman's mind where they took root and bloomed.

"Yes."

"I will flush them out like rats from a sinking ship. When the wards fall, take her."

Marius flashed his eyes to Draven, who was stirring. "Kill any who stand against you."

"It will be done," Roman said, his voice pitched low to mask his roiling emotions.

The Great Dragon extended his wings, the breadth of ten men from tip to tip. He launched into the sky with a roar that shook the earth.

Roman watched him circle the coven's land.

The red scales lining his serpentine body glinted in the moonlight as he banked hard and dove toward the earth.

Filling his lungs, Marius released a river of fiery breath. Flames smashed against the wards protecting the coven's land. A sea of molten heat curved around the barrier, forming a dome.

The Great Dragon's wings beat in the night air, his passing a dull thunder as he positioned himself to expel another firestorm.

Roman's eyes glowed as they reflected the awful heat radiating from his father's attack.

Trees within the borders of Gealach Forest squealed with eerie wails that radiated up Roman's spine. Animals poured out of the coven's ancestral grounds, streaming through the underbrush or flying through the air beneath the swelling flames.

He flinched as a hawk misjudged the molten heat encapsulating the barrier protecting the coven's land. It plummeted to the ground in a burning mass of feathers.

Marius swooped low and roared Gillian's name, punctuating each syllable with powerful commands to come to him.

Roman's head ached as his father's voice rang out over and over, each bellow followed by spitting fire.

The sky glowed orange, turning night to day.

It won't be long until the wards fall, Roman thought grimly, his mouth pulling down as a deer whose back was aflame streaked past him, bleating in panic.

It had only been moments since Marius began his assault, but it felt like hours. Time slowed as he watched his father circle and dive, unleashing his wrath.

The Great Dragon hung in the air above the Gealach Forest, wings beating slowly to fan the inferno.

Magical wards, created by Keridwen herself, strained against the onslaught, forming a glowing dome of protection as the goddess' magic fought Marius' fiery power.

Flames raced along the barrier shielding the coven's lands, burning themselves out as they followed the curves to the forest floor.

Another wave of fire shot from the Dragon's snout.

He bent his long neck, copper eyes scanning the chaos unfolding within the coven's borders, searching for witches. Searching for Gillian.

Chapter Eighteen

Gillian awakened with a scream lodged in her throat.

She sat up, her heart thrumming and sweat filming her body as the Dragon's powerful voice rang in her ears.

A sound, like rolling thunder, filled the quiet outside. "What is that?"

Morrigan tossed back her blanket and rose, cocking her head to listen. Her gray eyes narrowed, lips mashing into a thin line. "I thought we'd have more time."

The young witch went to her side. She followed the matriarch's stare, seeing nothing but the wattle and daub wall.

"He's coming," she said, facing Gillian, "for you."

A ferocious blast of wind raced across the landscape, bringing the Dragon's roar with it.

Witches leaped from their beds, flinging quilts aside and stuffing feet into worn leather shoes. They gathered around the matriarch of the coven in a silent ring.

Morrigan turned to them, studying each face. "We knew this day would come."

They nodded in unison.

"The Great Dragon has longed to breach our protections and take us prisoner. He will fail. Use your magic to sustain the goddess. Show her she does not stand alone."

"Yes, Mother," they replied, using the term as one of respect.

"Go, now. Fight with Keridwen."

As one, they left in a calm stream of bodies, each of them drilling down into the core of their power as they passed into the night.

Through the open doorway, the sky lit orange, casting the ground within the tiny village in fiery light.

Gillian walked stiltedly toward it, her eyes fixed on flashes of light the color of the setting sun. When she came to the threshold, heat blasted her face, and she stepped back with a yelp, slamming the wooden door. She pressed her back to the planks. Feeble planks that would burn within Dragon fire.

"We can't stay here," Gillian whispered, flinching as a roar shook the walls.

Morrigan walked toward her. Unhurried and calm.

"He cannot breach our defenses. Keridwen stands with us. Marius knows this. He seeks to instill fear and flush us out."

She cupped Gillian's cheek. "Watch and learn. One day, you will take your place among us."

The high witch slipped out the door and into the blood-red night.

Gillian took a few halting steps toward the opening, her gaze fixed on the coven's matriarch.

Morrigan spun in a slow circle, arms outstretched, lips moving rapidly. White light sprang from the ground in a ring, growing brighter and larger with each sweep of her hands. Planting her feet on the earth, she thrust her arms toward the sky, opening herself to the goddess.

They were one, Keridwen's power taking in Morrigan's and twining them together like the threads of a tapestry.

The circle of light blasted into the air, sinking into an invisible barrier high above and then spreading in every direction. Dragon fire and the witch's protective light collided in swirls of color, heat, and power.

Gillian stumbled outside, every fiber of her being fixed on the high witch who shouted into the sky, her words clashing with Marius' roaring.

It was deafening.

Clutching her ears, she careened toward the matriarch, falling to her knees when the Great Dragon spat a river of molten fire through the sky directly above. Gillian's teeth ground together hard enough to crack a molar. Her jaw ached as she clenched her eyes, fingers digging into the soft flesh around her skull.

Marius made another pass, wings fanning the flames, and bellowed Gillian's name. The sound lanced her mind, fracturing it as she knelt on the ground, keening.

The Great Dragon roared her name again as if he could feel her will shattering.

Blood caked the underside of her fingernails, where they dug into her skull as she tried to dig the Dragon's slick will from her mind.

Gillian screamed until her throat was raw. Until there was

nothing left but breathy whispers. She felt her body thrown to the side, slamming into the hard-packed dirt.

Still, her fingers curled, dug, scratched. Trying to dig him out.

Her heart raced in time with the roaring that filled the world. Her skin grew hot, blistering, as the white light streaming from Morrigan's outstretched arms buckled.

The high witch braced her legs and dug deeper into her well of magic, feeding it to the goddess as Keridwen flinched under the assault.

But the Dragon was too strong. Magical wards cracked.

Realization dawned, bright and ugly.

Morrigan turned to Gillian, who was curled on the ground.

"No," she whispered.

Tapping at Gillian's mind, the high witch found a psychic seed planted by the Dragon. It was a kernel of malignant power buried deep in Gillian's mind.

Morrigan's body trembled, sweat beading her forehead, cheeks, and neck. Her stark-white hair hung in clumps around her haggard face.

She watched Gillian writhing on the ground.

Unwittingly, she'd let the Dragon in, and Marius had done his work well. The seed he'd tucked into Gillian's mind was not meant for the young witch.

It was like a parasite, and she, the host. It was meant to be carried into the coven's land, its taint infecting the wards protecting the border as its host crossed them—a border created and strengthened by Keridwen.

Morrigan called to the goddess, receiving a muffled reply as though Keridwen were reaching through layers of rock that sought to smother her.

Through Gillian, the Dragon attacked the goddess, using her inherent link with Keridwen to destroy the wards keeping them safe. His ancient will slipped inside and corrupted the coven's power from within.

They were all linked—each of them to the other.

As Gillian and Keridwen succumbed under the Dragon's attack, so did they all. And there was nothing Morrigan could do to stop it.

In the distance, the high witch heard a faint scream. It floated on the hot wind.

"Gillian!" Morrigan shouted. "Gillian! Fight back. Don't let his power consume you! Get up, Gillian! Fight!"

If she heard the matriarch above the thunderous roaring of the Dragon, she gave no sign of it.

Gillian was lost to the assault Marius waged on her mind.

Using the psychic seed, he laid her bare, ripping into her mind, and, with that connection, exploited it. Like the roots of a tree, his dark will traveled along mental lines connecting each witch.

Marius stifled their power, draining it with tiny sips. The goddess struggled to fight him, even calling on her mate, Irylle, but she was too weak, and the god too drunk on power to save her.

The wards protecting the Gealach Forest crumbled, swallowing the Dragon fire encompassing their ancestral land as they dissipated.

The high witch of the Coven of the Silver Moon dropped

her arms in defeat. The screams of her sisters punched through the air as their homeland was exposed to the Dragon's wrath.

Witches raced through the heat and ash, gathering around the matriarch who stood her ground and faced the Great Dragon.

"Let her go!" she shouted, watching Marius soar in the sky, then hover like a hummingbird above the thirteen women.

Morrigan separated herself from her sisters. "Let her go before you kill her."

Leathery wings beat slowly, tail lashing, as the Great Dragon stared into the face of the high witch. "Long have you hidden from my rule, Morrigan. Behold, your sovereign.

"Kneel, and I will spare you and your sisters."

The high witch's hands balled into fists.

Olwyn stepped to her side. Her mouth thinned in a hardened line. "Don't kneel before that worm, Mother."

"You will kneel, witch," Marius warned. "Do not forget who I am and under whose command your land exists."

Morrigan grabbed Olwyn's arm, but the witch shrugged her off, her temper rising with each slow beat of the Dragon's wings.

"I kneel to Keridwen and no other!"

"If you wish to concede your lands, I accept."

He pulled in a deep breath of air, his chest expanding, gold scales glowing with heat and warning.

Olwyn's face contorted with old hatred, and she hurled a curse at him.

Marius' blazing eyes fixed on her as the spell slammed into his body, knocking him back.

Wings leveling out, the Dragon opened his mouth and spat.

A glob of molten heat shot through the air like an arrow and struck the witch in the chest.

Flesh burned, and fat sizzled.

Witches screamed and jumped back, their cries cutting through the chaos of Gillian's mind. Her eyes fluttered open, and she watched in horror as flames consumed Olwyn in a ball of fire.

It was over in moments. Gillian sobbed and crawled away from the pile of ashes.

"Observe the cost of defiance," Marius' voice boomed.

"Murderer," Morrigan hissed and braced her legs, hands whipping through the air.

Her remaining sisters mirrored the action.

Together, they harnessed their dwindling power and hurled it at the Dragon. It struck him head-on, tossing his scaled body into the sky.

He recovered with a steady beat of his wings and dove toward them, landing with a violent shudder. Black claws scoured the ground in deep ruts as he stalked forward, head lowered and tail lashing, slamming into outbuildings that burst into splinters and clots of dirt.

When he was ten feet away from the coven, Marius stopped, neck curving in a blood-red arch to look down at them. His attention flicked to Gillian, who sat curled in a ball on the ground, eyes wide and staring at him.

"I could've wiped your kind from the earth when I killed the mage who spawned you. But I let you live.

"You are beholden to *me*, not the puling goddess whose indifference took the very mate who begged me to let your kind live!"

He glared at Morrigan, flames dancing in his eyes. "Bear witness to my compassion. I spared you.

"Give me the girl, and I will let your sisters live. I will allow you to rebuild. To remain in these lands under my dominion."

He flicked his tongue and tasted the reek of fear and anger permeating the air as he pinned Gillian in his ancient stare. "Are you willing to sacrifice every witch in this coven? I will have you with blood or without."

Gillian's eyes welled, skipping from face to face before landing on what was left of Olwyn. She planted her hands on the ground and got to her feet, swaying slightly under the weight of his assessing gaze.

Her fingers curled into fists as she lifted her chin and faced him. "You are a murderous beast, but I will not be the cause of more killing."

Morrigan reached for her. "Daughter," she whispered, wanting to beg Gillian not to give in but unwilling to condemn the sisters to death.

She took the matriarch's hand and squeezed her fingers, then let her arm drop to her side.

A threatening rumble shook the ground as Marius dug a toe claw the length of Gillian's arm into the dirt.

"I'll go with you." Cries of protest rang out, and she waved them away. "I'll live in your prison. On one condition."

The Dragon's nostrils flared, emitting sulfurous plumes. "You think you can set conditions?"

Gillian glared balefully at him. "I could slit my throat. I've heard you're familiar with that line of escape."

Marius' eyes dilated, becoming thin, vertical slits. "It appears my son has a loose tongue. Speak your condition."

"Save my brother. Do that, and I'll—" she swallowed the lump crawling up her throat, "I'll stay with you."

"And bear my young."

Her head dropped to her chest as she whispered, "Yes."

The red scales along his snout shifted in a subtle wave that traveled around his spiraled horns, down his neck, and along his spine. "I haven't the power to save your brother."

His words threatened to bring her to her knees.

He'd destroyed wards that had stood for centuries, protecting the coven. Wards whose power came directly from Keridwen. But even with his strength, he couldn't stop the Wasting.

Or was he simply too callous to try?

"You can't help him, or you won't?"

Morrigan tried to warn her not to rile the Dragon, but Gillian ignored the high witch and took a step closer to the beast.

He chuffed, the heat making the air around his snout shimmer. Marius looked at her with a glimmer of respect. "You will make strong sons."

"I will do nothing if you refuse to help me."

"Very well. I spoke the truth when I told you I could not save him. But I have no wish to be mated with a woman who reviles me."

His eyes narrowed as he felt the frayed magic that ran through the witches' veins. Keridwen was a faint glow in their blood, depleted but not destroyed. The goddess still had the power to rise against him.

"There is time before the ceremony. I will permit you to stay with the sisters. Remain in Gealach Forest and dabble in spell craft to save your brother. Should your efforts prove fruitful, Morrigan herself can cross into your homeland and deliver the remedy."

He paused and lowered his massive head. "You, on the other hand, shall not leave my realm. The eve before the lunar eclipse, you and your sisters will join me in Valon, cure or no, where they will bear witness to our union and kneel at my feet."

Gillian nodded stiffly.

"A warning," he said slowly, "Attempt to escape your fate, and the lives of the coven will be forfeit. To ensure your obedience, my son will remain with you."

Roman melted from the shadows and stood at his father's side.

The Great Dragon swung his head to Morrigan, reptilian eyes flicking to Olwyn's remains. "Hide her, and there will be nothing left of your coven but ash."

The high witch's lip curled, gray eyes hard and cold like stones as they fixed on him. "Keep your son on a short tether while he remains with us, or I will return him to you in pieces."

Wickedly sharp teeth winked in the Great Dragon's mouth. "Careful, Morrigan. Lest your boldness be your sisters' ruin."

He spat a glob of molten fire.

It landed at Edith's feet, igniting the hem of her dress. The witch yelped and fell to the ground, rolling in the dirt as another threw herself on her legs to douse the flames.

"Next time, I will not miss," Marius said coldly.

Morrigan dipped her head, eyes sparking with controlled fury. "I yield."

"A wise decision."

Roman separated himself and moved toward Gillian.

The high witch watched him closely before lifting her chin to the Dragon. She was subdued but not beaten.

"Your wormling may take the form of a man, but I know better."

The high witch turned and gave Roman a look of disdain as she said, "Be warned, Dragon-spawn, I'll brook no interference. Mind yourself while you're in our realm."

Roman smirked, lips quirking on his handsome face.

He bowed with a flourish, the billowy sleeves of his black tunic fluttering like tiny wings. "I am your servant."

She snorted, waved a dismissive hand, and turned her back on the Dragon. "Leave us to mourn, serpent."

He chuffed a warning and backed away, turning his massive body around when he was clear of the broken outbuildings at his sides.

Marius spread his wings and flapped, the force of his wind bending trees and knocking Gillian onto her backside. She stayed on the ground, watching him swoop into the night sky until all that she could see was the winking out of stars as his black shadow passed.

She felt Roman watching her.

His feral eyes tracked her movements. He sniffed the air.

Gillian rose and faced him, feeling the heat of his stare as it consumed her. She balled her hands into fists and stalked away from him.

But he remained. Watching. Waiting.

Chapter Nineteen

J ust before dawn, the Coven of the Silver Moon took Olwyn's ashes, those that hadn't been lost to the Dragon's wind, into the heart of the Gealach Forest—the Darach Grove.

Roman followed, unobtrusive, though all felt his presence. A ring of ancient oak trees formed the sacred copse, their branches drooping in sadness as the witches passed beneath the bowers.

At the center lay a flat stone like an altar, carved with knotwork and intricate symbols. Five-pointed white flowers sprang from the surrounding grasses, spiraling around the rock, echoing the tangled carvings on the stone.

Gillian hovered along the perimeter, unsure what to do, afraid to utter a word in the solemnity. She felt Roman's eyes on her, crawling over her body. Gritting her teeth, she shut him out and focused on the high witch who wore a flowing white gown that dragged on the ground behind her in a gossamer drift of fabric.

Morrigan held a clay bowl in her hands. All that remained of Olwyn. She set the bowl in the center of the stone and dipped her head, lips moving though the words were lost to the wind.

Moving slowly to the eastern side of the altar, she pulled the Ashrune Dagger, a magical blade, from a sheath attached to a leather belt hanging low on her hips.

Edith filled in the spot opposite the matriarch, the west, carrying a shallow bowl of water. Helga carried a dish with a small mound of earth and stood to the north while Imogen, a shy witch Gillian had spoken little to, went to the south with a bowl holding a lump of coal with orange flames dancing around it.

Morrigan touched the end of the Ashrune Dagger to the earth and whispered words too low for Gillian to hear.

Shifting her body, the high witch stretched her arm to the sky, the tip of the dagger glinting in the pale light, holding the blade in the air, east. Lowering it, she rested the point of the dagger in the fire, the south, before leaning forward and resting it in the water, west.

At an unknown signal, the rest of the coven formed a circle around the altar, Edith beckoning Gillian to take her place among them.

She moved woodenly into the ring of women, clasping hands with the sisters at her sides. Gillian's shoulders relaxed as her fingers twined with the witches', their warmth and welcome radiating through their skin, easing her uncertainty at joining the mourning of their sister.

Her eyes fixed on Morrigan, who'd laid the Ashrune Dagger

on the stone and lifted her arms to the sky, palms open to welcome the gentle touch of the goddess, Keridwen.

A thrum of energy pulsed through the wood as the coven chanted, their voices blending into song.

Gillian listened, feeling the words, their power and longing.

Their music called to their lost sister, Olwyn, celebrating her life and grieving her loss. Her arms lifted in time with the chanting, still clasped by the sisters at her sides.

She looked up at the lightening sky, pale pink and orange as the moon, Keridwen incarnate, let go of her nighttime dominion.

In the last moments of the night before dawn blanketed the earth, Morrigan took the bowl of ashes and held it high, spinning in a circle so they flowed out in a wave, sprinkling the sacred ground where they would become one with the earth.

The coven's voices drifted as the sun burst over the horizon, their hands releasing their hold, letting go of one another, as they all must let go of Olwyn.

Roman stood beneath the bough of an ancient oak and watched the coven perform their rites. But his eyes returned to Gillian time and time again.

He saw her look of uncertainty bleeding into awe when her hands joined with the women at her sides and she felt Keridwen's power.

The soft fall of her pale lashes as the words the coven sang pulled at her heart. Her lush curves and innocence permeated every movement. His body ached with need.

But she was not for him. She could never be for him.

Reining in his lust, Roman breathed deeply, the cool morning air mixing with his heat. Tendrils of steam slipped from his nostrils. Nearly imperceptible as they dissipated.

He shut his eyes and his senses, refusing to allow his body to catch her scent as she shifted her body in time with the coven.

When he opened them, the witches drew apart, their farewell over in the fall of Olwyn's ashes. He kept his distance as they filed silently from the sacred grove, frowning as they came to their ruined settlement.

Only two structures remained unscathed from his father's wrath—the communal house where the coven slept and the kitchen. The rest lay shattered in piles of wood, thatch, and dirt. The belongings inside them were scattered in heaps beneath the debris.

He watched as Morrigan directed the women to the tasks of repair and cleaning. She asked nothing of him, ignoring his presence completely.

But as the day wore on, he found himself stepping in to lift a heavy plank of wood or scale a wall with a hammer and crude nails. The sisters of the Silver Moon said nothing. Only handed him the tools he requested or accepted his aid as though he were a hired hand.

Of Gillian, he saw little.

Morrigan kept her tucked away. But he could sense her, feel her mind when he reached for her presence, but her thoughts were shrouded and hard to read. She was hard at work alongside the high witch. Learning the rudiments of the craft.

Whereas her sisters in the coven had practiced magic since they could walk, Gillian was new to it. Her power was untapped and untrained. He wondered what she'd be able to do when she delved into the core of it.

They toiled into the early evening. Sweat poured from their bodies despite the chill air.

It was Edith who went to Roman at the day's end, a ladle of water in her outstretched hand. He dipped his head and accepted her offering, sniffing the liquid before gulping it down.

She watched him and said wryly, "If I'd a mind to poison you, I'd offer you something to mask the scent."

His mouth curved on one side. "I shudder to think what poisons you'd offer to speed my death."

"Oh, the most painful, of course," Edith told him with a chuckle and took the dipper.

Roman put his hands on his hips and shook his head.

He'd never been close to a sister of the Silver Moon. Not even Maud, Draven's mother, though she'd lived among them for decades.

She'd been a fragile thing, and her captivity broke her. In her last days, she'd become a lost soul. Drifting from room to room, her face rarely reflected awareness of the world around her.

When she'd raced up the stairs to the parapet, he hadn't tried to stop her. He'd let her slip past him, a dagger glinting in her fist, her thoughts churning so loudly he'd heard them as though she'd spoken aloud.

It was a mercy, he'd told himself.

And now Gillian would take her place. Would he see it as a mercy if he allowed her to take her life? Would he stand aside and let her slip past him, knife in hand?

Her image replaced Maud's.

It was Gillian's hand gripping the blade. Gillian's blood spraying as she screamed in triumph. Her body tumbling in the air to the unforgiving ground.

Roman shook his head, dispelling the foul imaginings.

It won't come to that, he told himself. But he knew it could, and if it did, he'd be unable to stand aside and watch her die.

He lit a fire for the evening meal, ignoring the grousing of a couple of the elders who huffed and threatened to refuse the food cooked above the flames he'd coaxed. Edith cajoled them after she gutted two hares one of the sisters presented and sliced up the tender meat, adding the chunks to a simmering cauldron of water, spices, and root vegetables.

By the time the smells of the stew wafted in the air, even the staunchest of the witches capitulated, though none would sit near the Dragonborn as bowls were passed around.

He took his meal from Edith's hands and stared at the dish for a moment, knowing it had been Olwyn's. Roman darted glances at the women, marking those who eyed him, their eyes flicking from his hands to the clay bowl.

While not immune to the glares they passed his way, Roman's hunger and refusal to shrink from the women had him dipping his spoon for a hearty portion, chewing slowly, and meeting every hostile eye.

Gillian sat far from him. Her body turned away, so he saw little more than her back. Despite his promise to himself to ignore her innocent allure, he sniffed the air, briefly shutting his eyes to savor her scent.

Let her spurn him. She could pretend she didn't see or feel him. He knew better, though he wished he didn't.

Three days passed, and aside from the reconstruction of the smokehouse, oven, and an outbuilding for storing grain and drying herbs, little progress had been made in spell craft to aid Gillian's brother.

Thumbing through ancient texts handed down through generations had garnered little insight. Morrigan and Gillian poured over the fragile parchment, reading histories and spells bound in old magic.

The high witch instructed her on the rudiments of spell craft, building on her knowledge of healing while drawing out the magic in her blood to strengthen remedies. But there was no one to test them on.

Instead, Gillian filled vials and satchels with herbs and tonics, hoping one would have the power to help Rory.

When they'd browsed the last text, Morrigan pressed her hand on the thick paper and looked at Gillian. "If I had the power to save him, I would give it."

She nodded, a ball of misery lodged in her throat.

"The Wasting is rooted in the connection between Keridwen and the Great Dragon. We cannot stop it, but perhaps we can buy him more time."

Not allowing her to give in to defeat, Morrigan pushed Gillian, pressing her to learn all she could in the short time they had. The young witch had a wealth of untapped, raw power. No doubt it was part of her allure.

Gillian played the part of a good student. She wrestled with failures and realizations of her limitations but remained steadfast. When exhaustion or frustration took its toll, she left Morrigan's company to wander within Gealach Forest alone.

Roman dogged her steps.

He was reluctant to let her out of his sight. Not for the sake of his father but for the fact that with the fall of the barrier protecting the coven's sacred land, the dark creatures of the Shadowlands could infiltrate the virgin territory.

Should she find herself face-to-face with a vauger or myrax, Gillian would be ill-equipped to fight it off.

So, he watched and followed, accepting the indefinable tether that bound him to her. That she didn't feel it was clear. But he did and was unable to sever it.

Her favorite brooding spot was a small waterfall that filled a clear pool, the water so crystalline she could see the rocks and sediment lining the bottom.

Roman's footsteps were little more than whispers on the pine needle-littered ground as he came upon her haven.

She sat on a rock that hung above the pool, legs dangling toward the icy water. Her head was bowed, shoulders hunched with the weight of the world. He crouched against a tree, hands hanging limply on his knees, copper gaze feasting on her form.

Gillian sighed. "I know you're there."

"Aye."

"Why do you torture me?" She craned her neck and found him. "I have four days left of freedom. Four days to find a spell to halt the Wasting consuming my brother. Four days..."

Gillian shook her head and shifted her body to stare into the pool. "Hounding every step I take makes everything worse."

"I didn't realize my task was to make things easy."

Her mouth pulled down. "If it were, you'd be terrible at it," she muttered.

"True enough."

He got up, went to a rock a foot from hers, and sat. They said nothing for a while, just listened to the babble of water and the twittering of birds.

"I wish I'd never come here," Gillian whispered and tucked her knees to rest her arms and chin.

Roman didn't look at her when he said, "I know."

"If you let me go—"

"Don't," he warned. "Don't finish that thought."

Gillian huffed and shifted her body to show him her back.

He shook his head. "Why do you wander alone and avoid your sisters?"

It was the first time he'd directly stated her connection to the coven.

"I'm not avoiding *them*."

"I see." Roman picked up a small stone and chucked it into the water. "Tell me of your life in Rudgarde."

She turned her head with a hooded look. "Why? So you can poke fun at it? I'd rather not."

"I have no intention of mocking your life."

Gillian turned around fully and faced him. "All right. But first, tell me your story."

His pupils dilated, shifting from round to serpentine slits like his father's. "Very well. What would you like to know?"

"How old are you?"

He thought for a moment. "We don't account for years as you do. Our lives are long, and I am young for my kind. If I had to guess, I'd say not more than a hundred fifty of your years."

Gillian made a face. He looked so young. Not much older than her eighteen. She wondered if he was always the callous ass he was today.

Roman chuckled, picking her thought from her head like he would a ripe fruit. "Draven would say so."

"Stop doing that," she grumbled. "It's annoying."

"Shield your thoughts, and I won't be tempted to read them. As it is, you may as well be shouting them at me."

"If I knew how to do that, I would," she snapped. "You know, Draven is a much better companion than you."

His eyes grew stormy, shifting from orange to red. "He's young and easy to manipulate. It's no wonder you like him."

"I see your opinion of me is just as complimentary as mine is of you."

"You've no idea what I think of you," he muttered, voice pitched too low for her to make out.

"What?"

Roman shrugged. "Just an errant thought. You asked me about my life. What would you like to know?"

"Tell me something about yourself. Something not... awful or disturbing."

"That seriously limits what I can say," he told her with a smirk. "All right. I can't eat cheese."

She made a face. "Why? Is that a Dragonborn thing?"

"No. I just can't eat it. Not anymore." She crossed her arms with an expectant look on her face. "The whole story?"

She nodded. "In detail."

His lips twitched. He leaned back and launched into a story of when he stole a wheel of cheese from the kitchen. How cook had run after him with a wooden ladle, hurling curses as that wasn't the first time he'd filched something from cook's domain.

His eyes lit with the telling, revealing a young man not so different from Rudgarde's youths.

Roman leaned back, regaling her with a time he'd hidden from the cook, and proceeded to eat the wheel of cheese in its entirety. He groaned, recalling the stomach ache he'd had for hours after and the other unsavory ailments that had lasted two days.

Gillian grew uncomfortable when he got to the part of the story where his father looked in on him, worried and frantic for something to ease his bowels.

Once again, she was given a glimpse of humanity within the Great Dragon. And she didn't want to see it. He was a monster. He needed to stay a monster.

When he finished speaking, the youthful glimmer receded from his features.

She watched his face become cold and hard, replaced by the mantle of a Dragonborn son. Gillian wondered if he'd ever truly embodied the carefree person he was when he spun his tale. Or if the aloof and guarded man had always completely taken over.

She goaded him into telling another story, watching the shift in his face, the looseness in his frame. Thinking that if she could tap into that part of him more fully, maybe he'd see her as more than his father's property. If successful, he might turn away from the Great Dragon and let her go.

Foolish thoughts, but pervasive ones.

Gillian gave him a sidelong glance, hoping her musings hadn't been plucked from her head. He appeared unfazed, and she relaxed, listening to the sound of his voice and plotting.

Chapter Twenty

Gillian cursed loudly and threw the pot on the floor, kicking it and cursing more as pain flared in her foot.

She'd been working on a potion for two days. Two days! Wasted with nothing to show for it but blackened sludge clinging to the bottom of the small cauldron.

Morrigan entered the kitchen, folding her arms when she saw the pot on its side, viscous liquid spilling out of it and onto the floor. "You added too much farrow root."

Plopping onto a wooden chair with a huff, Gillian leaned over, gripped her head, fingers massaging her skull, and groaned, "I know."

She leaned back and looked at the high witch. "Every time I get to the last step, it all goes wrong. I can't do this!"

"Aye. You can," Morrigan told her, bending down to pick up the cauldron. "You're not saying the correct words."

Gillian frowned. "I'm saying exactly what you told me to say."

"If that were true, it wouldn't look like that." She held the pot under Gillian's nose. "Do it again. This time, as I showed you."

Scowling, she grabbed it and stalked outside, ignoring the pointed looks from the sisters as they stopped to stare.

Roman caught up with her, and she picked up her pace, snapping at him when he increased his stride to match hers. "Can't you just leave me alone?"

"I could, but what fun would that be?" His full lips curved into a smile, making him too handsome, which only served to add to her irritation. "Besides, it's entertaining to watch you spit fire."

"I'm not the fire-spitting kind. That's your job, and I'd prefer you go off and do it somewhere else."

"I'll stay. If it's all the same to you."

Gillian muttered, her grumbling interspersed with curses directed at the entire Dragonborn race.

Roman laughed, peppering her with humorous jabs until she spun on him and threw the cauldron at his head. He ducked, but not before a glob of the noxious liquid was hurled in the air and landed with a splat on his face.

Gillian giggled.

She smacked a hand over her mouth when Roman swiped his fingers across his face to clear his eyes, smearing goo onto both cheeks. He glared at her as she bit her cheeks and tried to contain her laughter.

"Happy?" he drawled.

She snorted, losing herself again to a fit of mirth when a blob of the potion dripped from the tip of his nose.

He flicked fingers coated with the goo at her, grinning

boyishly when they landed on her face.

Gillian's eyes went wide as he bent over, dipped his hand into the discarded cauldron, and grabbed a fistful of sludge.

"Don't you dare!" she yelled, then darted away.

He gave chase, lobbing hunks at her, each landing with a splat on her back. Gillian tripped on a root and went down, sides aching with laughter.

Roman slid to a stop and stood over her, his hand blackened with the remains of the liquid.

"Enough," she panted. "I can't laugh anymore. My sides are going to split."

"You surrender?" He rolled his fingers, forming a small ball of sludge.

She jutted her chin. "Never."

"I was hoping you'd say that." He pulled back his arm to lob it at her, pausing when she held out her arms.

"I surrender!"

"Ha!" He dropped the ball and wiped his hand on his leather pants before sitting next to her.

Gillian caught her breath and lay on her back, looking at the sky between the breaks in the forest canopy. The soft hum of the nearby stream filled the quiet as she tried to ignore Roman. But it was a fruitless pursuit.

His presence was felt with every fiber of her being. She didn't know what that meant and had no desire to think too long about it. But it was undeniable all the same.

He'd gotten under her skin. His surly, stubborn self had slipped past her defenses. The thought annoyed her, quickly dousing the mirth from moments before.

She couldn't afford to spare any feelings for him. He was an obstacle, nothing more.

Gillian eyed him beneath her lashes, wondering if he was genuinely ignorant of her true thoughts or if he was playing her as deftly as she was playing him. The moment of reckoning would come soon enough.

As far as she knew, Morrigan's real training had gone unnoticed, relegated to healing craft they practiced in private, not that he had time to spy on her. The sisters kept him busy, hounding him with menial labor he reluctantly performed, accompanied by eye rolls and grumbling.

When his attention was firmly fixed elsewhere, Gillian and the high witch would slip away to Darach Grove, where the magic squatting within Gillian like a spoiled child refusing to rise from bed was drawn and molded.

It was a slow process, leaving the young witch with a headache and nosebleeds most days. The training should've begun when she was a child, slowly shaping her as she grew into womanhood. Trying to learn its nature at eighteen years of age was a task in itself.

It had always been there.

She saw that now, but it was raw and buried too deep to be of much use. Morrigan was determined to change that in the short time they had, though she was always quick to remind her pupil that the work they did was only the beginning.

She also cautioned her against using it too soon, warning Gillian that her attempts could be met with retaliation.

On reflection, she realized Roman and Marius had sensed her unwitting attempts to tap into their minds. The Dragon had gone so far as to admonish the effort, though she hadn't understood what he'd meant at the time, being unaware she'd used such power.

"It's a dangerous gift in the wrong hands," Morrigan told her. "Even more dangerous in inept ones. Understand your opponent and accept that they may understand you."

If she aimed to truly harness her power, she would need years at the matriarch's side. But even in their short time, Gillian felt her core of magic fluttering open, revealing itself like the petals of a flower.

Mentalism was the focus of her training.

"You will never be able to aid your brother if you fall into Marius' hands, and all of your healing work will be for naught. Your mind is the most useful tool against Dragonborn, and your only chance to escape should you be caught. Therefore, we shall hone that skill into a weapon," Morrigan told her early on.

"Wouldn't controlling the elements be a more powerful tool?"

"In time, my daughter, in time. Calling the wind to your hand does little if the Dragon already has your mind under his control."

The skill of defending her mind was a painful process.

Morrigan slipped into it, in the beginning, with a subtle touch as she fumbled to block her out, then later with brutal force. It was exhausting, leaving her thoughts a jumbled mess.

But time was a luxury they did not have, as the high witch often reminded her.

Though she didn't know it, Gillian learned to shield her

mind more quickly than Morrigan had anticipated. Likely, the young witch had been using the skill all her life without recognizing it. Learning the nature of guarding her thoughts was the first step.

Diving into someone else's was another matter entirely.

In the beginning, her magic recoiled when she plied it into a fingerlike projection to tap at Morrigan's, slipping back into the pit where it had sat for all the years of her life. But the high witch kept pushing, repeating the same technique over and over, forcing her to learn to draw it out. Even as she panted and grew dizzy from the strain, the high witch forced her to pull it free.

When it finally responded to her commands, she tried it on the high witch's open mind, grinning when she felt it take root and pull thoughts from Morrigan's mind.

Roman was another matter.

When she tested her skill on him, she was wary, each time wondering if he was allowing her to pluck surface thoughts from him while shielding himself from her intrusion.

While mentalism was her most useful tool, Morrigan permitted breaks in the intensity of her training to dabble in the art of harnessing the elements.

It was the true power of the coven, she'd explained. Wielding mental power born of the Dragon blood running in the veins of every sister of the Silver Moon.

Drained from flexing her power in mental combat, Gillian blundered through the ability to call on the wind or tame the flow of water, her efforts often ending in a fit of anger when a gust threw dirt in her face or water particles drawn from the air rained on her head.

Morrigan said little, only gently directing her hands to sweep through the air just so or offering advice on enunciating the words to draw the elements.

"What about fire?" Gillian asked, proudly standing above a small stack of rocks she'd lifted and moved with magic.

"While the blood of the Dragon flows through us, the gift of fire does not."

Morrigan raised her hand and picked up the tower of stones, lifting them into the air. The rocks wobbled but remained stacked.

Speaking too low for Gillian to hear, the high witch separated each stone and formed the lot into a circle. It spun in the air.

"All life is balance," she said, keeping her mind fixed on the spinning rocks. "One action can destroy it to the ruin of all."

The largest stone stopped midair, all others crashing into it and falling to the ground in soft thumps.

"The Wasting is a result of the loss of that balance. Whether or not it is reclaimed is within your hands."

While her training with Morrigan continued, other preparations were made in the shadows—a task to which Helga was ideally suited.

Quiet and unobtrusive, she proved a perfect intermediary.

The middle-aged witch moved freely to and from—an inconspicuous messenger—while Roman was kept occupied. It was risky, but time was running out, and the risks were all they had left.

Roman stood and held out his clean hand.

She took it, allowing him to haul her to her feet and using

the contact to test the shields protecting his mind as the high witch had taught her.

He blinked and looked quizzically at her, but she reached for him, distracting him as she wiped a drying clump of spoiled potion from his handsome face. He gave her a lopsided grin and chuckled.

She slipped into his mind then.

In and out before he knew she'd been there. A broad smile lit her face when she withdrew her mental needle unnoticed.

Roman's eyes shifted to her mouth, tracing her lips with his gaze. She let his thoughts linger there for a moment, then pulled away, relieved and emboldened.

The plan would work. It had to.

Now all she had to do was get that damn potion right.

The next afternoon, Morrigan sniffed the potion bubbling gently in the cauldron. Dipping a wooden spoon into the liquid, she ladled a taste into it, dipped her finger, then popped the digit in her mouth.

Gillian scanned her face and fidgeted, sighing with relief when the matriarch nodded.

"Well done."

Setting the spoon aside, she gathered a small vial and slipped it into Gillian's hand.

"Fill it to the brim. This evening, when you dole out the meal, mix it into the stew."

She took the vial, dipped it into the potion, and stoppered it.

Gillian stared at it sitting in her palm. "Are you sure about this?" Her fingers curled around it as she looked at the high witch. "The Dragon warned you what he'd do. I can't put you and the sisters in danger. It's not right."

Morrigan's face softened. "Aye, the Dragon warned me, and, no, you won't be altering your plan."

"But he said he'd kill you. Look what he's done already?"

She waved her hand towards the open doorway where the rest of the coven was repairing the broken buildings.

"I know what he can do. It is he who misjudges us. He believes his Dragon-fire is capable of unmitigated destruction, but it is not."

"How can you say that? Marius destroyed the wards protecting Gealach Wood. He killed Olwyn." The last was said through a clog in Gillian's throat. "When he finds out what I've done, his wrath will be terrible."

"Have faith," Morrigan said, stroking Gillian's arm. "The wards surrounding our realm may have fallen, but we are not without power. By the time word travels to Valon, our magic will be stronger."

"How?"

"Magic lives within us. It is not a separate thing. Rather, it is a symbiotic relationship.

"We are like two organisms living together. And like any organism, magic changes over time. In this case, it learns. The Great Dragon has never laid siege on our sacred land before. Not even when he railed against our refusal to give him a mate."

Her eyes drifted as though remembering. "Marius made our lives uncertain and challenging for a time, but he never used his full power. Until the other night. When he returns, Marius will not find us so easily defeated."

"That sounds like you're telling me you'll still be defeated in the end."

"I don't believe he'll kill us all. Though his wrath will be great, he knows from whom his ability to sire sons lies. We may be too old to become his mates, but we are not without the ability to ensure none of our sisters in hiding crosses into his realm."

Gillian bit her lip. "I want to believe you, but I worry. He's so strong."

"Worry does nothing but make your head ache. Pour your energy into learning what little you can in the time we have left."

She pulled out the vial and tucked it into the pocket of Gillian's apron.

"You'll have no time to waste when it takes effect," Morrigan warned.

Gillian nodded, trying to project an air of confidence. "I'll be ready."

The high witch cupped her cheek. "I shall miss you, my daughter. Take care of your brother. Ease his passing into the next world."

Discovering her mother, Naeve, was wrong, that there was nothing Morrigan could do to aid Rory, had been like the twist of a knife in her chest. It was not the answer she'd wanted.

But there was no hope.

The Wasting was beyond the coven's ability. The disease would take her brother as it had taken so many others. And it would continue to plague the young. Perhaps until all that was left in the village of Rudgarde were the old.

Tears pooled in her eyes, and she brushed them away.

Mourning would come later when Rory lay cold in the ground. Until then, she could only do what was within her means. Escape.

Gillian tucked her worry for her brother's fate into the recesses of her mind. It was time to face the next few hours with a clear head and put her plans into motion.

The sisters would be safe. Morrigan would protect them.

In the evening, she would say her goodbyes and leave the Shadowlands. Perhaps, one day, one of them would find their way to Rudgarde.

After... Images of Rory raced through her mind.

She shook them away with a jerk of her head. Now was not the time for sorrow. She focused her attention on deception and escape.

Chapter Twenty-One

Gillian ladled stew made of roasted chicken and vegetables into Roman's bowl. Setting aside a helping of thick broth, she slipped the vial from her pocket and added it to the liquid, stirring until it was mixed before pouring it over the food.

She filled the bowls of the other sisters and passed them around, keeping Roman's tucked in the crook of her arm. Gillian took her food and sat next to Helga, perched on one of the stumps surrounding the central fire. She dug into her food, barely tasting it in her effort to keep from looking at Roman.

As usual, he was quiet, only adding to the conversation when spoken to directly.

Gillian stilled her mind as Morrigan had taught her and listened with her inner ear. The high witch told her she'd feel the moment the potion took hold of the Dragonborn male, and once it did, there'd be no time to waste.

How long the magic held depended on Roman's strength, a

thing that remained unknown despite the subtle taps at his mind.

She felt Roman's eyes on her.

His attention had the same weight she'd felt for days. Though it galled her to admit it, she'd miss the feeling of him watching her. The longing she glimpsed when he let down his guard.

Guilt weighed on her shoulders. She was betraying him. Part of her admitted she was betraying herself.

With a mental shake, she smothered such thoughts and opened herself to the churning of his mind as he watched her in the flickering of the fire.

Gillian focused on that link, giving the appearance of attentiveness to the hum of conversation, nodding now and then as though she heard what the sisters were saying in the waning hours of the evening. Helga did much of the talking, as they'd agreed that morning, leaving Gillian to prowl around Roman's inherent mental shield, waiting for the moment when the potion took over, and it cracked.

Roman watched her as he chewed his food, hardly tasting the savory broth.

She was at home within the ring of witches, at ease among the sisters in a way she hadn't been since he'd taken her. How unfortunate that she'd come to the Shadowlands, ignoring the stories told by the people of Rudgarde to keep her away from the dark forest.

He swallowed a mouthful of stew, eyes fixed on Gillian's profile.

Like a switch, his mind went blank, and his mouth stopped working.

As though outside himself, he saw Gillian turn toward him and set down her bowl, saying something to Helga, who followed her gaze.

Gillian rose and stalked toward him, leaning forward, strands of pale blond hair tickling his face, though he could do nothing to scratch the itch.

His mind opened like a blossom, unfurling before her as she stared at him, into him, stabbing at his brain with a needle of thought. Her will smothered his, as he'd smothered hers on their journey to Valon.

Roman became a puppet, and she, the master.

He found himself standing, tethered to her, not by a thread but a chain of iron.

Gillian turned to Helga, "The satchel is at the foot of my bed."

With Morrigan's help, she'd gathered foodstuffs and supplies. The high witch had also blessed the most potent healing tonic they'd made using one of the coven's old texts.

The likelihood of its success was dim, but it had the potential to slow the Wasting's steady progression.

Morrigan went to Gillian, giving Roman a passing glance as he stood like a statue at her side.

From her apron, she pulled out Gillian's medallion. It hung from a strip of leather, slowly spinning in the firelight.

The face of the disc was carved with new symbols, powerful sigils to protect and guide her. The high witch slipped it over Gillian's head and pressed her palm to the clay, whispering a spell.

Warmth radiated from the disc to the point of pain, then dimmed as Morrigan withdrew her hand. Magical etchings carved into the medallion would grant her passage out of the Shadowlands. But they would not permit her return.

Once she crossed that boundary, the magic would wither.

Cupping Gillian's face, she said, "May Keridwen bless you, my daughter." She bent Gillian's head forward and kissed her brow. "Be safe, my child."

Gillian nodded through the thickness in her throat and swept her eyes across the faces gathered around her.

Eyes tinged with sadness, they looked back at her.

As though a signal passed between them, the coven formed a ring around Gillian, neatly cutting Roman off from the sisterhood so that he stood outside it, unable to do anything but watch.

The Coven of the Silver Moon said goodbye to their young sister, gifting her with spells of protection through bonds of sisterhood.

When the circle broke, Gillian felt a palpable loss. She'd known them for a span of days, yet felt as though they'd been with her through her entire life. Nodding at their well-wishes, she hefted her satchel across her shoulders and pulled the red hood of her cloak over her head.

The powerful medallion thrummed with energy as she turned and walked away, not allowing herself to look back.

With a mental command, she bid Roman to follow her, feeling his presence at her back and the battle he waged in his mind to reclaim control.

She would lead him beyond the borders of Gealach Wood and escape.

Draven waited at the predetermined location along the southern border of the coven's realm. Helga had given him explicit instructions. The soft-spoken witch would make a good spy.

As he paced, he could feel his father's presence in his mind like a tick that lodged itself in his thoughts, growing bloated with the false information he fed it.

While he wasn't strong enough to keep Marius out, he was not without the skill to warp and mislead the words and images he unwillingly passed to the Dragon.

For now, Marius believed he sought to redeem himself by spying on Gillian and ensuring her obedience in the face of his demands. Should his father discover his deception, his mind would be laid bare, and no mental shield would protect him.

He understood the risks of aligning with the coven but refused to see Gillian succumb to the same fate as his mother, Maud.

The witch-wife had loved his father once. He wanted to believe that love sprang from something real, not the persuasive power his kind possessed.

But that love had soured like all the others of her kind.

The sisters of the coven were not meant to spend their lives tied to a being who could never be their other half. There had been only whispers of a mating bond between his father and Maud. The true bond had been for the Dragon's mate, Ashael.

Instead, Marius had given each witch-wife a sliver of himself, never allowing for more, not after the loss of Sorya, the first witch-wife and perhaps the only witch he'd felt genuine love for.

Punishment for his betrayal would be swift, but Draven knew Marius wouldn't kill him.

The Dragon loved his children as any father did. Unconditionally. Despite their flaws and rebellion.

It was Roman's wrath he dreaded.

When Gillian arrived with his brother, he would take him far from the Shadowland border, a distance great enough to guarantee her escape when the potion wore off. The betrayal Roman was sure to feel when he realized what Draven had done made him shudder.

His ribs ached, recalling their recent tussle. He rubbed at his chest and scanned the line of trees marking the edge of Gaelach Wood.

The snap of a twig and rustle of leaves announced Gillian's approach.

She broke through the undergrowth, her dark red cloak swirling around her slim form and eyes sweeping the landscape. She found him in moments.

Smiling, she quickened her pace, Roman trailing at her heels.

Draven watched his brother follow the young witch and marveled at the completeness of the potion's effect. The Dragonborn male was devoid of emotion, eyes blank, though Draven felt his will churning below the surface.

When he escaped Gillian's hold... Draven shook his head, cutting off his imaginings of rage and retribution.

"I don't know how long we have," she said, referring to the potion and glancing back at Roman, who stopped walking the moment she did.

Draven studied his brother, seeing a flicker of red flame in his copper eyes. "Not long."

He looked down at his feet, then at her from beneath his brow. "Will you be all right? There are dangers in the forest beyond those of my kind."

"I have to try. Are there... others... like you out there?"

His eyes flicked toward Valon, though the stronghold was leagues away. "Not that I've felt."

Gillian's shoulders relaxed, and she shifted the strap of her satchel into a more comfortable position.

Draven watched her and tried to disguise his hunger.

Like his father, her blood called to him, and with every interaction, it grew more difficult to resist. He knew he could use the power of his scent to sway her, overwhelming her senses until she was little more than a slave.

Though his power was not as strong as Roman's. None of his siblings had his brother's strength.

And he sensed that Roman had yet to plumb the depths of it. He hoped his brother didn't choose to explore that power when he perceived Draven's part in this subterfuge.

"Are you sure you want to do this?" Gillian asked.

"Yes."

"Why? You owe me nothing and risk everything."

"Because I believe my mother watches me still. She would approve."

"Draven," she whispered, "He could kill you." It wasn't Roman she spoke of.

He curled his hands into fists. His name on her lips was intoxicating.

Getting a tight grip on his control, he told her, "My father won't kill me, though he may wish to." He grinned, though it didn't reach his eyes. "He'd have to get in line after Roman."

She smiled sadly. "You're a brave man. Thank you."

Draven nodded and watched Gillian face Roman and saw her lips move as she used her connection with him to command him, weaving magic as Morrigan had taught her to strengthen the words. His brother's face froze as it took hold, eyes blank slates.

When she grew silent, Roman turned stiffly toward Draven and stepped to his side.

"As long as the magic holds, he'll follow you," she said, glancing at the dark sky.

"Do you know which way to go?" Draven asked, wondering how she'd travel through the dark forest with no stars to guide her.

Gillian tugged the medallion from where it hung between her breasts. She looked at it, gently cupping it in her palm. "Morrigan imbued it with a spell that will lead me home."

Sadness and worry tinged every word. Her actions could doom the coven, and she'd never forgive herself. Although if she made it to Rudgarde, she'd never know their fate. Doomed to wonder and regret.

Draven eyed the disc and reached for her, giving her an awkward hug. Heat radiated from his body, growing stronger in his embrace.

She held her breath, knowing what his scent could do— acknowledging that Roman's scent was far more powerful and alluring.

Releasing her with a quick pat, Draven stepped away. "I hope your brother lives a long life."

She nodded, averting her eyes so he didn't see the grief in them. He couldn't know there was no hope. If he did, he might decide it wasn't worth it to let her go.

"Thank you."

Pulling her cloak tighter around her body, she stepped away from him. "I have to go. I hope... I hope Roman understands. It had to be this way."

"Goodbye, Gillian," Draven said, a note of sorrow in his voice.

"Goodbye."

She glanced at Roman, passing the parting word to him as well. It hurt to leave him.

How strange.

He was not the monster she'd thought him to be when he'd captured her in the forest. But he was no hero, either. Like she would've been, he was a slave to the Great Dragon. Maybe one day, he, too, would break free.

Turning her back on the brothers, she felt the pull of the medallion and took her first step toward freedom.

Chapter Twenty-Two

It was well past midnight when Gillian felt the link with Roman sever.

She stumbled and looked to the north. He would hunt her now.

Grabbing her dress and cloak, she hitched them up and started to run, focusing on the tug of the medallion as it led her home.

Gone was her ability to quiet her movements through the dark woods. There was no time.

Roman could outrun her in moments, as she had no sense of how far he and Draven had gone before the connection broke.

Every rustle of branches and leaves had her heart leaping in her chest, quickening her pace until she was careening through the trees. Her pulse thundered in her ears, blood rushing so forcefully she heard nothing but the pounding.

Not even the shrill wail of the myrax that followed her progress.

Its wings beat against the starry sky as it homed in on her, the black pools of its eyes tracking her movements, waiting for the moment she passed beneath a break in the trees.

It dove at her. Deadly talons extended, wings tucked tight.

Gillian felt the wind stirred by the flap of its wings as it angled its body to slow its descent and snatched her off the ground.

The world tilted as she left the earth, limbs flailing. She screamed—the sound of her voice drowned out by the myrax's screech of triumph. The forest unfolded beneath her, swaths of oak, pine, and ash spreading into the horizon on all sides.

She grabbed at the talons and tried to break free.

The myrax squawked and tightened its hold, wickedly sharp talons piercing her clothes.

Gillian wriggled, knowing if she broke free, she'd plummet to her death.

Better to die from the fall than be torn apart piece by piece, she thought with panic.

The myrax banked hard to the right, aiming for a craggy peak among the trees.

She twisted, watching in horror as the unforgiving rock drew closer.

It was a nest.

The dark forms of the creature's young were tucked within folds of rock. Nearly invisible but for their screeching.

They were hungry. And she was dinner.

Digging into her satchel, she swung in the myrax's grip and pulled out a dagger. Lifting her arm, she made to swipe at the creature's leg.

Her blade found nothing but air.

With a primeval sixth sense, the creature dove for the earth with such force that her breath was knocked out of her.

Her eyes widened as the ground swam before her, getting closer with every second.

It's going to crush me, she thought in panic.

At the last moment, the myrax spread its wings, slowing the wild descent enough to toss her onto the ground, where she rolled violently before coming to rest against the trunk of a tree.

Gillian groaned and flopped onto her back, her shoulder aching.

The myrax landed a short distance away and clacked its beak.

Her head lolled as she watched it approach. It looked like a vulture, only five times the size, with a serrated beak and dagger-like talons.

Maybe that's what it was at one time before the Dragon's darkness consumed the Shadowlands, twisting animals who lived within it into monstrous things.

It tapped the elongated middle talon of its left foot on the ground and cocked its head.

She rolled onto her side and tried to rise, but her shoulder flared blackly, and she crumpled.

The myrax hissed and bobbed its head, wings opening and closing.

What's it waiting for? she wondered, trying to think around the pain wrapping around her shoulder and into her back.

Gillian tried to reach for her satchel, but the animal screeched threateningly, and she stilled, watching it watch her.

She shrank from the myrax as it lowered its head and took a step toward her.

Snapping its beak, it stilled and swung around, fanning out its dark wings fully.

Gillian tried to see beyond it, but her eyes grew cloudy the more she focused. Blinking rapidly, she tried to clear them.

Through the haze of her vision, she saw the myrax adjust its stance as though facing a predator. It shrieked and lunged at something she couldn't see, though her mind conjured the hulking mass of a vauger.

Sound was muffled, as though cotton batting were stuffed in her ears, so all she could hear were faint roars, shrieks, and snarls. Blinking slowly, Gillian tried to rise, fighting the blistering pain that consumed her body.

Head swimming, she clawed at the ground, dragging herself a few inches, trying to escape the nightmarish images playing out before her in a macabre dance.

The last thing she saw was the myrax, wings spread, hurled backward, and the crunch of its bones when it landed.

Roman cradled Gillian in his arms and raced through the forest.

It wouldn't take long for the myrax's mate to discover the creature's body and catch his scent.

The beast would hunt him down no matter how long it took.

His only chance was to mask his scent with Gillian's and find shelter.

Roman knew these woods. He'd explored every inch of them in his youth. He veered away, aiming for a cave he'd played in for hours as a child, then later used as a refuge to escape his father's grief.

Gillian whimpered and thrashed in his arms. He tucked her closer to his chest, cursing his brother, who was most likely still unconscious two leagues away.

The mate of the dead myrax howled in the night, quickening Roman's pace. He would slay it, too, though there was always risk when battling such a creature.

If he fell under the monster's talons, so too would Gillian.

The ground was a blur beneath his feet as he leaped over rocks and roots, racing toward the cave. When they neared the entrance, he sent a mental flare into the dark space, slapping at any living things within its walls and sending them scurrying.

He slowed as they passed into the mouth of the cave, hitching Gillian up when she went limp—not stopping until he was deep into the cavern, where it rounded in a shallow bowl.

Holding out a hand, he lit a flame along his palm to illuminate the darkness and laid her gently on the ground. Racing out, he gathered an armful of dry wood and ran back into the cave, building a small fire in moments with the skill and speed of his kind.

Rolling Gillian onto her stomach, he yanked her cloak aside and ripped her dress, exposing her shoulder.

Her skin was purple below the deep gouges from the myrax's talons. And within the puncture wounds was a swollen swath of flesh, bulging and angry.

Venom.

Like many creatures in the Shadowlands, the myrax had a venomous barb on its talons, capable of immobilizing its prey.

He held his hand above the wound, a black claw extending from his index finger, the point needle-sharp.

Roman punctured the blistering injury and leaned forward, closing his mouth around the tiny incision. His lips clamped over her skin, and he sucked, pulling the venom out and spitting it on the ground. It couldn't harm him, but the taste was sour, like rotted meat.

He started a rhythm, drawing out the toxin and spitting it on the ground, over and over, until her clean blood flooded into his mouth.

Roman paused, face hovering above Gillian's exposed back, and tried to spit out the blood.

It coated his tongue, making his throat ache.

His body shook, and he breathed deeply through his nose to regain control. But Gillian's scent hung in the air, growing stronger with every soft puff of her breath.

Curling his hands into fists, his throat bobbed without swallowing, his arms trembling with the effort, and he looked down at her unconscious form.

His pupils dilated into narrow slits, curls of smoke spilling from his nostrils.

He fought a war in his mind, her blood, the enemy's army, pooling on his tongue. It was a battle he couldn't win.

With a shudder, he swallowed, feeling it slide down his throat and into his stomach, where it flared white-hot. His muscles locked, and the world tilted on its axis, righting itself as Gillian's blood fused with his.

Invading every cell. Every thought. Every part of who he was.

His hands shook as she stirred. Roman slowly turned her

over, nostrils flaring as a breathy sigh slipped from her lips. His pupils narrowed and widened, fixing on her face.

Leaning forward, he cupped her head. "Gillian," he whispered harshly.

She groaned, head flopping to the side.

Roman rubbed his thumbs on her cheeks, tilting her face to look up at him. "Gillian."

Lips parting in a quiet mewl, her brow wrinkled, lashes fluttering. She blinked, her eyes slowly focusing on his face hovering above hers.

"Ro—" she started and cleared her clogged throat.

"Hush. You're safe."

Her eyes swung around, taking in the darkness of the cave before returning to him. He hadn't moved from his position above her. Every part of him reflected a fierce hunger she hadn't seen before, tugging at her.

She licked her dry lips, seeing his eyes flick to her mouth. A faint tendril of smoke wafted from his nostrils, and she stilled. "Roman."

His eyes closed slowly as the use of his name had weight.

When he opened them again, the look of longing was tinged with something else, something softer. Deeper. More powerful.

She'd seen that look before, many times. But never with such aching need.

Gillian tugged at the shoulder of her dress and shifted, trying to ease a kink forming in her back.

Roman moved with her, holding out a hand to pull her into a sitting position. His skin felt hot.

Gillian looked at her hand in his.

I can't care about him, she told herself as she'd done dozens of times.

But she didn't let go.

Even when she'd scooted to the wall of the cave to prop her back, she held onto him.

He saved me, she thought, and looked at him, really looked.

How many times had she tried to penetrate the arrogance and stoicism? How many times had she seen glimpses of something raw and lonely?

He wore no mask now.

Somehow, it had been stripped from him. He was laid bare before her. Vulnerable.

She squeezed his fingers, and he glanced at their twined hands. "You saved me. Again."

He nodded. "I'll always save you, Gillian."

"How did you find me?"

In her mind, she screamed, *Why? Why had he done it?*

The looks he was giving her went far beyond duty to his father. What she saw was so much more.

"I heard you scream," he said harshly, body shuddering with memories of the fear that had stopped his fist as he pummeled Draven. "I followed the shrieks of the myrax."

"You must hate me for what I did."

She looked down, pulling her hand away, though it pained her to do it. Gillian glanced at him. "But I'd do it again."

It was on the tip of her tongue to tell him Rory was going to die, and she wanted to be there to say goodbye. She thought he'd finally understand. But she stayed her tongue.

"I have to get home, Roman."

Again, his name on her lips rocked him. Names had power.

"I don't hate you. I could never hate you. I understand why you did it. If I were you, I'd have done the same."

It was the first time he acknowledged her plight.

"You'll... you'll let me go?"

The words came easily, but felt so awful. Why was part of her begging for him to say no?

He hung his head. "Why did you have to come here? You turned my life upside down, and I can't—"

Roman shook his head with a quick jerk. "I can't let you go."

He looked at her, eyes turning into molten flames. "I've tried. I told myself that I accepted you were not for me the moment I caught you in the forest. But it was a lie. And now..."

His body trembled.

Gillian stared at him, thinking it was her first time seeing him.

Really seeing him. "What's changed?"

"Everything."

She didn't understand. Yet she couldn't deny it.

The air felt charged. Her skin prickled with awareness as the truth of his words took root.

Something was different. "Roman? What's happening?"

"Let me show you," he leaned forward, hands shaking with restraint, and cupped her face, stopping when his mouth hovered inches from hers.

"May I?"

She nodded, eyes wide, heart thundering.

Roman's dark lashes swept down, and he leaned forward, pressing his mouth to hers.

Her body rocked at the contact.

Warmth raced along her skin, down her throat, and into the pit of her stomach, where it exploded in a ball of blistering heat and need. Gillian threaded her fingers in his hair, feeling them curl and grip his head, pulling him closer.

She needed to get closer.

Roman growled low in his throat, the sound going straight to her stomach, where it tickled and swirled.

He nipped the tip of his tongue, drawing a bead of blood, and kissed her thoroughly.

Hating himself as he did it. Knowing what it would mean and yet unable to stop.

His tongue twined with hers, his blood mixing with her saliva.

She swallowed the mixture, heat flooding her body in a raging fire. She felt herself falling as heat bloomed. Erupted. Flooding every cell, every follicle, every thought.

It licked down her throat in fingers of need that spread to her womb. Her breasts ached where they brushed against his chest as he delved deeper into her mouth, nipping playfully at her lips, his tongue darting in and out, mimicking a dance she had yet to experience.

His maleness called to her in a primal song, and she answered it, snaking her arms around him and molding her body to his. Desire built. Cresting in a tidal wave of need she didn't understand.

Roman felt it and groaned, shaking violently as he ran his hands up her arms, unhooking them from around his neck.

He pulled away from her, his body aching fiercely, eyes dilated to hungry slits. Pressing his forehead to hers, he panted, reining in his lust with each scalding breath.

Gillian whimpered and tried to reach for him, but he held her still. Knowing that if her lips found his again, he'd claim her in every way. He didn't want it to be that way. To be driven by base animal need.

She must understand what happened between them and make her choice.

And he must accept. Though it would kill him, should she refuse.

"Gillian, stop," he rasped as she tugged at him again.

He breathed heavily, the sawing of his chest matching hers.

"I want..." She stopped. She didn't have the words for the sensations racing through her body.

"I know. I do, too, but not now. Not here."

Roman took a shuddering breath and drew away from her. Raising one knee, he rested his arm and slowly regained control.

"I feel strange," Gillian whispered, plucking her dress and twisting her legs to ease the ache between them.

His nose twitched as he caught the scent of her desire.

It took all of his effort to tamp down his lust. Clenching his hands into fists, he clamped his lips shut and breathed deeply, opening his mind to hers. *Can you hear me, Gillian?*

Her mouth fell open, eyes growing wide. She looked at his lips, but they remained still. Again, his voice echoed in her head.

She sputtered. "How did you do that?"

We are linked, you and I. It is the bond.

"What?" She rubbed her ears and stared at him. "I don't understand what you're saying."

Roman paused, unsure how she'd take the truth but unable to lie. *You can hear me because we are mated. Speak to me with your mind.*

Brows knitting, she asked, "Mated? Did we—?"

She ran her hands over her bodice as if she'd feel it splayed open like the rip in her shoulder.

No. He chuckled and shook his head.

He uncurled his fingers and let his hands dangle. "When I cleansed your wound of the myrax's venom, I drank your blood. I didn't... it wasn't deliberate. I—"

He sighed and dropped his head. *You were not for me. You could never be for me.* He looked up at her. *And now you are.*

Gillian tested his words and felt the truth of them.

He was part of her as she was part of him. There was a connection, stronger, more profound than before. But it had always been there.

Somehow, it had been there from the start.

Yes, he said as if she'd spoken her thoughts aloud. *I felt it, too, and fought it from the moment I found you. But I can't fight it anymore.*

A fierce need to go to him, wrap her arms around him, and feel his mouth on hers filled her, and she rocked forward, catching herself before her hands reached for him.

He sensed the need raging in her body. It mirrored his own.

"What you feel is the mating bond," he explained. "Tenuous now, but if we..." Twin flames glowed in his eyes. "If we come together, it will be sealed."

But it means more than that, doesn't it? she asked with her mind.

The flames in his eyes guttered. *That's why I couldn't take you. I want you to choose me. Not because your body yearns for it, but because I'm what you want.*

Her stomach roiled.

The thought of never seeing her brother again was a dagger in her heart. But equally as painful was the idea of leaving Roman and never knowing his fate. Never feeling the weight of his eyes on her, the softness of his touch.

How could she face such an impossible choice?

"You can't come with me." Her voice sounded so small.

"No."

Of course, he couldn't.

Keridwen had ensured that. His kind couldn't cross into her world. If she left him, she might never return.

That's what Morrigan had told her. The medallion would permit her to pass through the barrier, but once it did, the magic imbued in the clay would wither. It would be nothing but a gray disc carved in etchings that no longer held any power.

It wasn't fair.

Chapter Twenty-Three

They stayed in the cave until the promise of dawn lit the sky in pink, purple, and orange hues. Their bodies yearned for each other, but their wills resisted.

Roman led her out, his fingers laced with hers. Her need for him hadn't lessened, but she could control it. For now.

If he kissed her, she'd surrender completely. And she had to appreciate him for that because she knew he was aware of the power he could wield over her body, and he chose not to use it.

Through the wee hours of the night, he'd kept his distance, only touching her when he couldn't refrain any longer. And only her hands and face.

Never claiming her mouth, though she'd ached for him to kiss her again, longed for some part of him to claim her deeply.

The need for him was too strange. Too new.

She wrestled with it, wondering if he sensed her inner turmoil. Knowing, somehow, it mirrored his own.

Why didn't you just let it happen? she asked, staring out across the landscape and tapping at his mind as they stood at the mouth of the cave, stomach tingling when she recalled the feel of his lips on hers.

He looked at her and tilted her chin up to meet his eyes. "It wasn't easy, but I knew how you'd feel if I took advantage. The betrayal such an act would evoke. I couldn't do that to you. Your body would ever be mine, but your heart…"

Her hand traveled beneath her cloak to the torn shoulder of her dress.

The rip was like their relationship, all jagged edges with threads still clinging together. The dress could be repaired, but it would always show the tear like a wound that never heals.

"You betrayed me before when you stole me away to Valon."

"I know. If the bond had been in place at that time, I wouldn't have been able to do that."

She watched his expression, wondering how far the bond went in controlling his actions.

"It's not because the bond makes me incapable of betrayal but because I wouldn't want to spend my life with someone who would grow to hate me. I'm not a monster."

Gillian looked away. "I know."

She bit her lip, not wanting him to see the tears pooling in her eyes. She couldn't stay with him and let her brother die without seeing his sweet face again. Gillian needed Rory to know how hard she'd tried, how much she loved him, before he left the world.

She didn't need to tell Roman her decision. He knew. He accepted it even though it would haunt him for the rest of his days.

It would haunt her, too.

Roman breathed in her scent, letting it fill his lungs, feeling her essence invade every part of him.

When she left him, when he let her go, the gaping hole her leaving would create would likely kill him.

If not, he'd welcome the Wasting.

He'd court the deadly ailment and let himself wither and die rather than live for eternity without her. But she didn't need to know that.

Let her live in her world, believing he lived on in his.

"Will I still be able to speak to you, with my mind, when I cross the border?"

He swallowed hard, jaw ticking. "I don't know. It's never been done."

"If... if it works, would it be all right if I did?"

Turning toward her, he reached up and traced the line of her cheek, letting his finger curve around her chin.

His touch left a trail of jangled nerves as though he woke them up simply by pressing his skin to hers. Her lashes fluttered as he traced the perfect bow of her lips.

"Yes. I would like that."

"I'm sorry, Roman. If there were another way, I would take it."

"This is the only way, Gillian."

The sound of her name on his lips sent a wave of molten heat through her belly.

"It's not safe for you to remain in the Shadowlands. My father will never allow us to be together. You were never supposed to be mine."

They'd traveled half the day when Draven caught up with them.

His eye was swollen, and he walked with a limp. "Brother!" he shouted, stopping them in their tracks.

Roman tucked Gillian behind him. She clung to his back, fingers digging into his tunic.

"Forget you saw us, Draven."

The younger Dragonborn male stalked toward them, the scales along his cheek and neck pulsing.

"Let her go," he warned.

Gillian poked her head around Roman's shoulder, but he pushed her back.

"No."

Draven stopped and cocked his head. He sniffed the air, nostrils flaring and eyes growing wide when he scented their bond. "What have you done?"

"Back off, Draven."

His brother mashed his lips. "Do you have any idea what you've brought down on you both? Does she?"

Pushing against his protective grasp, Gillian walked around Roman and faced him. "What does he mean?"

The young male snarled. "You mated and didn't tell her of the danger?"

He charged at Roman, anger sparking in eyes that took on the appearance of flames. "How could you? You know what he'll do!"

Roman shoved him back and grabbed Gillian's wrist, pulling her away from his brother. "We didn't seal the bond."

Draven paused, and Roman held up his hands, dropping them in defeat.

"I didn't mean for it to happen. When it did, I couldn't... we didn't—"

His eyes flashed to Gillian, who stood awkwardly a few paces away. "Father will never have the chance to harm her. I'm taking her to the border. She's going home."

Draven looked from one to the other, finally landing on the older male, face contorting. "You know what this means."

Roman nodded brusquely.

"And you did it anyway?"

"Yes."

Gillian went to his side and clutched his arm, ignoring the flare of need the simple gesture induced. "Roman, what is he talking about?"

"It doesn't matter." He glanced at Draven, sending him a silent message. "We need to leave. If you found us, it'll only be a matter of time before he knows."

"He already knows," Draven whispered. "He commanded me to find you."

"How much does he know?" Roman demanded, glancing at the sky as though he'd see the Dragon sweeping toward them.

"Everything."

Draven hadn't meant to tell Marius. But he wasn't strong enough to keep the Great Dragon out of his mind. He'd grown weak over the years, so much weaker than before.

From the moment Gillian's potion had released its hold on Roman, Marius had known. He'd watched through his eyes and listened.

And, now, he was coming.

"You've doomed us," Roman said, horrified.

He whipped around and slung Gillian over his shoulder.

She yelped, wanting to ask what was wrong, but he took off at a sprint. Trees, shrubs, and rocks flew by in a blur as he raced toward the border, Draven at his heels.

They crashed through the trees, heedless of the noise of their passing, sending birds flying and small animals scurrying.

Branches smacked Roman's face, slicing his cheeks, but he ignored it, fear lending him strength as the border between Dwyer Forest and the village of Rudgarde drew nearer.

From behind him, Draven yelled a warning, his voice cut short by a thunderous roar.

The Great Dragon had found them.

Gillian whimpered and clutched Roman as wind from the Dragon's wings blew through the trees, snapping limbs. He held on tightly, his grip painful as he pushed himself to his limits, straining to outrun a creature he had no hope of thwarting.

Marius roared as he sighted them and sent an arrow of fire in their path.

Trees burst into flames.

Roman shifted course and kept running, Draven close behind.

He almost stopped when the younger male crashed to the ground, shrieking and clutching his head. Blocking out the pain he felt spiking through their brotherly bond. He barreled through the underbrush, Gillian bouncing painfully against his back.

The boundary between their worlds shimmered subtly like a mirage.

And like a mirage, it revealed its ugly truth, its false hope of escape, when the Great Dragon dove, landing between them and the barrier.

The ground shook violently, felling trees and causing small rock slides.

Marius swung his body around, lashing his tail, smashing everything in its path. He hissed, his tongue tasting the air, and lowered his head.

Hate-filled eyes fixed on Roman, who stumbled to a halt, chest heaving.

Gillian slid down his body and stood on shaky legs, tucking herself behind his back.

The Dragon chuffed and gouged the ground in deep furrows with his claws.

"You dare!" he roared.

Gillian grabbed the sides of her head and crumpled to the ground.

Roman's body tensed. He glared at his father and crouched low, shielding her. "Let her go!"

Marius came toward them, each step shaking the earth. "I'll see her squealing like a pig beneath me while you watch," he snarled.

Rage, unlike anything he'd felt before, thrummed through Roman's body.

He rose slowly, bracing his legs to stand guard over Gillian, who curled on the ground, keening, as Marius stabbed at her mind with daggers of thought.

His skin felt hot, the breath flowing from his nostrils igneous blasts.

Claws tucked deep within his fingers split his skin, extending to their full length. Fangs erupted from his gums while the scales he'd kept hidden, even from his father, slicked over his body in black waves, covering his skin.

Roman bent his knees in a fighting stance, arms out at his sides in readiness. "You'll have to kill me before I let you touch her!"

"So be it."

The Great Dragon opened his jaws, fangs dripping liquid heat, and came at Roman.

He glanced at Gillian, a myriad of emotions swirling in his eyes. "Run."

They clashed in a chorus of roars and snarls.

Roman leaped and spun, slashing at his father, but he was no match for the Dragon.

And he knew it.

Marius swung his massive head and snapped wickedly sharp teeth, cleaving the air around his son in warning.

Roman narrowed his eyes and scrambled onto Marius's back, racing along the Dragon's spine and bending low to trail his claws, scraping scales along his path. But they remained whole and unblemished.

Marius hissed and whipped his body to the side, launching Roman into a tree that snapped in half with an eerie shriek.

The Dragonborn male landed hard on his back in a cloud of splinters and leaves.

His father pinned him beneath his forefoot and pressed down. Marius arched his neck into a deep curve, the tip of his snout hovering above Roman's prone form.

"I could kill you."

Gillian screamed and staggered to her feet. She ran toward Roman, all her attention fixed on him.

Leave me! he shouted through their mental connection. *Run!*

She batted away his command and slid to her knees at his side, glaring into the Dragon's face. "Let him go, or you'll find another dead witch-wife."

Her words had their desired effect.

The Great Dragon flinched, images of Maud's broken body filling his mind.

He tapped a toe claw on Roman's chest and narrowed his eyes. "You have yet to seal your bond."

She bowed her head. "Release him. Please."

"Gillian, no," Roman pleaded, the scales covering his body melting away to reveal skin.

Something in her shriveled when she looked at him. "I can't let you die."

"Please. Don't do this."

Gillian got to her feet and faced Marius. "Free him, and I'll go with you."

The Dragon slowly lifted his foot, letting it hover menacingly in the air.

He could slam it down, ending his son's life, and she knew it. She heard the unspoken threat.

Equally clear was his voice in her head, nearly eclipsing Roman's silent plea for her to run.

Eyes swimming, she looked down at the mate of her heart and walked toward the Great Dragon.

Each step hurt.

She wasn't only leaving Roman. With her surrender, she was also leaving her young brother to die without hearing her voice or seeing her face before he took his last breath.

Talons curled around her body, and she grabbed hold of one of them, never letting her eyes stray from Roman's. Knowing she'd never forget the agony she saw as the Dragon flapped his wings and launched into the air.

Gillian clung to Roman with her eyes as long as she could. Watching as he stumbled toward her, reaching.

Watching until he was nothing more than a dim figure amidst the dark woods.

Chapter Twenty-Four

The air was biting as the Great Dragon hurtled toward Valon.

Gillian clenched her eyes shut and held on tightly, hearing Roman's voice in her head. It broke her to feel his wrath and grief as she was carried away from him.

I'm sorry, she told him over and over until it became a numbing chant.

He understood.

He raged, but he understood.

She couldn't watch him die. It would've killed her to see him split open on the ground.

He'd rather she were a slave to his father than think of her on her deathbed.

Roman found Draven lying in a stupor. Blood dripped from his nose, remnants of Marius' violent invasion into his mind. He swiped it away and took Roman's extended hand.

"He took her?"

Pain flashed across his face, and Roman looked away. "Yes."

"I'm sorry. It's my fault. I couldn't keep him out." He dropped his head. "If I hadn't found you."

"Stop." Roman's face tightened. "She was only mine for a moment. That was all we were ever going to have. I just hoped."

The muscles in his face jumped. "I wanted her to have peace. To be among the people she loved. I failed her."

"We'll get her back."

Roman looked at his brother, marveling at how his sibling could risk his life after what he'd done to him. "I'm sorry I hurt you."

Draven shrugged. "I would've done the same in your place."

He clapped him on the back. "You would've *tried*."

They spoke quietly, making plans, knowing time was short.

If Marius were able to sever his bond with Gillian, the Dragon would use all his power to overwhelm her senses and take her to wife.

Darkness had fallen, another day come and gone, when they crested a ridge and looked across at Valon.

"Can you still feel her?" Draven asked.

Roman gave a curt nod.

He could, but she was weak, as though her mind was battered.

Imagining what his father had done to wear her down over the long hours they'd traveled tormented him.

He flexed his fingers and glared at the castle. Once inside the gates, they'd have to avoid detection.

His father would be expecting Roman to devise some kind

of rescue. Entering the stronghold was a fool's errand. Draven's mind was too open, the younger male too weak to hide their approach.

But he couldn't leave Gillian. He had to try. Some things were worth dying for.

The cragga lowed plaintively as Draven and Roman ran, ducking in and out of groups of the bovine creatures, blending with the nighttime shadows and their hulking forms.

The village outside the castle was cloaked in darkness, quiet save for the intermittent sounds of snoring as they hugged the walls of huts, avoiding the sharp eyes of the guards prowling the wall walk.

Skirting the outer wall of the stronghold, Roman led them to a cellar door, partially hidden by curtains of ivy trailing from the black stone wall.

Roman paused and looked at his brother, his copper eyes glowing in the moonlight. "Do you sense him?"

Draven lowered his head and focused, searching his mind for the tenor of his father's thoughts. Lifting his lashes, he said, "No. But he could be masking his presence."

Gritting his teeth, Roman debated their next move, worry for Gillian overriding caution.

He nudged the door open, wincing when it squealed on its rusty hinges. Slipping inside, they paused in the darkness, allowing their eyes to adjust to the gloom.

Trailing his fingers along the damp stone, Roman led them to a narrow opening that connected to the root cellar. From there, the brothers took a short flight of stairs toward the kitchen.

Pressing his palm to the wood separating the dark stairwell

from the larder on the other side, Roman breathed deeply and sent out a mental probe, searching for the minds of anyone on the lower level of the keep. Brows knitting, he glanced at Draven and tried again.

Nothing.

Not even the cook, who slept in a small room off the kitchen. He drew back from the door, skin prickling.

His brother gave him a questioning look.

He frowned and turned his head toward the door. Tightening his hands into fists, he stared at the wood and listened with his ears and mind, but nothing came to him. Loosening his fingers, he let out a slow breath and grasped the latch.

The door swung away from the frame inch by inch. His hand gripped the metal, keeping it from opening too loudly. He craned his neck to look at Draven when the door was wrenched open.

Roman fell forward and into the hands of a contingent of his father's most loyal guard.

Behind them stood the Dragon, arms folded, an ugly sneer marring his darkly handsome face. "Did you think I would allow you to sneak into my keep and steal her from me?"

At Marius' side stood Ansel, his face wiped clean of the hostility he wore as a cloak.

With a blank stare, the Dragonborn lunged toward Roman, swinging a club and knocking his brother senseless with a brutal strike and a whispered word of power.

Roman went down, never hearing Draven's yell.

Never seeing his brother smash through the guards, throwing them to the ground as he went for Marius.

Roman was in darkness.

Trapped in his mind, while Draven writhed on the floor, screaming in pain, as the Dragon tortured him into servility.

Roman woke in iron chains, arms suspended from thick anchors set in a massive wooden beam.

He blinked, trying to clear the raging headache pounding against his skull. His tunic was gone, along with his boots, leaving his feet bare on the cold stone of the floor.

He craned his neck and flexed his arms, testing his bonds. The effort sent flares of pain shooting through his head.

The iron cuffs were carved with symbols to sap his strength.

He was soon panting, body sagging, pulling on the iron links fixed into the rafter. Roman's head dropped, and he reached for Gillian, visualizing the mating bond connecting their minds.

A flicker of awareness answered. Dim and weak.

He ground his teeth and balled his hands into fists, yanking on the metal bindings. Sweat poured down his body as he fought to free himself, knowing it was a fruitless effort.

Chest heaving, he stopped struggling and roared, his voice bouncing off the walls.

Time ceased to exist.

He had no sense of day or night, the only light came from braziers fixed into the stone.

He raged and fought the chains that leached his power and drained his energy. Roman drifted in and out of consciousness, coming to awareness by the sound of feet scraping the floor.

He lifted his head, strands of limp dark hair clung to his

face, sticking to the shadow of the beard covering his jaw. Lifting his eyes, he met his father's cold stare.

"Where is she?" he rasped.

Marius angled a brow. "She is no longer your concern."

Roman lunged toward the Dragon, the thick muscles of his arms and chest straining against the iron. "You bastard!"

Pain flashed in Marius' eyes, gone as soon as it came.

He hardened his jaw and breathed out in puffs of smoke, the wide sleeves of his robe billowing out at his sides.

"You betrayed me. It is I who should be cursing you. It is my hand that should cut your throat and sever the bond you forged with my future mate."

"Then do it!" Roman spat, heaving against the metal. "Without her, I'm dead anyway."

The Great Dragon's eyes grew molten. Flames danced in them, each flicker a warning.

"Sever our bond, Father. Force her hand, and she will grow to *hate* you."

"That is a risk I am willing to take for the sake of our survival."

The Dragon stepped toward him and reached for his face.

Roman jerked back, but his father gripped the hair plastered to the side of his head, forcing his face to remain fixed.

"Does your hate run so deep that you would see our line ended? Would you rather I spend eternity bereft of a mate?"

Within the Dragon's eyes were millennia of grief.

Chasms of darkness.

Marius slipped into his son's mind, showing him memories of Ashael. Filling him with the sounds of dragonlings. The peeps of young.

The images shifted.

Ashael's broken body bleeding out on the unforgiving ground. A cold, silent rookery.

Roman fought his father's mind, but his strength waned, no match for the Dragon.

Marius pummeled him with a taste of his grief. Centuries of emptiness. Flickers of hope when he coupled with human wives, only to be extinguished when they didn't quicken.

And finally, young.

Not Dragons, but sons who carried pieces of him within their veins.

Marius flooded every thought and smothered every emotion warring within Roman with his own.

Anguish. Loneliness. Yearning. Joy. Continuance.

Roman's mind buckled under the onslaught, body crumpling even as his limbs strained in the chains.

The bond between Gillian and him wavered. It was fragile —a thread pitting itself against the iron will of the Dragon.

A thin trail of blood slipped from Roman's nostril, curving over his lip and down his chin, dripping onto the stone floor.

Marius tracked it, following the path it carved along his son's face. He bent his head when the blood fell, loosening his hold on Roman's mind as he stared at the spot where it landed, the contrast of deep red on cold gray.

"You could've had any woman within my kingdom, and I would've blessed the bond. But instead, you took mine."

He paused and stared at his son.

"Gillian was never yours," he whispered, letting his words fill his son's mind.

Turning his back, Marius strode toward the door, pausing at the threshold.

His hand gripped the frame, fingers clenching, digging into stone and wood. Splinters and grit fell to the floor as he craned to look once more at the Dragonborn male. The favorite of his children, though Roman could not know that.

Releasing his hand, he left.

Part of his ancient heart remained in the cell behind him.

Chapter Twenty-Five

Gillian sat by the fire, awaiting the inevitable visit from Ansel. She'd grown to hate the sullen male—his clipped voice and cold eyes.

Every exchange was caustic.

Since her return to Valon, he'd come to her room twice or thrice daily, rousing her from bed or her frequent catatonic states before her chamber's narrow window. Not leaving until she accompanied him to the solar, where Marius would eventually join her.

"Get up. It's time to go," Ansel said, swinging open the door with barely a knock to announce his presence.

"No."

He sighed. "I tire of this routine."

"I tire of you."

She mashed her lips and stared at the fire, gripping the arms of her chair.

"Even the lure of your blood isn't worth the trouble of

trying to win you. I don't know why my father tries," he muttered, striding towards her and stopping at her feet.

She ignored his outstretched hand, knuckles turning white as she tightened her hold.

Dropping his hand, he stalked around the back of her chair, picked it up, and marched to the open doorway.

Gillian squawked with outrage and swatted at him. He took advantage and tipped the chair forward. She hit the ground and stumbled into the doorframe.

"Has anyone ever told you that your character is as ugly as your face?"

Her words were like a poisoned arrow.

They hit Ansel, their deadly tips burrowing deep into his mind. "Lucky for you, I'm not here to win your heart."

"You could never win someone's heart."

Ansel's eyes flickered, momentarily revealing the shadowy things he kept hidden beneath layers of disdain.

He motioned to the open doorway, lips clamped together in a thin line.

Gillian glared at him for a moment, then stomped out of the room, turning up her nose at the guards she passed in the halls.

Ansel was an angry shadow at her back, dogging her steps until she reached the solar. She took pleasure in slamming the solar door in his face. Snatching up a pillow, she plunked herself onto the cushioned seat of a chair and scowled.

Four days had passed since the Dragon had stolen her from Roman, and in all that time, she'd felt only echoes of him through their bond. Whispers as though he were too far to reach her.

She'd stopped asking Ansel if he was on the castle grounds.

Frowning, she plucked at her gown, a sumptuous dress in emerald green embroidered with tiny dragons throughout the bodice. A similarly exquisite gown had arrived each day through her maidservant, Mary.

The woman would bustle in and lay the clothing across the bed, oohing and ahhing as she stroked the silky fabric.

Gillian's passive face followed the displays, often leading to gentle pats and promises of better days if only she'd accept her life among them.

But she could not embrace her lot.

She made promises to Marius that she couldn't keep. Her brother lay dying outside the Shadowlands. He could be asking for her, wondering where she was and why she wasn't at his side as the Wasting ate away his body.

Roman had been willing to let her cross the border, knowing what it would do to the bond she'd felt since their blood mixed so exquisitely.

Roman.

He haunted her thoughts as much as Rory did.

Her mate, though their connection was tenuous. If he'd taken her when she'd clung to him, would she have been able to leave the Shadowlands? She thought not.

He'd known it, of course. It was why he'd gently pushed her away when she longed for more.

Gillian clung to the bond with Roman, feeding her magic into it. Shoring it up even as Marius sought to weaken it. Thus far, he'd had no inkling she worked against his efforts, but she had no illusions that her efforts would remain undetected.

When he discovered what she'd been doing all along, he'd begin a new campaign to wear her down and claim her.

Her face shifted toward the flames in the hearth.

Even now, having done nothing but sit and stare, she was tired. Worn in mind and body.

How much longer can I keep fighting? she wondered. *How much longer do I need to hold on until Roman comes for me?*

In dark moments, she imagined the Dragon had killed his son. That what she felt when she reached for the bond was an illusion. That she was trapped there, holding on to hope when there was none.

The solar door opened, and her body tensed, readying for the mental battle she was forced to play each day. But it wasn't Marius who entered.

It was Draven.

He walked stiffly into the room. Gillian rose, mouth parting, only to close when she really looked at him.

The scales along his neck and left cheek looked pale, the deep red tinged with sickly orange. Purple lined the underside of each eye as though he'd had no sleep for days.

He came to her, stopping when he was a foot away. She lifted her chin to face him.

He looked haunted. Lips tight, eyes flickering from light copper to muddy brown.

"Is he here?" she asked, hands twisting at her waist.

He gave a curt nod. "We—" he cleared his throat. "We were trying to rescue you."

Gillian swallowed hard. "Where is he?"

"I don't know."

"But he's here?"

Draven looked away. "I can feel him. I know he's close, but I can't..." His brow wrinkled. "Father blocks my thoughts. He's in my head."

Her lips thinned in anger. "If Roman's here, I'll find him."

She made to brush past him, but he grabbed her arm. She glanced at where his fingers curled around her limb. "Don't try to stop me, Draven."

"He'll never let you go."

She didn't need to ask who he meant. Marius had made his possessive nature clear. "And I'll never submit."

"Gillian," he dropped his hand and hung his head. "He'll kill him."

Draven's voice cracked. He lifted his lashes and met her gaze. His face was a mask of anguish. "He'll kill Roman if you continue to resist."

Her heart stuttered in her chest. Marius would kill him?

The notion was so evil that she recoiled. How could a father kill a son? She didn't want to believe it.

Her mind warred with the idea that a parent would intentionally harm their child. It was so foreign. So against what she'd glimpsed in the Dragon's mind that she became suspicious.

Was Draven toying with her? Playing on her compassion at the behest of his father?

She tapped at Draven's mind using the skills Morrigan had taught her. They were nothing compared to what they could be if she'd had the time to truly learn the craft of mentalism.

Gillian circled his thoughts. They were shrouded in darkness so thick she had no sense of him.

It was as though, like Marius, he'd armored himself against

her. She was about to withdraw when she felt a fluttering of awareness. Following it, she caught a glimpse of Draven's will struggling against the Dragon's control.

Gillian flicked her eyes to his.

He beseeched her. Saying what he couldn't utter with a look.

She opened her mouth to ask a question, and he shook his head. Snapping it shut, she stepped toward him. So close she could feel the heat of his body.

He dipped his head to look at her.

Lifting her arm, she cupped his cheek, feeling the smooth scales on his face shift beneath her palm. She pressed a finger to his temple and gave him a sip of her magic.

Magic lived within her as Rowena's child, as one of Keridwen's blessed daughters.

Morrigan had revealed the power to her. In the time she'd spent beside the high witch, she'd learned the basics of how to harness it. Its full, untapped potential remained nestled within her.

But she knew enough of its nature to call it forth.

Draven blanched, scales paling and yellowish, as the magic sank into him. His head buzzed, the darkness enveloping it retreating infinitesimally.

She closed her eyes, using her thready connection to slip deeper into his mind.

A needle of thought pierced the retreating darkness, illuminating the landscape of his thoughts. She felt his will reach toward hers and opened herself to it.

Had she more skill, had Morrigan trained her longer, she would've sensed the cold presence of the Dragon.

Like a spider, he waited and watched, sensing her intrusion while cloaking his awareness.

When the small portal to her mind opened to Draven's questing, Marius slithered out of the darkness. It was too late when she felt him.

Gillian yelped and collapsed on the solar floor.

Once again in the Dragon's control, Draven stared dispassionately at her.

Marius entered the room, sweeping his son aside to crouch at Gillian's head.

Such a strong creature, he mused, tracing a finger along her brow.

He could use brute force and cut through the fragile shields she threw up, but if he unleashed his full power, he'd hurt her.

His hand hung limply on his knee as he considered what to do. Using Draven to batter her defenses had limits. It was up to him to win her.

Opening her mind, claiming it, took time. She needed to let her guard down and unfurl like a blushing rose. Only then would he be able to claim her, mind and body.

But his nature was born of fire, and patience was for those whose blood did not flow with Dragon flame.

Marius breathed deeply, letting her scent fill his lungs.

It's foolish to fight me, Gillian. In the end, you will be mine, and together, we will usher in a new generation, he told her, smothering the last of her will.

He rocked back on his heels and glanced at his son, who stood immobile at her feet.

With a casual thought, he sent Draven from the room and

scooped Gillian into his arms, carrying her to a chaise near the window.

Buttery sunlight spilled through the glass as he sat, stretching her body out and cradling her head in his lap. He brushed tendrils of pale hair from her face and touched her lips, feeling a soft puff of her breath.

The door to her mind stood open.

He'd stolen his way inside when she'd reached for Draven's trapped will. His lashes swept down as he delved into her thoughts, feeling for the mating bond.

When he found it, his face contorted with deep and bitter envy.

In his mind, he saw their possible future. Their happiness. The young they would bring into the world. Young who would bear the stamp of their intertwined blood.

He saw himself outside their union, alone.

The Dragon's eyes turned flinty. His ancient mind balked at the theft of a future mate.

He was eternal.

It was his right to continue his bloodline no matter the cost. If he were gone from the world, it would cease to exist.

Marius grabbed a mental hold of the mating bond.

It was not the weak thread he'd anticipated.

Somehow, she'd forged a magical shield around it that even now protected it. He prowled the bond, poking at it with his mind. It repelled him.

Brows wrinkling, he cupped her head and drove a mental spike into her.

Gillian's body twitched before heaving upward, her back arching.

Marius held her in place and stabbed at her mind again and again.

She thrashed. But the bond held.

With a growl, he pushed her off his lap and stood up. Marius scowled at her, then lifted his head and looked out the window, seeing past the forests around Valon to the seat of the Coven of the Silver Moon.

Morrigan was responsible for Gillian's ability to repel him.

He'd warned the matriarch of what would befall her and her sisters should she defy him. It was time the high witch felt the cost of that defiance.

Marius stalked through the halls and up to the battlements.

Guards saw his expression and bowed before ducking out of his way. Brisk breezes tossed his long black hair as he stood on a parapet and faced Gealach Wood.

He climbed the low edge of the stone and lifted his arms, his robe flowing behind him. Angling his body toward the earth, he fell, shifting in the air, becoming Dragon.

He roared as he tore through the sky, sending villagers scurrying into huts or cowering in the shadows.

Sunlight bounced off his scales, giving the appearance of fire streaking across the horizon as he aimed for the coven's realm.

Leathery wings beat in a meteoric rhythm fueled by rage.

He shot through the clouds, banking hard when the coven's forest spread out below. The scorched earth of his last attack lay visible through the trees. Marius opened his wings, slowing his body, and circled the witches' lair.

With the sharp eyes of a falcon, he watched the sisters of the Silver Moon stop their work and gather in a ring around the high witch.

Morrigan tracked the Dragon.

Without wards shielding their realm, they were more vulnerable but not defenseless. Since the last attack, the high witch had drilled into the core of her power, readying herself.

Her lips moved as she called on powerful defensive magic to protect them.

The Great Dragon roared at her and whipped his tail in the air, cutting through a low-hanging cloud. Diving for the matriarch, he spat a jet of molten fire at the witch.

It struck the protective spell the high witch released into the air like a soldier's shield and flowed outward in rivers of heat.

The sisters raised their arms in unison and called to Keridwen, asking for the power to beat back the Dragon fire.

The goddess stirred, her celestial gaze fixed on the serpent.

Marius hissed as he swooped over the land, watching the flames recede and flicker under the witches' magic. Angling his body so that his tail dipped toward the ground, he hovered above the coven and released another stream of flames.

It hit their magic in waves of scalding heat, scorching the ground around the coven before shifting to black and then gray and dissipating in plumes of smoke.

Skin blistered and hair curled, but they did not waver.

Rage filled the Great Dragon.

He spun in the air and dove, ejecting streams of fire and globs of molten heat over and over in a barrage.

The goddess herself thwarted each attack as she poured her energy into the witches' spellcraft.

Marius' fire blackened the earth, consuming trees, singeing the hems of their dresses, and boiling water sitting in buckets.

Still, the coven, strengthened by the power of a goddess, stood defiant against him.

"Morrigan!" he roared, the sound ripping across the sky.

"I hear you, worm," she said, "and I know why you've come."

"Then you know your days have ended," he warned, loosing another sea of fire.

"That may be. You can destroy us, but not even you can defeat Keridwen. Tell me, Dragon, what do you think the goddess will do if you slaughter her chosen?"

The Dragon hovered for a moment, her warning filling his mind.

He tilted his massive wings and aimed for a sharp peak jutting through the trees. Flapping slowly, he landed on the rocky outcropping, sending shards tumbling as his body shook the earth.

Rage burned in his ancient heart as he glared at the witches through breaks in the trees. But he couldn't ignore what the high witch said.

Her words were like a tiny insect burrowing into his brain.

He watched as Morrigan separated herself and left her sisters to face him. Her confidence renewed his wrath.

"How dare you defy me!" he screamed into the wind.

She paused and craned her neck to look at him. "I do not answer to you."

"I am the earth itself! Without my gifts, you and your kind would be nothing but cosmic dust floating across the universe!"

"And this is how you treat your children?" she challenged.

The Dragon snarled, puffs of smoke blasting from his nostrils.

Morrigan ignored his bluster and walked slowly through Gealach Wood, allowing the Dragon to feel her contempt.

She knew of the mating bond between Gillan and Roman. And she knew what Marius had done to them.

The moment the young witch was captured, she'd felt a rift.

It grieved her to stand helplessly as Gillian was taken from the Dragonborn. She'd even felt pity for the Dragon's son.

He must have paid a steep price for claiming Marius' future mate, she thought to herself.

Leaving the shelter of a line of trees along the border, Morrigan swept back her white hair and lifted her face toward the Dragon.

His narrow pupils fixed on the witch, tendrils of smoke filling the air around his snout. Digging his black claws into the rock, he stretched his neck toward her. Sunlight bounced off the golden scales of his underbelly.

"Unhook your vile will from my future mate, or I will burn her to ash," he snarled in flecks of scalding spit.

"My will?" She shook her head. "Unlike you, I do not pit my will against my sisters and steal their minds. If she defies you, it is her doing, not mine."

A hind leg dragged across the ground, creating deep furrows. Tail lashing, he chuffed, flames dancing along a line of fangs. "You lie."

She shook her head. "You have never understood our sisterhood."

"Release her!" he roared, each word punctuated with power.

Morrigan studied him, seeing beyond the rage to the pain buried deep within it. "I cannot. I have no hold on her."

He flung his head skyward and fanned his wings.

Taking a deep breath, he released jets of fire into the sky. They hit the atmosphere, lighting banks of clouds in hues of orange, giving the horizon the appearance of dawn.

When his anger was spent, he lowered his head and glared at her. "I'll kill her."

Her chest squeezed.

She knew the Dragon wasn't dissembling. He was on the cusp, so filled with rage and loneliness that he was prepared to burn his realm to the ground before he'd give Gillian up.

The high witch envisioned Gillian's death, allowing her mind and body to feel the grief of such an act and knowing she'd do nothing to stop it if it came to pass.

She'd let Gillian go, knowing the risks. Even then, Morrigan had accepted the possibility the young witch would never reach her homeland.

The finality of what she knew might be the only path forward was a bitter brew to swallow. One life was a sacrifice she would have to bear to protect the lives of her sisters.

"Is your anger so great you would kill any hope of a future?"

The Dragon growled softly.

"Hear me, serpent. If you doom Gillian to die, I do not have the power to stop you."

Marius rumbled low in his chest, the sound vibrating through his stone perch. His tongue flicked the air, tasting the truth of her words on the wind. He scraped a claw along the rock, sending shards in every direction.

"But I don't believe you want her blood, or the blood of

your son, on your hands." She sighed and looked at the ground, adding softly, "Ashael sees you still."

Her words sank into the Dragon like a poisoned arrow. He rocked back, eyes dilating, wings snapping.

"Go now. Return to Valon and face the consequences of what you've wrought."

Morrigan looked at him sadly, then turned and disappeared into the forest. Trees bent as she walked beneath them, shielding her entirely from the Dragon's baleful stare.

He remained on the bluff overlooking the coven's land for many minutes, considering her words and feeling the weight of Keridwen's eye fixed on him.

Ashael sees you still, she'd told him.

Her words were an unwelcome reflection, as though he leaned over a still pool of water and saw what he'd become.

Marius' neck bent in a graceful arch, and he looked down at the ruined ground beneath his talons. He tapped a toe and watched rock crack and flecks tumble, permanently scarring the peak. Perhaps those scars were also a reflection of himself.

Sighing with a gush of smoke, he leaped into the air and flew toward Valon.

Chapter Twenty-Six

A kink in her neck woke Gillian, and she rolled to her side on the chaise in the solar, nearly toppling to the ground when she misjudged the edge.

Her head was fuzzy, echoes of the Dragon lingering like a stain.

She felt for the mating bond, sending a thought to Roman along the thready connection and sagging in relief when he weakly tapped back. Running her hands down her gown, she rose and looked through the leaded panes of the window.

It was well past midday. Men and Dragonborn trained on a field in the outer bailey.

She scanned the horizon, her muddy thoughts recalling the sound of the Dragon, expecting to see Marius furiously circling the keep. But all she saw were puffy white clouds hanging above the mountains of Valon.

The door swung open, and she turned, coming face-to-face with her captor.

Marius looked haggard, his normally striking face gaunt and

pale. He watched her from the doorway like a wounded predator.

But even she knew that an animal was at its most dangerous when injured. Gillian stood still, forcing her hands to her sides, and met his gaze.

"Where is he?"

The Great Dragon's eyes shifted to the floor. "Where you can't find him."

Her hands balled into fists. "Let me see him." He glanced at her from beneath his brows. "Please."

Marius lifted his chin and strolled toward her, hips moving in a loose gait. His black robe flared behind him, the deep V of his tunic showing glimpses of his muscled chest.

He stopped when he was a handbreadth from her. Marius tilted his head and captured her gaze, resisting the urge to crush her body to his. He let out a soft breath laced with the primal essence of his being.

Her pupils dilated when she caught his scent, returning to normal in moments.

Her will was too strong. The bond was too fixed for him to sway her.

She craned her neck to look up at him.

He was fire itself standing before her. Copper eyes shifting to molten flame. Heat dripped from his pores and made her skin flush.

Her legs shifted restlessly, trying to ease the aching his nearness provoked. Gillian gritted her teeth and clamped down on her physical response, severing the need growing within her before it took root.

Had the mating bond been absent, she would've been

consumed by the Great Dragon. Lost in the universe of his eyes. Her body bent toward his like a supplicant. But the bond prevented him from enveloping her senses fully.

Gillian took a step away from him, pleased to see his lips curve down. "I am not for you," she told him quietly. "Let him go."

Marius' nostrils flared, eyes shifting to deep red. "You were mine before he claimed you, and you shall be mine when he is gone."

He grabbed her wrist and hauled her from the room.

"This ends now," he snarled as he pulled her along passageways and down flights of stairs to a lower level of the keep.

They passed numerous doors, some open to reveal empty cells or rooms filled with old relics. Ducking around a dimly lit corner, Marius tugged her to a stop and released her hand. He unlatched the heavy wooden door before them and then beckoned her inside.

Roman hung from iron chains in the center of the cell, his body limp, legs dragging on the floor. His bronze chest was layered with sweat and blood.

Deep marks from a whip oozed blood across his back. Head hanging, damp strands of black hair covered his face.

Gillian shoved past Marius and ran toward Roman, only to be snatched around the waist and swung away from him in a swirl of skirts at the last minute.

She lunged again, raking her nails down his handsome face when he held her back.

The Dragon wiped the blood from his cheeks with the back of his hand as she glared at him, her eyes flicking to the wounds that knitted together in moments.

She ducked to the side and tried again to reach him, but Marius anticipated her move and kept her at bay. She screamed at him, the sound bouncing off the stone and rousing Roman, who lifted his head.

His eyes went round through tangles of hair, becoming cold, narrow slits when he watched his father push her away. Roman got his feet under him and stiffly righted himself.

Arms stretched and shackled, his chest heaved, the pads of muscle flexing with rage. "Take your hands off her," he snarled.

Marius gripped her arms and jostled her to face Roman, keeping his powerful hands around her limbs in an unbreakable hold.

She wriggled, yelping when he flexed his fingers, nails digging into her soft skin.

Roman's eyes turned red, pupils dilating to slits. Along his body, scales flickered, trying to surface, but he was too weak and the iron too strong.

Roaring, he lunged toward Marius, spitting curses at his father. Arms straining against his bonds, he jerked at the chains until his wrists bled.

Gillian sobbed as Roman's blood ran down his arms.

As though summoned, Ansel entered the room, a whip with metal points on strips of leather dangling in his hand. His face was a mask of anger as he looked at her.

She spat at him, sneering when it hit his cheek.

Patches of deep red scales on cheeks and jaw flared outward and then lay flat, accentuating the ugly look he leveled on her.

Ansel swung his arm, twirling the whip as he circled his brother.

Roman swept his leg out when Ansel got too close,

knocking him onto his back. Before his brother could rise, Roman slammed his bare foot onto his sibling's chest.

Ansel snarled and curled the fingers of his free hand, forming a small ball of fire that he flung at his brother.

His power was depleted. The flames struck Roman's chest, scorching his skin. He stumbled back as far as his chains allowed, his face a mask of pain.

"You were always afraid to challenge me, brother," Roman panted, slowly rising to his full height. "It took putting me in chains to make you brave enough."

Ansel rolled to his feet and leaned in close. "Long have I lived in your shadow. Those days are ended."

His arm whipped through the air, leather whistling before it landed on Roman's blistering chest.

Skin split, blood sprayed.

Gillian screamed and writhed in Marius' arms, jerking her body so forcefully she wrenched her shoulder.

"Stop!" she cried as Ansel raised his arm again and looked toward his father, pain flashing in the Dragonborn's eyes. "Please," she begged, "please stop."

Roman stood panting, his body wracked with pain. She locked eyes with him.

I can't watch you die. A tear slipped down her cheek. *Forgive me.*

"No!" Roman yelled, his voice hoarse and pleading.

Her body shuddered, and she closed her eyes, envisioning the tenuous mating bond.

Gillian's heart fractured when she snipped it, severing her link with Roman.

He howled in anguish and dropped his head to his chest.

Knees buckling, she hung in Marius' grip, eyes clinging to Roman. It broke her when he met her gaze. The death-like emptiness. A mirror of her agony.

The Great Dragon nodded to Ansel, who lowered his arm and dipped his head, retreating from the room with a look of accusation when he passed Gillian.

Marius relaxed his grip, letting Gillian sink to the floor in a puddle of silk.

She crawled to Roman. He tried to lower himself, arms straining against the iron chains. Rising to her knees, she wrapped her arms around his waist and pressed her cheek to his burning, bloodied chest.

Whispering a word of healing, she tried to mend the skin, fumbling for strong enough magic, but the wound remained.

The Dragon walked slowly toward them.

He said nothing, only watched them hold each other for a few moments before leaning down and pulling Gillian away.

She went, too bereft to fight.

"I'm sorry," she sobbed over and over as Marius led her from the room.

Gillian looked back at the threshold. What was left of her heart twisted.

Roman's eyes were dead. Devoid of the fire that had always lingered within them.

What hung from iron chains was an empty shell.

My fault, she told herself. Turning away, she left Roman and let the Dragon take her hand.

Chapter Twenty-Seven

Marius closed the bedchamber door, pressing his palm to the wood, imagining it was Gillian's quaking form he soothed and not the rough plank.

He'd won.

She'd severed her bond with his son, freeing herself to become his mate. But it was an empty victory, and the price was steep.

His arm dropped to his side. How could she grow to love him now?

He'd killed their future before it had even begun.

After a thousand years of finding mates among the Coven of the Silver Moon, he understood that he could not simply take what was not freely given. There must be more than an animal bond between mates.

There must be love.

Not the same love he felt for his true mate, Ashael. Every mating bond following her death was a pale shadow of what they'd had together.

But the witch-wives of the past filled something within him when he claimed them. They each conquered a piece of his heart, that thing that had grown cold when Ashael passed into the next life.

He turned away from Gillian's door and strode through the dim hall, letting his feet take him where they would while his mind dredged up memories.

Sorya, his first witch-wife, was a brilliant flame in his memories. Her red hair had blazed in the sunlight like dragon flame, and her gray eyes looked past his aloofness to his damaged heart.

But the lives of witches are short, and too soon, she was taken from him, her death reopening jagged wounds.

Other witch-wives had come.

The matriarchs of the coven believed he'd stolen them. That his heart was a blackened pit where mercy went to die.

He paused mid-stride and turned his head toward Gillian's chamber. They had a right to believe that of him now, and it shamed him.

But not then.

In earlier days, he'd only loosed his Dragon song into the wind, and they'd come, each needing to be won. And he'd done it, peeled back the hardened scales of his being to reveal his vulnerable underbelly.

They could've refused him. He wanted to believe he would've let them go.

But each had remained, sharing their minds and bodies. Bearing young.

Decades passed. Centuries.

The cycle of birth and death played out over and over. His sons grew.

His young were the anchors tying him to this world. If not for them, he would've let his ancient heart burn out years ago.

They were not Dragon, but their songs twined with his, and through them, he carried on.

Once, it was enough. In the beginning, his offspring thrived in the early days, leaving the keep and finding mates among Valon's humans, raising their own families. His blood lived within the children of those matings, too.

But it was weak. Diluted. Hardly a whisper of Dragon.

When the Wasting crept into his realm, crawling across the peaceful meadows of Valon and into the lives of his Dragonborn young, he thought them impervious. Even when his sons sickened, he believed they would recover and live on as he did.

He was wrong.

Sons died in his arms, surrounded by their children and their human wives. Believing his ties to the world he'd created were fraying in the face of such loss, he looked to the witches, taking mates and raising true Dragonborn.

But the Wasting did not abate.

Maud, Draven's mother, had broken something in him when she'd taken her life.

He'd had no sense of her intention. Had not felt her mind fracture. But he should have known. She'd always been fragile. Too fragile.

In his grief and desperation, he'd shifted into his true form and flew to the coven's sacred land. He begged the high witch to give him a mate or show him the way to reach the sisters who'd fled the Shadowlands and hidden among mankind in Mirynn.

She'd refused.

Morrigan had stood defiant and told him it was unnatural for a witch to become the Dragon's mate. To give birth to male young and live beyond the touch of their goddess, Keridwen, in the Dragon's realm.

It was why their lives were cut short. The high witch would not betray those who'd fled. She would not sacrifice one of her own.

He'd cursed her for it.

Marius reached his chamber and entered, closing the door with a soft click. A massive bed with red velvet curtains hanging from the posts and beams stood against a wall opposite a blazing hearth.

He had no need of the fire. His blood burned hotter than the flames.

But the flickering was soothing as it danced on the dark walls, the light catching the seams of gold in the dark stone.

The Great Dragon slumped in a stuffed chair before the fire, arms dangling from the padded arms. His face was blank as he stared at the flames.

Marius' mind wandered to a room on the opposite side of the keep, pulled by the sorrow that lived within its stone walls. Morrigan had been right to keep Rowena from him. If he'd known of the existence of Gillian's mother, he would've torn the coven's lands apart to find her.

Now, he had Rowena's only child. And she hated him.

Marius rested his head on the back of the chair and closed

his eyes. Somewhere in the bowels of the keep, his son anguished.

He knew the pain Roman felt, though it was a dull thing compared to the agony of losing Ashael.

In time, Marius would be forgiven. Once Gillian became his wife, Roman would have no choice but to let go.

Until then, he would remain bound.

Gillian was an empty husk as she sat at the narrow window.

Mary came and went, tidying the room and delivering meals—plates of food that would remain untouched. She would look on her charge, worry creasing her brow as she tried vainly to elicit something more than glimpses of awareness.

But beneath layers of indifference, Gillian was drilling into the core of the magic Morrigan had shown her. She slowly drew it forth, each thread of power an effort.

The high witch had so little time to teach her how to shape it, hone it, and use it to defend her mind. What little she'd gleaned in their days together wore her down as though she were fighting herself as she sought the magical armor.

It had been enough to strengthen her bond with Roman, but that was gone now. Sundered by her hand to save him.

Had it saved him? Or did the Dragon kill his son as she sat in her room, waging a losing battle?

Her heart twisted.

Watching helplessly as Ansel tortured his brother under the Dragon's command was awful. Severing the link was devastating. But even in those terrible moments, she'd felt Marius' anguish buried deep with his rage.

He was powerful, but he couldn't shield every emotion, even with his vast strength. They flowed out of him, as untamable as a river.

He didn't want to kill his son. But that didn't mean he couldn't be pushed to such a depraved act.

She had to be careful.

Morrigan would be aghast if she knew about Roman.

The high witch hadn't taught her how to tap into her magic only to see her in the arms of a Dragonborn. For all Gillian knew, any future with Roman would be cut short, their bond unnatural like those who'd become mates of the Great Dragon, slowly sapping her life from her.

It hadn't mattered when she'd fallen into Roman's arms, and it didn't matter now.

She loved him. That's all there was.

As the days passed, she'd tapped into the core of her power, drawing it out, and learning its nature. She fortified her mind, hoping it would be enough when the Dragon's patience ended.

Marius came often and sat with her. His dark presence filled the space, though he kept his distance, speaking quietly, unconcerned when her face remained blank.

At times, his ancient mind would tap at hers, the flame of his heart burning through the fog. She saw him then, eyes flickering to life only to gutter moments later.

He grew restless, visiting more often, his voice tinged with frustration.

The afternoon he took her arm and pulled her from the chair, she hadn't realized she'd left the chamber until they'd passed the solar on the way to the stairwell. Blinking, Gillian slowly turned her head and met his gaze, expecting to see anger. What she saw was worse.

Longing. Regret. Resolve.

Her eyes skittered away. The warmth of his hand on her elbow sank into her skin.

She wanted to cringe. She wanted to burrow into it.

Part of her longed to surrender to the emptiness that fluttered in the periphery of her mind. To lose herself entirely to it.

But she'd never surrendered, not even the day she'd walked away from Roman and into the Dragon's talons, walked away from her last chance to see Rory before he died.

It was not in her nature to give up.

So, she blocked her mind from the Dragon, drilling into latent power and hoping it would be enough. Praying he didn't know what she was doing, and if he suspected, that he didn't use that knowledge to punish her through Roman.

Her lashes swept down as she let him guide her down the narrow steps and into the great hall.

The rushes smelled sweet, her skirts trailing over them, releasing wafts of lavender and sage.

Marius didn't speak, only led her gently out of the hall. His guards bowed as they walked through the inner and outer baileys. She briefly wondered where he was taking her, then decided it didn't matter.

They made their way up a small hill, finally stopping at a familiar sight.

Beneath layers of time stood the temple of Keridwen. The door she'd slipped into when she'd run from her fate stood ajar, obscured by leafy vines.

Marius ran his fingers down her arm, leaving trails of sensation, and took her hand. Shoving the door open, he pulled her inside and paused.

The air was thick with memories as he took in the ruined temple.

"When Maud died," his voice was gravelly, "when she killed herself, I cursed Keridwen."

The Dragon released her and walked toward the mural on the wall where the goddess' depiction gazed at the interlopers.

"But it was not her fault."

He turned his head and looked at her, where she stood rooted to the floor.

"It was mine."

She didn't want to hear this. Her hands twitched at her sides, and she clenched them, wrestling with the urge to cover her ears.

He was a monster. He'd taken everything from her. Gillian bit the inside of her cheek as he continued.

"I should have known Maud was suffering. That her mind—"

He lifted an arm and let it drop. "She was with child."

Gillian gave a stiff nod.

"I felt the last shudder of our son's tiny heart as Maud lay broken. When her body was nothing but ash on her pyre, I came here.

"I defiled this temple—severing my last ties with Keridwen. Shortly after I desecrated this sacred place, the Wasting took hold as it never had before. It closed in on my realm like a hand into a fist.

"I am cut off from Mirynn, from the witches who hide

among mankind. From you." His eyes flicked to hers. "It is my punishment... for many things."

The Dragon came toward her, his potent figure seeming to grow beyond the bounds of the temple, robe flaring out and flapping like wings before tucking close to his body.

He stopped when he was mere inches away. Touching his finger to the underside of her chin, he lifted her face to his, the heat from his skin making her flush.

His eyes were molten.

"I will give you time. I am not a monster, though my actions say otherwise." He got to one knee and held her hand. "Please, Gillian. Let me show you."

Names had power.

When he said hers, each syllable laced with persuasion, she rocked on her heels, eyes dilating. Her body swayed for a moment, part of her wanting to move toward him, to his heat. His power.

She fought it. And won.

Gillian breathed deeply, keeping her hand in his, letting his scent and heat envelop her. Letting him see it. See his power swallowing her.

She saw a look of triumph crawl across his face like a shadow.

When it passed, she released his hold and stepped away.

"You have no power over me," Gillian told him, watching his eyes glow red. "I severed the bond with Roman to save him from you. His father. You would see your son die." Her face grew cold. "Only a monster would do such a thing."

Marius rose slowly, his body unfurling in a swish of fabric.

He towered over her, the temple dimming as his massive presence filled the room.

She held her ground and faced him. Her bond with Roman, though severed, still echoed in her mind. It gave her strength.

He studied her. "I've walked this earth since the dawn of time. I have watched civilizations rise and fall. I have welcomed travelers from across the cosmos and then barred the gates to this world. I am eternal..." Marius tilted his head, "but you are not. In time, you will stand beside me.

"I can wait."

In her mind bloomed images of years, spans of time during which she dwelled beside him under the shadow of his mountain, separate but together.

She watched her body age while he remained young and virile.

He layered the images with emotion. Loneliness was etched into every facet of that tentative future.

"Is that how you wish to spend the years of your life?"

Not waiting for an answer, he flooded her thoughts with different images.

They stood side by side at the high table presiding over the people of Valon, her belly rounded with their child. The soft glow of motherhood lit her face, a smile curving her lips as his fingers laced with hers.

She felt bereft when the image winked out, his mental touch receding to nothing but dim awareness.

"The choice is yours, Gillian."

He pressed his lips to her forehead and strode from the temple.

She stood where he left her and reached for Roman along the remnants of their sundered bond. But felt nothing.

Chapter Twenty-Eight

Roman sat against the wall of his cell, head bowed and legs stretched out. The wounds on his chest and back had healed, leaving behind strips of new skin and dried, blackened blood. His dark hair hung in his face in damp clumps.

The cell was cast in shadows, its braziers spitting out weak light that flickered on the walls in a mockery of figures dancing.

He shifted his body, wincing at the aches radiating through his limbs and torso. Chains dragged along the stone, the grating noise reverberating against the walls and bouncing off his skull.

The room smelled like old piss and misery. He rested his head on the cold stone and let it roll to the side.

Other than Ansel, who'd visited three days prior to loosen the chains—he'd left with bruises and a broken finger—he'd seen none of his family members.

Only maidservants came and went, offering plates of food or emptying the piss pot.

His mind was consumed with thoughts of Gillian.

When she'd severed the bond, it was like the air in his lungs evaporated. He understood why she'd done it but wished she hadn't. Despite the iron sapping his strength, he could've fought.

He would've fought until there was nothing left.

Roman closed his eyes and reached for her as he'd done a thousand times since she'd walked out the door at his father's side. At times, he thought he felt a pale response, but when he homed in on the tenor of her mind, he felt nothing, as though she were dead.

The thought hammered in his skull, and he gripped his head, chains thumping against his body.

She wasn't dead. She couldn't be dead.

The sound of footsteps moving down the hall outside his cell brought his head up. He dropped his hands in his lap and looked at the door, seeing the latch lift.

He expected to see one of the maids, but it was Draven who entered the room. His eyes were haunted as he stood in the doorway, his hand clutching the latch. Gaunt features and sunken eyes fixed on Roman.

Roman dragged his bare feet under him and rose, using the wall to brace his body.

"Brother," he whispered.

Draven's face contorted, and he looked away. "I brought this on."

Roman sighed. "No, you didn't."

He looked up, the scales along the side of his face turning a deep red. "If I were stronger, he wouldn't have known... he wouldn't have found you both."

Draven had delved dangerously deep into his power to visit

Roman, using that strength to fortify his mind. But he felt Marius skulking around the perimeter of his thoughts like a rat sniffing out scraps of food.

So he filled his mind with distractions, surface thoughts, easily plucked and analyzed, while his real intent remained hidden.

He hoped it remained hidden.

"It's not your fault," Roman told him. "I never should've touched her. She wasn't mine to keep."

He leaned against the cold stone and dropped his head. "Have you seen her?"

Draven stepped into the room and shut the door. "From a distance."

"Is she well?"

"How could she be?" Draven reached into his tunic and pulled out a chemise, handing it to Roman. "I pilfered it from the laundry."

Snatching the garment from his brother's hand, Roman pressed it to his face and breathed deeply. Her scent lingered in the fibers, sending heat flowing through his body.

Lowering his eyes, he inhaled her sweet smell. Tiny currents buzzed in his head as he breathed her in, zapping his mind, sparking parts of him the iron suppressed.

He opened his eyes, still holding the cloth to his face, and reached for her. *Gillian.*

Moments ticked by, hope dimming, then flaring to vibrant life when he heard her voice as though she stood at his side.

Roman.

He froze. *Gillian. Can you hear me?*

I hear you, her voice in his head cried. *I hear you, Roman. How is this happening?*

I don't know.

Roman sagged with relief, his back sliding down the stone, abrading his skin though he didn't feel it. "Gillian," he whispered.

Draven went to his side. "What is it?"

He looked at his brother. "I hear her."

He gripped his head and took a shuddering breath. *Gillian,* he called to her, *has he...? Has my father—?*

No. He has been patient. He hopes to wear me down.

He heard the chagrin in her thoughts when she added, *Marius doesn't know me very well if he thinks that will work.*

She shared a memory of herself as a child, the tilt of her mutinous mouth as she planted her hands on her hips and refused to move an inch when her mother, Naeve, wouldn't permit her to keep the abandoned wolf cub she'd found in the forest. Gillian had won that battle, raising the pup to adulthood. He visited now and then, though he had a family of his own.

Roman's lips quirked in a smile, *I'm not so easily tamed.*

Is that a challenge?

He chuckled and looked up at Draven, who hovered at his side. "She is well."

Where are you? she asked.

He scanned the walls of his cell. *I don't know. I have no recollection of this place.*

I'm going to help you escape.

His mouth turned down, eyes flicking to Draven, who watched the silent exchange.

Roman? Did you hear me?

Aye. I heard you, but the answer is no.

If silence had a voice, hers would be loud and scathing. Roman waited, shoulders slumping when Draven prodded him.

Fine. If you won't help me, I'll scour the castle myself. Maybe I'll beat Draven into submission and force him to aid me.

He shook his head, the corners of his mouth twitching. *I have no doubt you could. He's a weakling.* Roman glanced at his brother. *But you can't take that risk.*

I don't recall asking permission.

Gillian, he paused and leaned his head against the wall, *even if you could sneak through my father's halls unseen, do you really think he wouldn't find out the moment you freed me? How far do you think we'd get before he found us?*

"Enough of this silent dialogue. I know you're talking about me. You're wearing that face again," Draven said, folding his arms across his chest. "What's going on?"

"She's threatening to search the grounds to find and free me."

"And if she manages that feat? What then?"

Roman sighed. "I said as much."

His brother muttered and paced. "If she frees you, Father will know," Draven warned.

He nodded. Roman had no doubt Gillian would throw caution aside and poke her nose into every corner of the castle.

She'd shown the same defiance when she'd crossed into the Shadowlands despite warnings of its dangers. But he had no power to stop her.

He was trapped in his cell. Bound by iron that eroded his strength and sapped his body of its gifts.

He eyed his brother. He could ask Draven to watch her, to subvert her efforts. But a small, and very loud, part of him wanted her to try. He wanted to see her, hold her sweet curves against his body, breathe in her scent, and dream of a life he could never have.

If she managed to free him, would he be able to get her to the border? He needed a distraction, something profound enough to draw Marius' attention and hold it.

Roman mulled over the possibilities, his brow arching when he hit on one. He had no delusions that his life would be forfeit should he succeed. It was a price he was willing to pay.

But Gillian couldn't know.

"I need you to do something for me, brother."

Narrowing his eyes, Draven said, "Why do I have the feeling I'm not going to like whatever it is you have to say?"

"You're not going to like it, but I need you to do this."

Blocking Gillian from his mind, lest she sensed his thoughts and balked, he laid out a risky plan.

Draven frowned as he listened, shaking his head and arguing, before finally backing down.

Draven's hands curled into fists when he jerked his chin in reluctant agreement. "You know what he'll do to you if you succeed, not that you will."

He nodded. "I do."

"Are you sure?"

Roman looked away, lips pressing into a thin line. "Yes."

"Very well," Draven said quietly.

The scales along his neck and cheek lay flat, rust-red where they had been ruby bright.

"Thank you, Brother."

He shook his head. "Don't thank me for this."

Chapter Twenty-Nine

Draven chose his moment carefully.

Using the cover of darkness, he and Gillian made their way through a labyrinth of passages to the lower levels of the castle. Slipping into the hall outside Roman's cell with Gillian silent at his heels, Draven pushed open the heavy wooden door and darted inside, motioning the young witch to remain in the corridor.

Roman looked up, rising abruptly and murmuring a greeting.

Draven clapped him on the back and, using a stolen key, unlocked the iron manacles imprisoning his brother. The young Dragonborn held up his hand and tilted his head, the scales on his neck flaring out. He listened for the sound of feet, expecting to hear the Dragon's roars, when the iron cuffs dropped to the stone floor with a muffled clank.

Roman grasped his brother's shoulders and brought him in for a fierce hug.

Nose wrinkling, Draven pulled away and slapped him on the back. "You smell rank, brother."

Shaking his head, Roman sighed. "It's good to see you, too."

Draven grinned and motioned toward the door beyond which Gillian waited.

They had minutes only if their ruse failed. Minutes during which Roman and Gillian could embrace before Marius found them.

Roman followed Draven into the hall, grabbing Gillian to his chest.

She stood on her toes and wrapped her arms around him, her body silently shaking with suppressed sobs.

Pulling away, Roman brushed loose strands of pale hair away from her face, tucking them behind her ears as he pushed the hood of her red cloak off her head. He feasted on her with a heavy stare, his gaze traveling from the laced boots hugging her calves to the leather pants that had been Draven's in his youth. A dark brown tunic beneath a fitted vest hugged her breasts.

Their eyes locked, and Draven paused, unable to look away, sensing words were said from mind to mind, words too precious for him to hear.

If only his father could see what was so clear.

He shook his head. It wouldn't matter.

Nudging Roman, he grabbed a torch from the wall and led them through a maze of passages deep into the bowels of the castle.

They came to a small door set into the stone. Pulling it open, Draven bent into the narrow cell and handed his brother a stack of fresh clothing. "I figured you'd want to change in case this mad plan succeeds."

Roman's lips twitched. "I suppose I should wait until after I bathe to don them?"

"It's *her* nose," Draven said, flashing a look at Gillian.

She rolled her eyes. "I think we have more pressing things to worry about than Roman's stench."

Draven grinned at his brother. "See? I told you, you were ripe."

Roman punched him in the arm. "Are we just going to stand here and talk about how I smell?"

Raising the torch in his fist, Draven led them through a maze of neglected halls. The light from the torch bounced off the walls, casting ominous shadows.

More than once, Gillian found her heart beating too fast as she looked behind them and tried to probe the darkness that swallowed their passing.

Draven finally stopped and motioned toward a stairwell. "Take the stairs, then go right. You'll find an outer door that opens to the old kiln beyond the keep."

He stopped, his mind flipping through memories. He and Roman used to play in that patch of ground, pretending the massive kiln was the gutted ruin of their castle.

Glancing back at his brother, he said roughly, "You know the way from there."

Wrapping his arms around his brother, Roman whispered in his ear, words too soft for Gillian to make out. She watched them embrace, feeling their bittersweet goodbye.

When the brothers parted, she stepped toward Draven and took his hand. "Thank you."

She saw shadows in his eyes as he squeezed her fingers, but he only nodded stiffly and moved away.

Roman took one last look at his brother and strode into the darkness of the stairwell, Gillian's hand grasped firmly in his.

At the outer door, Roman poked his head out and swept the landscape bathed in moonlight. The abandoned kiln sat like an ancient sentry among the overgrowth.

Happier days, Roman thought as they slipped past its neglected frame.

Guards patrolled the wall walk of the castle.

Roman shielded Gillian behind his back and watched them for a few moments. No alarm was raised, and he loosed a long breath, craning his neck to give Gillian a look of relief. Her teeth flashed in the darkness.

Leaving their cover, Roman lifted Gillian into his arms and bolted into the forest beyond Valon.

Gillian slid from Roman's arms at the edge of a small pool of water and stretched her legs. He cupped her face and tilted her chin. His hands felt hot against her cheeks, their warmth spreading through her skin to wrap around her skull.

Tingles of awareness raced along her scalp as he bent and pressed his lips to hers. She wound her arms around his neck and pulled him closer, grumbling when he drew away and glanced at the still water.

"While it pains me to part from your sweet lips, even I'm offended by my aroma."

She giggled. "I'd complain, but your stink seared my nose, and I can't smell you anymore."

His eyes narrowed. "I'll have to think of a fitting punishment for that insult."

Gillian waved a hand at him. "Bathe while you think."

She strolled away and found a fallen tree. Climbing onto the trunk, she twisted her body to give him privacy and looked up into the night.

Stars winked through the branches of the trees as she listened to Roman splashing. The wind rustled the leaves, and somewhere in the distance, a myrax screeched.

A feeling of foreboding sank into her mind the longer she stared into the sky.

"He'll find us, won't he?"

Roman climbed out of the water and shook his head like a dog, shedding droplets in every direction. Running his hands along his body, he swept layers of water off his body the best he could, then bent for the small bundle of clean clothing.

"With any luck, you'll be beyond his reach when he realizes what we've done."

She glanced at him, eyes going wide and face bursting into flames when her eyes landed on his naked body. Her stomach flip-flopped, heat pooling there and spreading outward as her gaze wandered below his waist.

Roman's sultry chuckle broke through her mental fugue.

She stammered and forced herself to look away, but the bold sensuality of his natural form was stamped into her brain. Fumbling over her words when her thoughts finally clicked back into place, she averted her eyes and asked, "What...uh... what do you...uh...mean by *me* being beyond his reach?"

Roman said nothing, but she heard every movement.

The slide of his leather pants over his muscular legs. The whisper of his tunic as he lifted it over his head.

His bare feet padded softly on the ground, and he came toward her. Her lashes swept down when he touched her chin, gently tilting her face to meet his.

She meant to rephrase her question, to ask him what he meant when he told her she—not they—would be beyond the reach of the Dragon. But all thought flew from her mind when she looked up into his heated gaze.

His eyes glowed like twin flames as he stroked his thumb along her bottom lip. "I don't want to talk about the future."

Roman pulled her from her perch on the trunk, his body not moving an inch as she slid against him until her feet touched the ground. Trailing his hands on either side of her face, he memorized her features, drinking her in, knowing time was precious. Unwilling to waste it.

Her mouth parted when he bent and took her lips, nibbling along the tender skin.

"I want to live in this moment," he whispered, his tongue dancing with hers.

Hovering above her hungry mouth, he released a slow breath laced with his scent. "With you."

Gillian's eyes dilated, and she tilted her head back with a moan. He ran a hand along the line of her neck, fangs slipping from his gums.

He nipped her skin just above her thrumming pulse.

Two small spots of blood welled. His pupils went dark. He licked the small wounds, his body growing hard and hungry as blood flowed over his tongue.

Running a finger along the tip of a fang, he sliced his skin and slipped the digit into her mouth.

Gillian's lips closed around it with a gentle pull. Blood ran down her throat and into her stomach, where it exploded in blistering heat. Her hands dug into his tunic as she clawed at him, trying to draw him closer to ease the ache that spread throughout her in a fiery wave.

Her skin felt hot, and she whimpered.

Roman lowered her to the ground, his body covering hers with delicious weight. His hands were everywhere, each touch sending currents of energy along her limbs, causing her skin to pebble, heat pooling in her stomach before traveling lower, deeper.

Roman's lips followed his fingers, plying her body as his breath, rich with pheromones, filled her senses until all she felt was him.

Her mind was consumed, and the world slipped away.

Clothing disappeared before she even realized he'd tugged her free of it. She was lost in him as the bond of their mixed blood ignited and bloomed like a molten flower.

After, when their bodies cooled, heat dimming to satiated warmth, she rolled to her side and rested her head on his chest.

Power, as though newly awakened, hummed throughout her body in steady currents of energy.

She felt alive. Awake.

The bond, forged in blood and sealed with the oldest magic, amplified the power passed from mother to daughter, back and back, to the first witch, Cyrena, who sipped the immortal blood of a Dragon.

She could feel the bond like chains of iron anchoring her to Roman. It was so much stronger, deeper than what it had been before.

Trailing her fingers along his chest, she asked, "He can't separate us now, can he?"

Roman's mouth pressed into a thin line. He wanted to tell her that his father couldn't touch them now that their bond went beyond his power to sever. But there was one way he could sunder it, and before that happened, he would get her to safety.

"No. You'll be safe."

Lost in the glow of their union, she didn't hear the message in his words. "Good."

He tightened his hold on her and looked up at the sky. How much longer did they have?

He traced his fingers along her smooth back, relishing the line of her body. The curve of her hips. It wouldn't be long now.

Marius would learn what he'd done and hunt them.

Roman let Gillian doze for a couple of hours, gently nudging her awake before the first streaks of dawn danced across the sky. Her pale hair was a tangled mess as she batted him away with a grumble.

He nipped her shoulder, and her eyes flew open with a yelp. "Hey!"

He chuckled and drew her up, sweeping his eyes over her. She tried to shield herself from his hungry gaze, and he smirked.

"If we had the time, I would kiss every inch of you until you lost those inhibitions."

He sighed and handed her the rumpled tunic he'd discarded during the night. "But we must be going."

Gillian slid the garment over her head, then slipped on her borrowed pants and leather boots, finger-combing her hair into some semblance of order before darting into the bushes for a few moments of privacy.

Roman was waiting with a lecherous look on his face when she returned. Her cheeks flamed, and she stumbled on an exposed root, grousing when he chuckled.

"That was entirely your fault," she said, rubbing her toe.

"Mine?"

She sniffed and strode past him, grabbing her red cloak and slinging it over her shoulders in a wide arc so the hem brushed his chest.

"Yours."

He shook his head and followed, grinning when she tossed her hair over her shoulder and marched forward.

"Are you planning on returning to Valon?"

Gillian spun around. "You know, I'm not sure I want to be your mate anymore."

Roman growled and lunged for her.

She sprang away with a squeal of laughter, leaping over rocks and fallen branches.

He caught up and swung her into the air, hugging her to his chest and spinning. "What was that now?"

She wriggled as his fingers found a particularly ticklish spot along her ribcage and dug in. "I don't think I like being your mate."

"Hm? What was that?" Poke poke.

Gillian shrieked with laughter. "I love being your mate! I love it!"

He relaxed his hold, giving her one last tickle, before setting her on her feet. She clutched her sides and panted.

Pain suddenly ripped through him when she smiled into his face.

Would he ever hear her laugh again after today?

He masked it with a lopsided grin, gripping her hand and tugging her.

She fell into step beside him, and they walked in silence. Eventually, his brooding spilled over into her mind through their bond, and she stopped, listening to snatches of his thoughts he unwarily let slip.

"Where are we going, Roman?"

"Home."

Her brows knitted. "Home? What home? The coven?"

Roman looked away.

"What are you keeping from me?"

When he faced her, his mask fell away, revealing a look of anguish. "You won't be safe until you leave the Shadowlands."

Gillian tilted her head. It was the same plan they'd had when Marius had caught them before they reached the border, but she sensed something different now.

"It's more than that."

His mouth flattened. "You know I can't go with you."

She nodded. "I know."

This, too, was no different. She would return home and be

with her brother in his last days. It was all she'd wanted when she left the sister of the Silver Moon.

To be at his side and say goodbye.

Then she'd return. Somehow, she'd find her way back to him.

But looking at him now, seeing the shadow of grief lurking beneath his features, she knew he was hiding something.

Gillian reached up and placed her hand on his cheek. "Roman?"

His dark lashes swept down, shielding her from his eyes as surely as his mind closed, blocking her from his thoughts. He took her hand from his face and pressed his lips to her palm.

"It's nothing. Let's go."

Roman swung her into his arms and ran toward Rudgarde.

To his fate, whatever the cost.

Chapter Thirty

Morrigan arrived outside the gates of Valon hours after the moon reached its zenith.

She drew power from the celestial orb as it glowed brightly above the horizon before the dawn. It was Keridwen incarnate.

Cloaking her passing in shadows drawn from the night, she passed through the gates.

Guards manning the entrance startled, eyes darting from shadow to shadow, skin prickling with awareness. But they saw nothing, only pools of darkness.

The heavy door leading into the keep groaned as she pushed it open, revealing rows of braziers along the dim hallway that glowed against the black stone like the jaws and fangs of the Dragon.

Morrigan slipped inside and closed the door, shutting out the night and the prying eyes of guards who followed the sound of her passing, hands moving rapidly to ward off a fell presence they heard but couldn't see.

Inside, she stopped and wrinkled her nose.

It stank of Dragon, a dry and musky scent the herb-laden rushes couldn't mask.

She entered the great hall, avoiding the sleeping forms of two servants tucked against the wall on thin pallets by the hearth. Following the scent of the Dragon Lord, she made her way through a maze of passages and into the mountain—the true heart of Valon.

Drawing on spells of protection, Morrigan stood on the precipice of Marius's lair.

Entering could mean her life. It probably would.

She had no delusions about her fate when Draven sought an audience and pleaded with her. She'd agreed readily enough, accepting the consequences.

Keridwen had withdrawn from the world following the Dragon's attack. Though Morrigan and her sisters reached for the goddess, they felt nothing but flutters of awareness as though she had abandoned them. Even the moon shone less brightly.

The sisters of the Silver Moon were aging, the weakening of the goddess skimming years from their lives as it had done for decades. With each of them beyond their fertile years, there would be no more daughters among them.

Not within the Shadowlands.

Those who'd fled the Dragon's realm may not have fared any better.

There was only Gillian. The last daughter.

And she could not remain within the Dragon's realm.

Morrigan had doubts that her ruse would work and buy

Roman and Gillian enough time. But their fate would be sealed if she did nothing.

What choice was there, really?

Her dark cloak brushed against the black stone as she passed into the mountain.

The smell of Dragon hung in the air, sulfurous and rank with centuries of loneliness.

The Dragon's lair opened up before her in a black abyss. She lifted her hand and whispered, her voice swallowed by the vast emptiness.

A ball of light flared and hung above her open palm, chasing the dark until the space around her was lit in an oval glow. She craned her neck, her hood falling back to reveal her stark white hair. Stormy eyes swept the cavern, whose vast dimensions spanned into darkness so deep she couldn't see where they ended.

A low scraping sound echoed through the cavern, and she walked toward it, hand extended before her. The orb of light enveloped her form, fighting the blackness that tried to swallow her.

Morrigan stopped.

A wickedly sharp obsidian talon extending from a massive red-scaled foot sat under the magical light. She stared at it, slowly raising her arm, the darkness peeling away in layers to reveal the Great Dragon.

"You should not have come here, witch," Marius rumbled, his deep voice bouncing off the stone.

"What choice did I have? Your theft warranted as much."

Marius released a long breath.

Flames slipped from his mouth and curled around his

snout, illuminating his form as he bent his neck in a perfect arch and lowered his head toward the high witch.

"You let her go, did you not?"

Morrigan released the magic funneling into the light and lowered her arm. She looked up at the Dragon, felt his hot breath waft across her face, singeing her hair, and looked deeper into his ancient mind.

His mental shields were multi-layered scales, hard like diamonds but tinged with darkness.

She prodded at him as she said, "I am no tyrant. I do not rule my sisters. They have a will of their own, and I respect their wishes."

She tilted her head. "That must be foreign to you. Even now, I can feel you trying to sway me. Don't bother. I, too, have the blood of Dragon in my veins. Or had you forgotten?"

The tip of his tail twitched, its sharp barb gouging the stone floor.

Narrowing his eyes, he leaned closer, curls of smoke and tendrils of fire dancing along the edges of his snout. "Do not lecture me. It is by my will that you and your sisters live."

Molten flames dripped from the tip of a fang and landed on the ground at Morrigan's feet. She followed the tenor of his anger and found a tiny chink in his mental armor.

She drove her mind into it. "It is by the grace of your mate that you have sired sons, or have *you* forgotten?"

His mind was an alien landscape, and Morrigan knew she had only moments to delve into its sonorous depths before he sensed her and cast her out. She slipped past centuries of memories, searching for the voice of his true mate.

She saw Maud and the sisters that came before them, each a

tiny flame in his mind. They called to her at a deep level, but she ruthlessly shut them out.

"Ashael is dead," he spat, chest expanding as his neck shifted away, pulling his head up and into the dark cavern.

"She sees you still, Marius."

He flinched at the power woven into his name.

In that moment, Morrigan saw Ashael's image spark in the Great Dragon's mind. She dove toward it, heedless of her intrusion, and grabbed hold of spans of memories.

Using them, she called on her full power.

Morrigan raised her arms and blasted the Dragon's mind with Ashael's images and words.

He roared, claws scraping the stone, wings stretching then flattening against his form as if to shield him from the mental war she waged against him.

The high witch stepped toward him, jaw clenched, arms trembling. Amplifying her power, she drew on the memories of his mate and bludgeoned him.

Marius lashed his tail and took a step away from her. His eyes lit with fury, then dimmed, blending into copper as she came toward him, pushing him back until his flank hit the confines of the cavern.

"Ashael never wanted this!" Morrigan yelled, her voice doubling as she infused it with power.

Her body shook, strength waning. "You defiled her gift! You turned your back on the goddess who gave birth to your mate!"

The high witch flung her arms out and unleashed the last of her magic imbued with memories of the Dragon's mate.

It hit Marius in a blast, sending his head crashing into the stone ceiling. Shards of rock tumbled from the cavern, filling the dark space with dust.

The flames in his mouth winked out, and the room was enveloped in darkness.

Marius heaved once, then slumped to the ground, sending plumes of dirt and rock into the air.

Tiny chips hit Morrigan's face, slicing her skin. She fell to her knees and grabbed the hood of her cloak, covering her head. She felt for his mind, but it was sealed.

With shaking hands, she held out her palm and produced a weak light. It hovered, a dull yellow against the blackness.

She rose and walked toward the Dragon's head. He was aware of her presence and let her come. When she stood a few feet from the deadly tips of his fangs, she stopped.

"What would Ashael think of what you've become?" Morrigan sighed and shook her head. "I cannot defeat you, and I have no wish to. Our world would not survive without its creator. Just as it will not survive without the goddess who gives it life."

She retreated fully from his mind. "Tell me, have you not wondered why your sons are dying?"

"I am cursed," he rumbled, thinking of the desecration of the temple following Maud's death.

She lifted her chin. "That is true enough. You cursed *yourself* when you took your first witch-wife. You cursed the *world* when you renounced the goddess."

He lifted his head, eyes sparking. "My mate would not wish my line to end."

Marius rose, once again towering over her. The heat of his breath caused beads of sweat to pool on her body.

"If you have come to beg me to free Gillian, you've wasted your time. She severed the bond with Roman. In time, she will stand at my side and bear my young. Pleading with me changes nothing."

He tapped a claw on the ground, eyes narrowing to slits. "Why are you here?"

Morrigan's power was sapped.

If she hadn't spent so much delving into the Dragon's mind, she could've shielded him from her thoughts. As it was, her effort to repel him failed.

He saw Draven's face in her mind, heard his son's words, and felt their treachery. His nostrils flared, fangs winking between his lips as his forked tongue tasted her breath in the air, sour with guile.

"Deceiver!" he roared and swung his tail out.

It struck her full in the chest, sending her body hurling through darkness. The light in her palm flared briefly, then blinked out as she sailed through empty space, landing with a crunch against the side of the cavernous hall.

The Great Dragon smelled her blood and listened to the slow beat of her heart. He could split her open with one slash of his claws and bring her mangled corpse to the border of Darach Grove to remind the coven under whose domain they lived.

His pupils dilated as he stalked toward her, becoming thin strips of black against the flames of his eyes. A haze of smoke lingered in the air around his snout as he considered her.

He dragged a forefoot along the floor, considering what to do with the witch, his claws slicing through the stone like soft clay.

The urge to kill was strong, but it was tempered by fear of

killing Keridwen's high witch, further weakening the goddess to the point of death and plunging the world into chaos.

And there was also a sliver of respect.

She had risked much coming to Valon. He let out a rolling grumble and swung his massive body away from Morrigan.

Let her die in the heart of my mountain or live with the knowledge that she failed, he thought as he left her where she lay.

Moving through a deep tunnel that took him up a steep climb, he emerged from the mountain just as dawn chased the moon from the sky. Standing on a jut of rock, Marius spread his wings, the red of his scales glinting in Irylle's early morning light that bled across the horizon.

He flapped hard and lifted into the air, aiming his body toward the border of the Shadowlands where Rudgarde sat just beyond his reach.

Chapter Thirty-One

Gillian stood on her toes and clung to Roman, reveling in the heat that flowed from his skin into every fiber of her being. His breath was hot in her mouth, carving a path of delicious warmth down her throat and into her belly.

She couldn't get enough—the feel of his lips pressed to hers, the sweet release his touch elicited as he moved inside of her.

Roman cupped her buttocks, lifting her against his hardness and growling in his throat when she wriggled.

Loving her was too new. He felt like an untried youth in her arms, insatiable and frenetic.

"Come with me," she pleaded, biting at his lower lip when he slowly released her from his tight grasp.

Fangs sprouted from his gums, and he growled, ready to pull her to the ground and lose himself in her willing arms.

He was on the cusp of ignoring the danger that surrounded them, but enough reason remained, and he grabbed hold of it, gently pushing her away. Roman breathed heavily, pupils dilating as he took hold of his baser needs and forced his hands to let go.

"I can't," he said hoarsely, throat bobbing. She reached for him, and he clasped her hands together, keeping her still. "We can't. It's not safe."

Gillian pouted and pushed her body toward him. "I want you," she whispered.

His dark lashes swept down, and he clenched his jaw, the muscles ticking beneath shadows of stubble covering the hard planes of his face. He strained against his desires, his need to keep her at his side. His mate.

But time had run out. They had no future.

Roman knew Morrigan likely failed, that his father could be on his way to intercept them before she left the Shadowlands.

"You need to go, Gillian."

He said her name with power and a rush of breath laced with persuasion.

She blinked, mouth parting so the tips of her teeth flashed against the red of her lips.

Roman breathed out again, filling the air around her face with his scent. Through their bond, he told her, *You have to go. Please, Gillian. Go before it's too late.*

Her mind filled with his thoughts, but he wasn't strong enough to drown out her own. *I don't want to leave you.*

I know. You'll return. The last was a lie that tasted like ash on his tongue. *You need to see your brother. He should know what you've gone through to aid him.*

Roman knew his words hit their mark when he saw her flinch.

Her eyes welled, and she dropped her arms, taking a step from him. He wanted to close the distance, wrap her in his arms, and never let go. But he held his body rigid.

"I failed." She looked away with a gulp. "He's going to die."

"Yes. But he needn't die alone."

Her face twisted, and she nodded. "I'll come back af—" She swallowed and whispered, "After."

Pain shot like an arrow through his heart.

She believed she could return. That he would be there to welcome her back. He imagined her coming through the barrier and searching for him, becoming lost in the maze of the forest, hunted by vauger and myrax, screaming his name in the dark.

And he wouldn't hear it.

He was Dragonborn. Leaving him, leaving the Shadowlands, and going where he couldn't follow would kill him.

He hoped it was quick.

Her eyes narrowed, and she stepped toward him. "What was that?"

Roman sealed his mind from her, pasting a bland look on his face. "I didn't say anything."

"You'll die if I leave?" She lunged at him. "Why didn't you tell me? Why—"

Her words were cut off by a thunderous roar.

The Great Dragon flew across the sky above the canopy of trees that sheltered them from his piercing gaze.

Roman grabbed her arm and ran toward the edge of the forest, where the barrier between their worlds sat like the impenetrable front line of an invisible army. It remained a bulwark against the Dragon, with the last of Keridwen's power.

Sliding to a stop, he whipped her into his embrace and

kissed her feverishly before pushing her away and toward the border. "Go!"

Gillian shook her head, seeing clearly what he'd hidden since their bond was sealed.

He'd given her a piece of his heart. That's what she'd consumed as his blood ran down her throat. The barrier would sever that bond, killing it as surely as it would take his life, for the goddess would allow nothing of the Dragon beyond the Shadowlands.

And Roman had known. He'd known their time was fleeting, that she would leave, and he would remain until his heart beat its last terrible rhythm.

Anger flared and died.

She looked into his stricken face as the Dragon screeched through the sky, scenting them and banking hard.

"Gillian, please."

"I love you, Roman," she said, pulling his head down to her lips. Letting go, she stared into his face. "I'm not going anywhere."

He frowned, eyes flicking overhead where Marius was aiming for the trees. "It was never going to be forever."

He whirled her around and shoved.

She went flying toward the barrier with a yelp, her body propelling her with the force of her momentum and a gust of hot wind from Roman's hands.

Grabbing the leather strip around her neck, she ripped the medallion from her bodice, scoring her neck with deep red lines. Yanking hard, she broke the thong and dropped the medallion Morrigan had infused with sigils to allow her passage out of the Shadowlands.

It fell to the ground, and her body slammed into the barrier.

She crumpled, the breath knocked out of her lungs. Blinking rapidly, she rolled onto her back, her ears ringing with booming roars interspersed with vicious cursing.

Roman ran toward her, snatching the medallion from the ground. "You fool!"

He slung the medallion over her neck, but it fell to the ground, the leather cording torn. He bent to retrieve it and was thrown to his knees by a gale of wind from the Dragon's wings.

Trees shrieked and branches snapped, trunks were ripped from the ground, or shredded to strips of woody pulp as Marius landed.

The Dragon spat a glob of molten fire at his son. Roman dodged, and it struck the ground at Gillian's feet. Sparks shot from the dirt as dead pine needles erupted. Fire licked the ground and caught on the hem of her red cloak.

She jumped up, batting at the wool, her hands blistering.

Roman smelled her flesh singe and lowered his head, glaring at his father with feral rage.

His skin exploded into black scales as talons and fangs erupted from his fingers and gums. He charged the Dragon, hands curled into claws.

Roman leaped into the air.

Marius watched the arc of his body and flung his neck, smashing his head into his son.

A tree snapped when Roman collided with its trunk. Chunks of wood blasted outward.

Growling, he got to his feet and flexed his fingers. Charging at a full run, he sprang onto the Dragon's back and dug his claws into the line of scales along Marius's spine.

The Dragon roared and spun in a circle, trying to dislodge him.

Roman hung on and reached for a tender spot along the base of his father's wing. He tore at the flesh between the red scales, blood spraying like mist.

Marius flapped his wings, hindered by the remaining trees that broke and fell around him, pinning his tail beneath a fallen pine. The Dragon craned his long neck and released a jet of fire.

Roman dodged it but slipped on the slick blood flowing from the wounds he'd inflicted.

Roman flipped in the air and landed on his feet. He sprang at Marius, coming at the Dragon from the side, never seeing his brother, Draven, until it was too late.

Draven jumped from a boulder and slammed into Roman, wrapping his arms around his brother. They tumbled to the ground in a ball of leaves and dirt.

Gillian ran toward them, the burned hem of her cloak dragging on the ground. She whispered healing words as she raced to the males, mending her skin the best she could. Her skill was untrained and sloppy, leaving lumpy flesh on her palms.

But the pain was gone, and she focused on her mate, who stared at Draven through a fog of rage.

"Roman!" she screamed.

He jerked his head toward her, and Draven took the moment of distraction to charge the Dragon.

The scales along his neck and cheek lay flat, their color leached of their usual ruby-red. Now they were a sickly pink with splotches of yellow.

He gritted his teeth and shouted at his father. "Stop this!"

Marius's neck bent, his head swinging toward his youngest. "You dare side with him again!"

His chest expanded and let loose a torrent of fire.

It hit Draven full-on. He screamed but kept coming, his skin blackening. "I did not sire sons to betray me!"

Another jet of flames shot from the Dragon's mouth. Draven didn't bother to deflect or dodge. He was too weak to fight the battle and win.

"Run!" he screamed at Roman and Gillian before leaping into the air at the Dragon.

Marius's eyes turned to slits, fangs flashing.

He snapped at Draven and released a rush of hot breath that knocked him aside. Head whacking the ground with a crack, Draven blinked a few times, the scales on his cheek blanching.

Roman watched in horror as his brother's body shuddered and lay still.

He was dying and not just from the Dragon's blast. There was something older, deeper. The Wasting.

That's what Draven had been hiding. Why he'd grown weak over the years, unable to shield his mind from Marius or call on his Dragon blood to fight when they'd brawled.

Grief so deep it threatened to eclipse reason filled Roman's mind.

Tucking Gillian behind him, he raged at his father, "Murderer!"

Fixing Roman with a baleful glare, Marius stepped toward him, eyes flicking to Gillian, who hovered at his back.

"Mate stealer," he hissed.

Torn between saving his brother and his mate, Roman craned his neck and looked at Gillian.

Their eyes met. He slipped the medallion he'd hidden in his tunic into her hand.

Go. You have to go.

She shook her head. *I won't leave you.*

You have to. We were never going to have more than a few stolen moments. He gripped her hand. *I love you.*

He shoved her back and ran toward his brother, standing over Draven's prone form with his legs braced apart. "You may as well kill us both because I won't let you have her."

Gillian watched the exchange and fiddled with the leather strip, tying the ends together. She slipped it over her head and felt a surge of power from the sigils when the disc rested against her chest.

Summoning a memory, Morrigan's voice and face flared in her mind, as though she stood at Gillian's side.

"The power of Dragon lives in you as it lives in every sister of the Silver Moon. Beneath that power is the core of your magic. You feel it. You've always felt it, though you didn't know it for what it was. Your mother, Rowena, had great power gifted to her from a direct line to the most powerful witch, Cyrena. She drank from Ashael, taking in a piece of the Dragon's heart."

"It lives in you as it has lived in every daughter of Cyrena's line. It gives you strength that surpasses even my own. Use it, my daughter. Listen to the voice of Cyrena, she is with you just as she was with your mother.

"Listen, Gillian. Listen, and you will hear her."

Gillian closed her eyes, blocking out the angry threats between Roman and Marius.

She couldn't help Draven, though the witch in her longed to heal him if only she'd the time and talent to use the craft.

And she couldn't stop Roman from facing his father.

But she could do as Morrigan had told her. She could listen to the voice of her ancestor.

She could open herself to Cyrena.

Chapter Thirty-Two

Gillian's eyes appeared otherworldly when she opened them and turned to the Dragon.

Walking slowly, she passed Draven's prone form, noting the slow rise and fall of his chest, feeling the thready pulse of his life.

She touched Roman's shoulder, hand trailing down his arm, her touch draining him of rage and leaving him immobile.

Gillian! he screamed at her through their bond.

Robbed of his voice and will to move, his eyes rounded, shifting to flames that guttered when she turned her head to look at him.

She was someone else.

Her steps were slow and measured.

The Great Dragon watched her progress, smoke trailing from his nostrils, his fangs winking in his snout.

"Have you come to sever the bond with my traitorous son?" he snarled.

She lifted her chin and caught his gaze, holding him there. "You will not have her."

The voice coming from her lips was full and tinged with an unusual burr.

Marius started and scraped his claws.

Narrowing his eyes, he tapped at her mind, flinching when he felt a response. *Cyrena*. "What magic is this?"

Gillian jerked her chin at Draven, who lay unmoving. "Are you so full of rage that you're blind to the monster you've become?"

He huffed, his breath a blast of igneous heat.

She scanned his features and shook her head. "Ashael would turn away from you if she could see you now."

"Do not speak her name. You know nothing of my mate!"

Gillian tilted her head. "I know what you have forgotten."

She went toward the Dragon until she stood between his deadly talons. The golden scales along his neck and chest flared out and then lay flat, sealing his body from her.

He wouldn't strike her down.

She knew this, though he blustered, flames dancing along his snout.

Arching her neck to meet his face as it hung over her like a cobra about to strike, she lifted her arms and lay her palms on his scaled chest.

He hissed and shifted, moving away from her. She followed his movements, keeping her hands in place.

"You risk much, touching me," he rumbled.

"I risk nothing." Gillian leaned forward and closed her eyes.

His scales glowed beneath her fingers, the color rippling outward from her hands like rings of water.

She hummed as she drew upon memories, pulling them from the past and breathing life into each image and word until they spun in her mind as though she were living them.

Raising her lashes, she stared up at the Dragon, a sad smile playing on her full lips.

"This was the only way," Gillian said softly in the voice of another.

Ashael fell from the sky like a meteor—blue scales glinting in the failing light as she tumbled through the air and slammed into the rocky ground.

Men cheered, banging swords against shields, the din momentarily blocking out the roar of Ashael's mate.

Cyrena motioned to her sisters to remain and wove through the rocks and underbrush, shielding the witches and humans fighting with them.

Marius, under siege, streaked through the sky, spewing streams of fire over a sea of soldiers that devoured the landscape like a locust swarm.

Climbing a short hill above Ashael's landing spot, the high witch pressed her body to the ground and peered over the edge. Strands of red hair blew around her face, freed from her tight braid after hours of fighting.

Fatigue and grief shadowed her stormy gray eyes as she scanned the stretch of land around the Dragoness' fallen body.

Tapping at her magic, Cyrena frowned.

Days of battling a sea of men who sought to overthrow the Great Dragon's rule had taken its toll. She didn't think she had enough power in reserve to heal Ashael, and if she died... it didn't bear thinking.

Springing from her vantage point, she ran over the lip of the craggy hill and down its steep side, rocks and dirt spraying into the air and pelting her leather-clad legs as she slid down toward Ashael.

The Dragoness' eye was little more than a pain-ridden slit tracking the witch's progress.

Above her broken body, Marius circled, roaring in fury and dodging the same spears that had pierced his mate.

Morfran's army was too great in number. Tens of thousands of swords wreaked havoc and protected scores of their Great War machines that hurled iron weapons at Marius and those who fought with him.

The men fighting Morfran's banner came from every corner of the kingdom, soldiers and knights who paid fealty to nobles thirsty for power, land, and titles.

They resented the Dragon's reign, believing his death would ring in a new era for mankind, one where men ruled.

Marius and Ashael could've ceded the land sought by King Morfran, retaining their rightful supremacy over all living things while allowing the illusion of rule to the corrupt king, but Marius was unwilling to bend his neck to beings he'd allowed to flourish in his world.

The Great Dragon spied Cyrena making her way to his mate and let out a plaintive roar.

The witch looked up at him and nodded, letting him know she'd do all she could.

In an effort to draw the enemy away from his wounded mate, Marius dove toward Morfran's army, engaging them until they fell back, intent on waging a battle on the Dragon.

Cyrena raced to Ashael, leaping over rocks and listening for the approach of soldiers.

A battle cry rent the air, and her skin prickled as the sisters of the Silver Moon unleashed their waning magic alongside the Dragon's army.

Too many witches had already fallen, and with Ashael wounded, they were all on the precipice of losing their lives. And if the Dragons fell, so would all people.

She'd considered seeking an audience with Morfran to plead with him, but the Great Dragon forbade it, telling her the king would likely hang her in the public square before listening to her counsel.

He would not risk the lives of the coven for such a man.

Ashael chirred when Cyrena crawled to her side, the sound pulling at the witch's heart as it was one used for Dragon young. A growing pool of blood covered the ground, cooling on the rocks like a black lake. It coated Cyrena's hands and legs, congealing in slick layers.

Pressing her hands to the Dragoness' side, the witch used her magic to feel out the injuries.

"I'm dying," Ashael whispered.

Shaking her head, the high witch gritted her teeth and focused, calling on Keridwen to lend her strength. She desperately mended organs and muscles, but there were too many wounds. Her body was too damaged.

The low thumping of the Dragon's heart was slow and ponderous. There wasn't much time.

"Cyrena," Ashael rasped, "drink."

The Dragoness lifted her snout toward a gaping wound in her shoulder where the tip of an iron-forged barbed spear pierced her blue scales.

"Take a piece of my heart and fight with my mate."

Her body shuddered, and she coughed bloody foam onto the ground.

"Drink," she pleaded, "share our blood with your sisters and defeat Morfran."

The witch's hands shook as she leaned forward. "I would give my life to save you if I could," she told Ashael.

The Dragoness closed her eyes and rested her head on the ground, too weary to keep it raised. "I know."

Cyrena closed her mouth around the edge of the wound. Thick blood coated her tongue and ran down her throat, burning a path into her belly where it exploded with heat.

She clutched her stomach and groaned, doubling over as the fire in the Dragoness' blood ran through her veins straight to her heart.

The high witch reared back and arched her neck, tendons straining. Dragon and witch blood fused and flooded every muscle, every pore.

Her skin felt hot, her face flushing to a deep red that matched her hair. A fevered mass settled in her body as she kneeled, rigid, at Ashael's side.

Slowly, the Dragoness' blood cooled in her veins, leaving behind currents of energy that filled her well of magic with new power.

Ashael rolled pain-filled golden eyes toward her. "My mate..." she wheezed, a bloody bubble forming and popping in her nostril, "he will grieve. His Dragon heart will rage. He will blame Keridwen. He must not... he must not turn his back on her. The coven—"

Her body seized, pupils dilating. She panted, the beating of her heart erratic and labored. "You and your sisters share this realm as—"

She gasped, the sound ending in a gurgle. "Equals. Tell him, I am with him. Through the goddess... I am..."

Cyrena's face twisted as Ashael's heart stuttered, then grew silent.

The Great Dragon roared, and it shook the earth.

Oceans swelled, and storms flashed across the sky, echoing his grief and rage.

He drew on the darkest parts of his power and unleashed his wrath on the army. Men broke rank and tried to run or covered their ears and screamed. Commanders rallied them at the points of swords, forcing them back to the front.

With a trembling voice, the high witch dropped her head and prayed to Keridwen, asking for blessings for Ashael and the sanctifying of the union of Dragon and witch blood. She felt the touch of the goddess in a breeze that blew across her face, cool like the kiss of the moon.

Standing, she gazed at Ashael's body, then turned and faced the legions of men crawling across the landscape.

Above them, Marius hovered, targeting their war machines.

He spewed torrents of fire, wings beating the flames, fanning them until they consumed everything in their path. He turned his head toward her, and she felt his ancient mind tap at hers.

The grief, raw and terrible, made her knees buckle.

She lifted her chin and spoke to him with her mind, *I am with you. The sisters of the Silver Moon are with you.*

In those words was a promise beyond the fell days of battle.

It was a promise to be at his side as Ashael had been. To ease his grief and help carry the burden of ruling such a world without his mate. Equals with the blood of Dragon.

Cyrena found what was left of her sisters in the melee.

Cutting her wrist, she bade them drink and take in Ashael's blood, knowing it would amplify their gifts. When all had consumed it, she led them onto the battlefield, and in the days that followed, they beat back the enemy, forcing them out of the Shadowlands.

Years passed in a blur of memories.

Marius was shown the birth of Cyrena's child, a daughter named Kenna, in honor of her Dragon blood. He was forced to see the babe, feel the weight of the squalling infant, and inhale the child's scent—tinged with Ashael's blood.

Memories of dragonlings mixed with the images she shared until they blended together, and through it all, Ashael's dying words, "You and your sisters share this realm as equals."

Gillian came back to herself and dropped her arm, stepping away from the Great Dragon.

She stared into him. *Is this the world your mate died for?*

Chapter Thirty-Three

The Great Dragon bowed his head, claws digging ruts in the dark soil.

His golden eyes flicked to his son.

Roman darted forward and tried to tuck Gillian behind his back, but she would have none of it.

Marius shifted his attention to her, smoke curling from his nostrils as the sharp point of a fang flashed in his snout.

"I see Morrigan's hand in you," he rumbled.

Gillian lifted her chin. "You saw more than that."

Roman glanced at her. *What did you do?* he asked through the bond.

What I had to.

Breaking away from Roman's side, Gillian stood her ground. "Your mate revered the goddess. She understood Keridwen's power as equal to Irylle's. She gave a piece of her heart so we could live alongside you, not beneath your talons. You sully her memory by preying on those who share Ashael's blood."

"My mate would not wish my line to wither and die," Marius countered. "But you have given me much to think on."

He swung his head to the sky, where the moon was visible even in Irylle's light. He had wronged the goddess. His rage had cursed the world and his sons.

Marius shifted his long neck and looked at Draven, who lay on the ground still as death.

"Is there no hope?"

It was more than his son's survival he questioned.

"Hope for whom? You? Your son? Those you rule?" Gillian tilted her head and waited.

Roman cocked a brow.

How had he won this self-assured woman? She fearlessly faced the Dragon where others would cower or run. It was as though she was lit from within by a fire of her own making.

Pride made his chest swell.

Marius' neck arched back, pulling his head away and up. Wings tucked tight to his sides, he folded in on himself, collapsing like a star.

He stood in the footprints of his true form as a man, black robe fluttering at his sides.

Striding to his youngest son, he knelt and laid his palms on Draven's chest.

"I have lost too many of my children."

He bowed his head and let out a long breath. "You were right to show me—" He swallowed hard, eyes turning to flames, red scales covering skin in waves, then disappearing. "If my mate stood before me now, I would be ashamed."

Rising, he looked at Roman and then let his eyes fall on Gillian. "I do not know the way forward."

"I do," Morrigan said, materializing from the forest.

She was haggard but whole, trailed by a white buck with black antlers the breadth of a full-grown man. Fian.

He'd walked the earth since the mage days. Magic-born and ruler of the hoofed animals that called the Shadowlands home.

The high witch stroked the buck's muzzle, whispering thanks. He dipped his head and looked at Gillian with liquid brown eyes before turning and bolting into the forest.

Marius eyed the witch and rose from his son's side.

There was no apology on his face, but the fires of rage had receded, leaving him unguarded.

She stared at him, seeing beyond the illusion of his form to the broken soul beneath it. Her sisters had often berated her for the pity she felt for the Dragon.

They did not understand.

They could not see.

But Morrigan had always known what hid under layers of time. Beneath centuries of grief and anger.

For the first time since the death of his mate, the Dragon let down his defenses.

Morrigan nodded and went to Gillian.

She clasped her hands and said, "With the blessing of the goddess, it has always been within your power to sunder the barrier between worlds. Your mother's sacrifice created it," she paused and glanced at the Dragon, who scowled at that piece of information. "As her blood runs in your veins, so does the power to raze what she wrought to protect you. The question is, is that what you want? Destroying it means bridging the two realms again and exposing those who sought sanctuary in the kingdom of your childhood."

She turned her face to Marius while still speaking to Gillian. "It means trusting those who have not earned it."

Gillian felt Roman step to her side as Morrigan released her hands. His heat radiated through the space between their bodies.

Craning her neck to look up at him, she saw his face tighten and then relax. "I am with you."

His words echoed those of Ashael as she'd lain dying. Uttering them had a visible effect on the Great Dragon.

Marius shuddered, his head swimming with memories.

An image of his mate grew in his mind, blue scales gleaming in the soft light as she gazed at him after their first joining.

"The future is ours," she'd whispered to the Great Dragon.

And it had been until he stood alone, facing it.

Time had worn away the edges of his grief, leaving behind rough corners that bled anger and retaliation against the world that had taken his beloved. But the men who'd launched the spear that stole her life were long dead.

There would be no more Dragons in the world. None, save him.

He hung his head. "Tear it down."

Gillian studied him, sliding her hand in Roman's.

Marius lifted his chin to meet her eyes. "I give you my oath, I will not betray you or the coven. It is time I accepted my fate. Past time."

He turned away and strode a safe distance before exploding into his true form.

They watched him soar into the sky and disappear beyond the tree line.

Morrigan went to Draven, healing what she could. The

Wasting had lived in him too long for her magic to rouse him, but when she drew away, he was breathing easier, the waxiness of his face fading.

Roman kneeled at his brother's side and spoke softly while Morrigan wearily moved away to find a place to rest.

She sat on a slab of rock and closed her eyes, drilling into the well of her power to cleanse her mind and prepare to aid Gillian.

"Are you well?" the young witch asked, sitting next to her.

"Aye. As well as I can be." Morrigan gave her a sidelong glance. "I can feel her lingering in you."

Gillian nodded and looked away.

She, too, felt Cyrena, as though her ancestor remained. Perhaps she had always been there. A voice in the back of her mind, leading her to this time. This place.

Morrigan rested her hands in her lap. "There is much I will teach you in the days to come."

"I'm ready."

"You will see your brother first. If he cannot be saved, know that the ferryman is kind and the river is not wide. You will see him again."

Gillian nodded jerkily, stuffing her sadness into the pit of her stomach where it sat like a ball of lumpy gruel.

Morrigan grasped her hand, her skin rough and calloused in Gillian's palm. "Since the day Keridwen cut off our world from your homeland, I prayed to the goddess that I would never see you. That you would remain beyond the barrier. Safe from the Dragon. Free to live and love on your terms."

Gillian looked at her. "And now?"

"I'm glad you came." She tucked a loose strand of pale hair

behind Gillian's ear. "You are your mother's daughter. I see her strength in you." Morrigan smirked. "And her reckless nature. It is a good thing her blood runs hot in your veins. You'll need it."

The young witch wrinkled her nose and made a face. "Thanks. I think."

Chuckling, Morrigan rose and went to gather some roots and flowers to shore up her strength.

Roman saw her leave and patted his brother's shoulder. Rising, he strode to his mate. He grasped Gillian's shoulders and turned her body toward his. Cupping her face, he kissed her deeply, breathing in her scent and sharing his own.

She inhaled, letting the essence of his being fill her nostrils and travel into her lungs. In moments, her head swam as though she were drunk.

Lashes fluttering, Gillian pulled away and gave him a lopsided grin. "You really shouldn't stun me when I have work to do."

"I wanted to inspire you to get it done quickly," he said in a husky voice, eyes turning to ruby flames.

Her stomach flipped, and she bit her bottom lip, a grin tugging at her mouth when his attention shifted to her lips. "You'd better get started."

Chapter Thirty-Four

It was midday when Morrigan and Gillian stood facing the barrier.

It shimmered in the sunlight breaking through the trees, shifting subtly as though it breathed. Roman crouched nearby at Draven's side, brows knitted as he watched his brother's shallow breathing.

It reminded her of her mother, Naeve, watching Rory sleep as the Wasting slowly ate away at his young body.

Morrigan nudged Gillian, bringing her attention back to the barrier.

Cocking her head, Gillian focused on it, delving into its structure and beyond to its source: Keridwen. Intermingled with the energy of the goddess was her birth mother.

Rowena spoke to her in the crooning of a mother's voice to her babe. Singing of the life she was leaving and the future that lay ahead.

The stain of death lingered in the protective shield, Rowena's life having been spent to aid its creation.

But it was not unpleasant.

There was hope within that sacrifice. Hope and love for the daughter it protected.

It was not for Gillian to bring down the barrier. That power resided with the goddess. But she had the blood of Rowena, and it was her mother who'd begged Keridwen to protect her child.

That connection was deep and powerful. It still lived in the pulsing energy of a power strong enough to repel the Great Dragon.

The high witch lifted her arms to the sky and prayed to Keridwen. Her lips moved rapidly, little more than faint whispers of sound.

The wind stirred, and leaves rustled, tree branches swaying with low creaks and groans.

Closing her eyes, Gillian listened to the trees.

They had voices of their own. Through their woody bodies, she heard the goddess, felt her presence in the breeze ruffling the loose strands of her hair and the rumble of oak, pine, and ash as tree trunks slowly undulated.

The skin on Gillian's arms prickled, and the tiny hairs on the back of her neck sprang outward. She clenched her eyes tighter, struggling to be in the moment, to resist the urge to look around and watch the forest bending its will to Keridwen.

"Sing with me," Morrigan told her and pressed her hands to the shimmering barrier.

Gillian raised her arms into the air, mirroring the high witch's posture.

Energy surged along her open palms like thin needles lightly stabbing at her skin. Gritting her teeth, she held her stance and opened her mouth.

It was a song Morrigan had taught her as they worked side-by-side in the safety of Gealach Wood. She'd hummed the tune and sang the words, twining her voice with Gillian's, teaching her the song her mother had sung when she'd given her life to fortify her baby daughter against the Dragon.

Within the words was a prayer, and within her blood was the power.

Silver Moon

Mother Moon

Their heads rolled back in unison, and the wind stirred in a gentle vortex around their figures.

Roman tore his gaze away from Draven and fixed his attention on Gillian.

She swayed, energy flowing through her limbs as the song spilled from her lips.

He caught snippets of it, each word imbued with power.

Keeper of the Cauldron

Gillian's arms trembled.

Morrigan sensed it and reached for her, twining the fingers of her left hand through Gillian's. The action anchored the young witch to the earth.

She stood straighter, neck arched, voice rising above gusts of wind.

Walk with me, Great Mother

Through the wood and plain

Speak to me in whispers

Roman's eyes shifted to the barrier.

It shimmered and stretched as if it reached for the witches. The surface bulged out, then in, bending with their song.

Morrigan gripped Gillian harder, pouring her magic into

her pupil. He crouched, frozen, as their voices rose in pitch, climbing into the swirling air above their heads.

The words doubled and trebled.

Fill me with your song

Gift me with your might

The veil between their worlds writhed, holding onto itself for a protracted moment, then shook. A thin fissure grew from the ground at Gillian's feet, snaking upward as Keridwen released the power that had forged the barrier.

As it fractured, a new voice blended with theirs. It was Gillian's voice, only fuller and deeper.

It was a mother's voice.

Daughter of the Silver Moon

Hear your mother's call

Listen to the whispers

Of the Cauldron Goddess

And your sisters

Beyond the wall

Roman rose slowly, drawn to Gillian as Rowena's voice eclipsed hers.

Tears streamed down her pale cheeks unchecked, though she did not waver. Did not lower her hands or cease her song. Her legs shook with strain, her heart racing as though she'd sprinted rather than stood facing the insubstantial veil between realms.

Morrigan's grip slackened, their palms slick with sweat. The matriarch's power waned just as Gillian's did.

Sensing her weariness through the bond, Roman came forward and stood behind her.

The wind tossed his dark hair as though trying to force him

back. He reached through it to place his hands on her shoulders. He heard the voice of Gillian's mother, clear and strong, the moment they touched.

Closing his eyes, he opened himself to his mate, willing her to draw on his strength.

Her voice hitched for a moment, the slight pause ushering in her mother's final refrain.

Live, my silver daughter
Live free and know
I am with you, always
In darkness and in light

The fissure raced up the barrier between the women's hands with a low rumble.

As their voices hung in the air, it flowed upward, becoming a gaping crack.

Roman followed it with his eyes, keeping his hands on Gillian's shoulders.

The crack ripped through the veil. Up, up, up. Arcing toward the heart of Valon.

He could see it now, the perfect dome wrought by Keridwen's will and Rowena's lifeblood, trapping everything within the Shadowlands.

All to protect her most precious possession. Her daughter.

A deep groan echoed through the sky as the barrier broke apart. Gillian's arms fell to her sides, and she leaned into Roman, chest heaving with strangled sobs.

Rowena's voice slipped into her mind, soothing and filled with love. Keridwen embraced her—a soft breeze brushing her cheeks and drying the tears that coated them. For a moment, she heard her mother's voice as if she stood at her side and felt a motherly embrace.

She closed her eyes and whispered to Rowena, feeling a feathery kiss on her forehead before the wind settled and all was still.

When Gillian opened her eyes, nothing and everything had changed.

Roman's fingers curled gently on her shoulders, offering her strength.

She took it, letting their bond encompass the places where her mother's presence lingered. Dropping her head, she took a step back to press against Roman.

He wrapped his arms around her and bent his head. "You're free."

She nodded. "We all are."

Part of her wondered if she'd done the right thing. Would Marius keep his word? Had she doomed the world of her childhood?

Gillian glanced at Morrigan, whose attention was fixed beyond the border of the Shadowlands, though little could be seen through the trees.

She was calling to her sisters who lived there. Those who'd sought sanctuary among mankind. In time, she hoped they would sense her and respond.

Turning slowly, Gillian wrapped her arms around Roman and buried her face in his chest.

"I have to go home."

She shared images of her brother Rory through the bond. Happy memories of him romping through the village turned dark with worry and sorrow when he began to weaken and grew ill.

"I hope I'm not too late," she choked into his chest.

He kissed the top of her head and breathed deeply, letting her scent wash over him.

"I'll wait for you. No matter how long it takes."

She nodded, her head bumping against him. Roman tightened his hold, testing his strength and the ability to let her walk away from him.

"You could come with me," she whispered.

He shook his head. "I can't."

"But—"

He leaned in and gave her a quick kiss, followed by a lopsided grin when he pulled away and saw her skin flushed.

"You have to go alone."

She tried to argue again, but he reached up and traced his thumb along her bottom lip.

"The barrier is destroyed, but that's only the beginning of the work to be done. There's a long history of hate and fear among our kinds."

He stepped back and rubbed her arms. "It will take time."

She frowned. "I'll worry."

"There's no risk to me now that you've sundered the barrier. I will still feel you. You'll still hear me."

"Promise?" Her voice wavered a bit.

"Aye. I promise not to give you peace as I invade your mind with unfulfilled wanting every moment we're parted."

Gillian smiled. "See that you do."

Morrigan chuckled and moved away from the pair to kneel at Draven's side.

She laid her hands on the Dragonborn.

Tilting her head, the high witch listened to his labored breath. There was a rattle in his chest. The Wasting had taken its toll.

Morrigan sat back on her heels and held her hands out, palms up, praying to the goddess to cleanse her mind and replenish her depleted power.

Gillian moved to Draven's other side and matched the matriarch's movements.

She felt weak, her body drained, as she closed her eyes and listened to the words humming from Morrigan's lips. Her magic sparked, faint but whole, and she grabbed hold of it, drawing it out and pouring it into her hands in healing waves.

Minutes passed while Roman paced, the scuff of his soft leather boots creating a rhythm.

Draven remained unconscious, his chest rising and falling. As the women whispered and chanted, the pale cast to his face faded to his natural color. The scales along his left side twitched, fluttering like the feathers of a bird. Their ruby-rich color had bleached to sickly yellow and pink.

As the witches' healing magic flooded his body, the scales shifted to a reddish hue, healthier, but lacking their normal vibrancy.

It would take more than words, magic, and the banishment of the barrier to repair his body if it could be healed completely.

Roman paused in his pacing when Draven's lashes fluttered. He fell to his knees at his brother's head and leaned over as the young Dragonborn male came to.

Draven's pupils dilated, the copper of his eyes a muddy brown.

Roman frowned and cupped Draven's head. "Brother?"

Morrigan and Gillian's chanting drifted to silence.

All eyes focused on the young male.

He blinked slowly, fighting against a haze of listlessness, struggling through the waters of exhaustion like a drowning man. His mouth dropped open, emitting a raspy noise.

Licking lips that had a purplish cast, Draven tried to speak but choked on dried spit. His efforts ended in a fit of coughing as he was rolled to his side.

The high witch harrumphed. "Save your strength, Dragonborn."

Roman glanced at her, and she got to her feet with a groan, muttering about age and old bones.

She caught his look and said, "We've done all we can. The rest is up to Keridwen."

Roman closed his eyes briefly, offering up a prayer to the fire goddess, then crouched at his brother's back and hauled him into a sitting position. Leaning Draven against the trunk of a tree, he kneeled at his feet and spoke softly.

Gillian watched the exchange, face softening when Draven's eyes shifted to hers, and he gave her a weak smile.

The young male nodded, and Roman patted his shoulder, springing to his feet and striding to Gillian.

Her face was turned from him. She looked toward Rudgarde, hoping the scene she found in her childhood home would be free of black drapes and weeping.

Roman wrapped his arms around his mate. "Go to him."

She craned her neck to look at him, twisting her body to burrow into his embrace. "I'll come back."

His chin bumped the top of her head as he nodded. "And I'll be waiting."

Chapter Thirty-Five

The thatched roof of her childhood home came into view when Gillian left the forest bordering the Shadowlands.

Laundry hung from twine strung between two saplings outside the front door. It flapped in the wind above a group of chickens that pecked and clucked the hard-packed dirt.

She paused, seeing shadows move beyond the thick, uneven panes of the single window on the outer wall. Her heart raced as she searched for signs of mourning.

In her head, Roman spoke to her, offering words of comfort through their bond. She took solace in the whisper of his voice and straightened her shoulders.

As her home drew closer, she broke into a jog, feet pounding on the ground, the hood of her cloak bouncing against her shoulders. Just beyond the threshold, she called out, "Mama?"

From inside came a happy squeal, followed by the sound of racing feet.

Naeve burst through the doorway and grabbed Gillian. The two fell to the ground, sending hens squawking. Her mother's hands were everywhere, checking for injuries, assuring herself that her daughter was well and safe.

Between sobs and hitched breaths, Gillian discovered that Rory lived, though he could no longer rise or feed himself.

"I think... I think he's been waiting for you," Naeve choked out, burying her face in her hands.

Lochlan joined them moments later, kneeling in the dirt to embrace the two women.

Unable to let her go, Naeve clung to Gillian's hand as Lochlan helped them rise and led them to the door.

Her body locked for a moment as they stood in the doorway, fear and grief clogging her throat. But there was Roman speaking to her through their mating bond as if he'd shared her reunion with her parents and knew she stood on the precipice of saying goodbye to her sweet brother.

It gave her strength.

Naeve squeezed her fingers, and they passed into the house.

Dust motes hung in the air like tiny stars reflecting the buttery sunlight pouring through the windowpane. The air smelled of fresh bread.

Clay bowls sat in the washtub, flies buzzing around the remains of food clinging in small globs. A muslin curtain separating the kitchen from a sitting area that had been turned into Rory's bed-chamber was pulled back and hung on a wooden peg.

Suddenly, Gillian couldn't wait a moment longer.

She bolted from her parents and slid to a stop at Rory's bed.

He lay curled on his side, a thin blanket covering his body up to his ears.

Red hair poked out from the top of the bedding. She studied her brother, seeing the subtle shift of his body as he breathed.

So like Draven, she thought, sending the image to Roman, who tapped at it with strength and understanding.

Gillian knelt on the floor, her red cloak billowing out behind her. "Rory. I'm home." She reached forward and gently touched him. "Rory. It's Gillian."

"Gil?" Came a small voice.

Her throat tightened, eyes welling. "Aye. I've come home."

Rory rolled over, aided by Gillian's hand. His cheeks were flushed, blue eyes fever-bright. "Gillian," he rasped, chapped lips splitting into a grin. "Where have you been?"

"I went to the Shadowlands."

His eyes rounded. "You did?" Rory glanced at his parents, who nodded solemnly. "What did you see? Were there dragons?"

Gillian smiled. "There was a Dragon and Dragonborn and witches and all sorts of creatures you've never dreamed of."

Rory grinned. "I knew they were real."

His expression was ruined by wet coughing that had him doubled over and gasping by the end.

Gillian patted his back and propped him up, bunching the pillow under his head and shoulders. Naeve handed her a cold cup of tea with honey, and Gillian held it to her brother's lips, watching his throat bob as he swallowed.

"Rory," she said, darting a look at her parents hovering at

her shoulder, then back at him. "I learned some healing ways when I was gone and want to try them with you."

He looked skeptical. "Are you gonna be a midwife now?"

"I might." Rory made a face, and she asked, "What? Don't you think I could do it?"

He shrugged his shoulders and picked at the bedding.

Gillian huffed. "Are you doubting my skill?"

Rory rolled his eyes and scooted back to ease the wheezing in his chest. "Maybe. I guess you couldn't make me worse."

She laced her fingers and splayed them outward with little pops of her knuckles. "That sounds like a challenge, and I always win. You do remember you've never beaten me in a footrace."

"That's cause your legs are longer than mine! It's not fair."

"It's because I'm faster than you." She winked at him and laid her hands on his chest.

She could feel her parents at her back, her mother's nervous energy mixed with tenuous hope and her father's incessant worry.

Blocking them out, Gillian drilled into her core of magic. It was depleted from bringing down the barrier, but she felt its threads and pulled on them.

It spooled out of her, humming through her limbs and into her hands. Her palms grew warm as she recalled the words Morrigan had spoken over Draven. They spilled from her lips, halting at first, then with purpose.

She let the healing spell flow from her.

Rory flinched as the warmth from her hands spread over his chest. Naeve stepped to his side and took his hand, her eyes fixed on her daughter's bent head.

Gillian ignored their movements and channeled her energy, pouring all she could into Rory's frail body. Minutes later, she slumped, head drooping and arms leaden. Sitting back on her heels, she lifted her chin and studied her brother, giving a wobbly smile when she noted the fevered flush in his cheeks had receded, and his breathing had eased.

Naeve gripped her shoulder with her free hand. "Where did you learn this?"

Gillian looked up at her. "I'll tell you."

They spoke in soft voices at the table as Rory slept.

Lochlan and Naeve sat side-by-side across from Gillian, who cupped a chipped mug of watered wine.

She wanted to tell them everything, but hesitated, settling for a version where she learned healing ways at the elbow of the matriarch of the coven. Of the Great Dragon and his sons, she said little, choosing to spin a story of meeting Roman and falling in love. Naeve looked stricken as she spoke, reaching across the table with a soft mew of complaint.

Lochlan rubbed her back, asking if she thought her daughter would forever remain a spinster. Her mother shook her head and chuckled, though her eyes were misty as Gillian continued speaking.

When Lochlan rose long after the evening meal, he hugged Gillian and assured the women he'd check on Rory, knowing there was more to be said and that they waited for him to leave. Naeve nodded and accepted a kiss, watching him pull the curtain and speak softly to their son, whose sleepy voice carried through the small house.

When they heard the soft click of the latch on their

bedroom door, Gillian turned to the only mother she'd ever known and said, "You've been keeping secrets."

Naeve dipped her head and nodded. "For your own good and at Finn's request."

Finn. The man Rowena had fallen in love with and made a child with. The man she had trusted to raise their daughter beyond the Dragon's reach.

Over the years, Naeve told her stories of the man with a young daughter she'd married. He'd been taken too soon when illness ravaged the town of Rudgarde, and she'd raised his child as her own.

When Lochlan proposed, it was on the condition that he was aware of Gillian's history and understood that some things must remain secret for the child to live a full life. Never had she imagined the sacrifice of Gillian's birth mother. Finn hadn't known it either.

All that his beloved had told him was that their daughter was in danger, and the only way to protect her was to keep her heritage secret. To keep her out of the Shadowlands.

And he'd done it. Even with his dying breath, he'd made Naeve promise to protect the girl.

"It was a heavy burden," Naeve said quietly. "But it was one I was honored to bear."

She held out her hand, palm up. Gillian glanced at it, then laid hers in it. Naeve's fingers curled around hers, rough from years of use. Familiar and warm.

"Finn loved you so much," Naeve said, voice wavering. "How could I not abide by his final wish?"

Gillian nodded. "You did what you thought was right. Even

if I'd known the truth, I don't think it would've changed anything. My life was here."

"Was?" Naeve asked, leaning closer.

It was Gillian's turn to peel back the layers of secrecy and tell her mother of the sisters, who were like family. Of Morrigan and how the high witch had embraced her as a daughter. While many things were kept hidden, she told Naeve about the coven's sacred lands, about Roman and Valon.

She spoke of Marius, but it was in simple terms, never alluding to the trials the Great Dragon had put her through. Perhaps in the future, she'd tell her. When the world was ready to hear such things.

If the land and its people were healed, and the Wasting was nothing more than an awful memory. Maybe then.

For now, they talked into the night, checking on Rory and speaking of little things until the time came when they ran out of things to fill the hours.

Gillian rose from her chair and embraced her mother. "I love you, Mama."

Naeve held her tight, then pulled away, tilting her chin. "Why does that sound like a goodbye?"

She gave her a sad smile. "It's not goodbye. Not yet."

"You're going back there, aren't you?"

Gillian nodded. Naeve tucked a lock of pale hair behind her ear and cupped her cheek. "I knew the day would come, but now that it's here, I'm not ready."

She turned her cheek into her mother's hand and kissed her palm. "It won't be forever. I'll visit often. I promise."

"And you'll bring your man."

Nodding, Gillian smiled and said, "Yes, I'll introduce you."

She turned toward the curtain separating the kitchen and sitting room and listened to the even breathing of her brother.

"Rory would love that, wouldn't he? Meeting a true Dragonborn."

Saying the words felt right. True. As if some part of her knew he'd recover. That he would get to live.

Naeve chuckled softly. "Aye. He'd brag to his friends, to be sure."

Gillian pressed a kiss to Rory's forehead and whispered goodnight before heading to her thin pallet in the small bedroom they'd shared until he'd fallen ill. She lay on her bed and thought of Roman, her mind drifting along their mental tether, smiling to herself when he responded.

His voice lulled her to sleep, and before she succumbed to slumber, she heard him painting vivid pictures in her mind of his arms around her, his heart beating strong and solid against her cheek.

She dreamed of him, her body humming with energy until the dawn.

Chapter Thirty-Six

A fortnight passed during which Rory struggled to fight the Wasting. By the end of that time, the disease that had taken so many lives over the years had let go of the child. In truth, it released its hold on every family it had taken root in, even those of the Great Dragon.

Keridwen was at peace.

Far from Rudgarde, Roman kept watch on his sibling, rarely leaving his bedside. The drone of his voice as he read from dusty tomes from his father's library was the first thing Draven heard after days of unconsciousness.

The young Dragonborn's lashes fluttered open. Gone was the muddy brown color of his eyes, replaced by buttery copper. He blinked and rolled his head to the side.

"I'd begun to think you remained asleep to avoid listening to me read," Roman drawled from the wide chair at the bedside.

Draven pushed himself up against a pillow and glanced at

the book stuffed against the arm of the chair. He cleared his throat. "I tried that for all the good it did."

Roman chuckled. "Shall I continue?" he asked, plucking the book from the chair and opening it. "I'll admit that it is a rather harrowing story of King Balor when he lost his entire army crossing the Red Wastes. You were never one to enjoy a happy ending."

"I'd rather hear the story of how I came to be here and what's become of your mate."

Closing the book, Roman cocked his head. "Alas, brother, you won't like that one either. What with those happy endings and all."

Leaning forward with his hands hanging from his knees, Roman told his brother what had happened since he'd lost consciousness. Gillian remained with her family, though she gave him regular updates through their bond.

Her brother was recovering, and soon she'd return to the Shadowlands, where they would make a life for themselves.

Marius had withdrawn, though he visited Draven often and enlisted the aid of the local healer who'd plainly told him there was nothing she could do.

"An old spitfire, that one," Roman mused. "She marched herself into this room and declared Father the cause of your suffering. I thought he was going to throw her out the window." He shook his head and looked at his brother from beneath his arched brows. "He's worried about you. We all are. Even Ansel visits daily."

Draven gave a shaky laugh. "I find that hard to believe."

Roman shrugged. "He's still a prick, no matter how many

times he visits." He rose and dropped the book on the chair. "I'll leave this here in case you'd like a bedtime story."

His brother snorted and swung his legs to the side of the bed. A sheen of sweat covered his skin, but the scales lining his left side bloomed a healthy red, indicating his recovery was imminent.

Roman slapped him in the back and strode to the door. "I'll fetch you some food. Cook will be pleased to hear you're awake. He's been hounding me to arrange a hunt and bring back a haunch of vauger meat."

Draven wrinkled his nose. "Don't tell me he believes eating that will aid me. The meat tastes as awful as the beast looks."

"Not only that. He thinks it'll increase your... uh... vigor." He waggled his eyebrows and ducked as Draven threw his pillow.

Opening the door, Roman paused and dipped his head, quickly standing aside. "Father."

Marius stood at the threshold, his long black hair swept back in a queue. Worry lined his face, and dark circles made his eyes look bruised.

He nodded to Roman and stepped inside. The Great Dragon studied his youngest child and let go of days of anxiety and regret.

His shoulders slumped with relief, the bell sleeves of his robe shifting. Marius walked to the bed with small steps until he reached the chair. Tossing the book on the ground, he pulled it toward Draven and sat so the two were knee-to-knee.

Roman closed the door with a faint click.

"It is good to see you awake," Marius said in a gravelly voice.

His eyes skipped around the room, unable to meet the level stare of his son. He dropped his head and took a deep breath.

"The Wasting that nearly killed you is my fault," he said quietly.

Draven tried to argue, but Marius shook his head.

"Stop. You have to know the truth. I turned my back on Keridwen when Ashael was taken from me. I cursed her, blaming the goddess for allowing my mate to die. It weakened her, though I didn't know it. I didn't care to know it."

He sighed and leaned back in his chair, a wry smile lighting his striking face. "It might surprise you to hear this, but I'm a rather selfish creature."

Draven chuckled and relaxed. "It's a family trait."

Marius nodded.

"For too long, I put my wants above all others, regardless of the cost. I cannot bring myself to regret those choices because they resulted in you and your siblings. But I carry the heavy weight of guilt."

He sat up straight and looked directly at Draven, eyes shifting to molten red. "I do not expect your forgiveness. In truth, I don't deserve it." His throat bobbed. "I'm sorry. For too long, you've stood in your brother's shadow. Perhaps you were content to be there. I'm proud of you, Draven."

The Dragonborn's eyes glowed with golden light.

"I haven't told you that enough. You're strong, my son. I hope, in time, you and your brother can look at me as a father again. Until then, I will work to earn that regard."

Roman moved away from the door he'd pressed his ear to.

Marius had said much the same after the scene in the forest, and while he didn't know the way forward, he knew they would find it eventually.

The day Gillian reached for him through their mating bond and told him she was ready to come home, he'd been standing in the great hall speaking to Draven, who sat before the large hearth.

His mug of ale slipped from his fingers and landed on the floor, soaking the rushes.

"What?" Draven asked. He was still weak, but food and rest had improved him greatly.

A smile split Roman's face, and he looked at his brother. "Gillian is coming home."

"Is she now?" Draven rested his elbows on the arms of his chair and tapped his fingers together. "And will I be an uncle soon? Perhaps I should tell her to make haste."

"Just because you're an invalid doesn't mean I won't beat you into silence."

The young Dragonborn chuckled. "Rein in that fiery temper of yours, brother. I have no wish to see the lady blush and stammer. I'll leave that task to you in your bedchamber." He jerked away as Roman snaked his hand out to whack the back of his head. "Touchy, aren't we?"

"Careful, Draven," Ansel drawled as he entered the room, an amused smile lightening the severity of his asymmetrically scaled face. "That one bites."

Ansel, like Marius, had come to both brothers.

Hidden behind his gruff exterior was a tortured man who looked at the world through jaded eyes. He'd never tried to find a human mate among his father's people. Women shunned him, afraid or repelled by his features.

When Marius had commanded him to whip Roman, he'd balked.

But the Dragon's rage was powerful, crushing his will and twisting his already dark mind into a tool of wrath. That Roman and Draven had forgiven so readily forced him to face what he'd become, and he didn't like what he saw.

Making amends would take time.

"I may not be able to beat the humor out of Draven, but I can certainly beat it out of you, brother."

Ansel waved him over with a grin, and Roman lunged. They tussled on the ground, laughing and digging furrows in the freshly laid rushes and causing a general uproar that brought the staff from their posts and eventually their father from his solar.

Marius loomed at the top of the stairs and bellowed, "I see, after decades, you're still little more than boys."

He walked slowly down the stairs and stopped when he reached the bottom. Folding his arms, he raised a brow and said blandly, "Do save his face, Ansel. You wouldn't want his mate to refuse him in their bed for his ugliness."

Ansel sniggered and released Roman, who sprang away, grousing as he fixed his tunic and plucked hay and herbs from his hair.

Tugging his clothing into place, Roman turned to his father. "I will be fetching Gillian tomorrow."

The Great Dragon's eyes shifted from gold to red flames, their fire dying slowly as he nodded. "She will be welcome."

Roman had no plans to reside within the halls of Valon.

Emotions were too raw, and he knew Gillian would be uncomfortable living under Marius' roof.

Instead, he'd spent days repairing an abandoned cottage on the outskirts of Valon. It had belonged to a farmer and his wife who'd died without an heir three summers past. It was far enough to lend them privacy and close enough to remain part of the world he'd grown up in.

When they were ready, if that day ever came, they could move into the keep. And if not, they could travel the world and find a place of their own.

There was such freedom now that the barrier was destroyed.

Dipping his head to the Great Dragon, Roman went to Draven and spoke softly, then left the castle to make last-minute preparations for Gillian's arrival.

Marius watched his son. Having the young witch within his reach yet so far from his possession would be a trial in itself. He didn't know if he had the strength to face it.

Draven sensed his turmoil and rose slowly from his chair by the fire. "It will take time."

Marius flicked his eyes to him, lips thinning. "Aye."

"Perhaps you should begin with Keridwen. The temple has been in disarray for too long." He left the hall, a slight limp in his gait that may never heal.

Marius followed him with his eyes, the words and their meaning hanging in the air.

The land had begun to heal, the Wasting sliding back to the dark place where neglect had birthed it.

He knew the Moon Goddess waited, the pale touch of her love ready to embrace her wayward child. In his heart, he knew Draven was right.

It was time. For many things.

Chapter Thirty-Seven

Saying goodbye was bittersweet.

Though it was not forever, it felt that way as Gillian embraced her family and turned her back on Rudgarde.

Hanging from her neck was the medallion Morrigan had created. She didn't need it now.

The way was open. The two realms were one.

As they were in the beginning and would remain long after she was dust.

Gillian looked back once to see her parents holding Rory between them, their arms wrapped around his small body and each other.

Her brother waved frantically, and she returned the gesture, blowing him a kiss that he caught and held in his fist.

Adjusting the strap of her satchel, she turned from them and walked toward a new future.

The border between the Shadowlands and the Kingdom of Mirynn was little more than a jagged line of old magic.

Gillian knelt, her red cloak, singed around the hem, spreading out behind her, and pressed her palm to it, feeling the fragments of energy that had held it in place for so long.

A twig cracked, and Gillian rose slowly, scanning the heavily forested landscape. Slipping her small knife from her belt, she gripped the handle and narrowed her eyes, trying to pierce the shadows.

"Where are you going all alone in the forest?" a sensuous voice purred from the darkness.

Gillian's mouth ticked, and she slipped her blade into its sheath. "I'm on my way to see a fierce Dragonborn who lives just beyond the border."

"Hm." Roman melted from the line of trees. "I may have to pretend I'm him and snatch you away."

She laughed and ran to him, leaping into his arms.

Roman swung her around and pressed his face into her hair, inhaling deeply. Setting her down, he slipped her hood from her head and whispered, "Did you miss me?"

"A little."

He growled and nipped at her lips, eyes turning molten.

Gillian leaned up and twined her arms around him, feeling his heat penetrate her clothing and cling to her skin.

Her stomach tightened as he ran his hands down her back to cup her buttocks. She wriggled and gasped, sensation racing down her spine when he laughed softly in her ear.

Swatting him playfully, Gillian pulled away, face flushed and pupils dilated.

Everything was too new, and they'd been parted too long,

the blood of their mating bond racing unchecked through her veins. She raised her eyebrows, pleased to see wisps of smoke curling from his nostrils, knowing he was just as affected as she was.

He clenched his jaw and balled his fists, staring into the trees until he'd wrestled control over his desire.

It was not the time or place. He could wait.

Lacing his fingers through hers, he pulled her under the cover of the trees and swung her up against his chest.

She looped her arm around his neck, recalling the first time he'd held her like that. It seemed so long ago, so much had happened since then, and so much more needed to happen in the coming years.

But change came slowly. She knew this, though patience wasn't her strong suit.

Giving him a peck on the cheek, she said, "Take me home."

Roman ran through the forest, her body bouncing gently in his arms. They stopped a few times so she could rest her legs or use the bushes, but by nightfall, they'd arrived.

Torches along the wall surrounding the stronghold cast an orange glow on the ebon stone, making the veins of gold glow in the darkness.

Roman set her on her feet, keeping his hand at her back, feeling her thoughts and emotions through their connection.

"You don't have to enter the keep. I have a place for us just over that hill." He motioned to a small ridge above the pastureland. "We could stay there, and you'd never have to see him. Or we could leave the Shadowlands. I've always had a mind to see the Red Wastes. To walk the land King Balor thought he could conquer."

Her mouth quirked. "I've seen it from a distance and can assure you it's nothing but a sprawling desert of red rock and sand. I imagine there are more welcoming places to visit."

Roman took her hand and kissed her palm, the feel of his lips on her tender flesh making her stomach flip.

She curled her fingers, trapping the echo of his touch on her skin.

"Your wish is my command. Tell me what you want to do. Where you want to go."

"Are you saying I can command you?" Gillian asked, lifting a brow. "What a tempting thought. Although I think I'd better save those commands for later, behind closed doors."

His eyes glowed red, black scales winking beneath the surface of his skin for a moment, making him look dark and dangerous. "I look forward to that."

She smiled and turned her attention back to the keep where Marius waited.

A range of emotions washed over her as she looked at the magnificent edifice. There was anger and betrayal, but also sorrow and a tinge of longing.

She didn't fixate on the latter, knowing that feeling was rooted in her by the Dragon's power. It wasn't real.

Gillian held Roman's hand, taking strength in his touch, and said, "I'm ready."

Marius was waiting for them as they entered the great hall.

He stood with his back to the hearth, Draven seated in a chair at his side. As always, the Dragon wore a black robe that fluttered at his sides like wings. His deep red tunic, so like the color of his scales in his natural form, hung loosely against his chest, the deep V of the shirt exposing padded muscle beneath tanned skin.

He stood with his legs braced apart as though ready for battle.

And perhaps he was. A battle within himself.

Gillian glanced at Draven, who winked.

He looked well. The scales on his left side were the colors of rubies. She was happy to see him recovering.

Unlike Rory, the Wasting had been rooted in him for many years. It would take time for him to be rid of the remnants of the disease if that were even possible.

With Roman at her side, Gillian crossed the hall, coming to a stop when she was a few feet from the Great Dragon.

The fire in his eyes flared before he banked them, their color turning to brilliant gold. "Welcome."

She tilted her head and studied him, feeling his mind tap hers. Gillian opened to his questing and heard him ask, *Are you happy?*

She showed him memories of her and Roman and let him feel her emotions. *I am.*

I am glad.

He released her and looked at Roman. "I am glad to have you home. You and your mate."

Roman nodded and put his arm around Gillian. "It's good to be welcomed."

Marius dipped his chin, then motioned to servants hovering in the hall. They entered the room bearing trays of food and glasses of wine.

More hungry than uncomfortable, Gillian dug into what was offered, eyes drifting to the Dragon, who watched her silently.

Ansel joined them, as did other Dragonborn and their families, each bearing the mark of their father with striking features and potent sensuality.

It was overwhelming after a couple of hours, and Gillian broke away from the melee and left the hall to sit on the stone steps outside the double doors.

The Dragon watched her slip out.

Roman lowered his chin to his father, granting permission to speak to his mate, but he lingered just inside the hall, listening.

Fabric rustled as the Great Dragon left the keep and stood on the top step next to Gillian.

The wind blew his hair and shifted his robe. He looked down at the young witch with an appreciation for what she'd wrought in her short time within his lands and deep envy for what he would never have.

Sweeping the folds of his robe away from his body, he sat an arm's length from Gillian.

She stared straight ahead, feeling the heat of his body from the short distance.

Turning her head, Gillian studied him, the sharp lines of his profile, the dark wings of his brows. The shadow of a beard along his jaw. Her stepfather, Lochlan, looked twenty years his senior, and yet Marius had walked the earth for millennia.

He turned to her, and there she saw it.

Age. Wisdom. Experience.

All of it intertwined with love, loss, longing, and regret.

"There will be no more Dragons. I am the last," he told her and looked away.

"I'm sorry."

He smiled sadly. "I know, and I would take that sorrow from you if I were a better man. But I hoard it. It's all I have left of you."

Gillian's hands curled, wanting to reach for him to ease the pain. It was the healer in herself and their connection, faint but undeniable, that his sadness called to, and he knew it.

He'd used it before, and she'd let him.

He breathed heavily, exhaling smoke and his own spicy scent that drifted into the air.

She inhaled it, feeling its presence in her mind and body. But it was dull now and tinged with resignation.

Twisting to face him, she opened her mouth, but he silenced her, holding up a hand. "Don't. I know what you would say, and the words would be pure and heartfelt. But I do not want your pity. I don't deserve it."

His eyes shifted from gold to red to copper flames. "I think I will leave for a time. Now that I can," he said with a crooked smile.

"You don't need to leave."

He tilted his head. "I've lived long enough in the shadow of my mountain. I must make peace with Keridwen. I have much to atone for. And it is time I see the world again. Who knows? Maybe one day..." His voice drifted off. "Be happy, Gillian. Take care of my son."

"I will."

Marius took her hand and kissed her knuckles, holding his lips there for a few protracted moments, then let her go.

Standing, he glanced at the keep, then strode down the stairs in measured steps.

He didn't look back as he left the castle grounds.

She rose, feeling Roman join her, and leaned into him as he wrapped his arms around her shoulders.

They watched the Great Dragon move through the village and out into the rolling pasture where cragga slept bunched together in shaggy herds.

His body shimmered when he shifted, erupting from the earth in a fiery ball of red scales and flapping wings.

Marius soared into the sky, a dark shadow against the fullness of the moon. They watched until he disappeared.

Roman gently spun her around, wiping a lone tear from her cheek and kissing the place where it had been.

Gillian snuggled against him, pressing her face into his chest, feeling the steady rhythm of his heart. An uncertain future lay before them, but it was different now.

The world was different.

And together, they would face it.

The End

<h1 style="text-align:center">*Acknowledgments*</h1>

As a young girl, bedtime stories inevitably involved magic, witches, dragons, and many other fantastical characters and worlds. My mother lent her voice to tales of good vs. evil nightly. I've never outgrown my love for such adventures!

When I began writing *Dark is the Wood*, I knew the story would unfold as all of my stories have: with the fragile promise of an exciting tale and a guarantee that it would go off the rails when I least expected it! Characters introduced themselves along the way, and, at times, they stole the scene and quickly demanded a book of their own. As a benevolent creator, I must acquiesce to their wishes.

My dearest reader, you will see Marius, Draven, Ansel, and Morrigan again!

No book is written without the love and support of family, friends, creators, editors, and book lovers. I'm blessed with all of these.

My husband and three sons allowed me to live in the world of *Dark is the Wood* for months on end without complaint, even listening as I rambled on about story threads and characters time and again. Their unwavering love and support are what keeps me going!

My designer, Lindsey, once again poured her artistic passion into the cover of the book, often spending hours texting or chatting with me about design elements. Of course, I would never publish a book without my editor, David. He's traveled every world I've created, always adding sound advice, drawing out the characters and story, and helping me thread all of the pieces together. My new friends at Crab & Bell followed his skills with this book. These lovely people added the finishing touches and loads of praise for the story!

Another essential group of people I want to thank are my ARC readers. Releasing a book starts with an ARC team. *Dark is the Wood* is unique because I have a new group of bookworms who fell in love with the story and truly inspired me to add more tales to Gillian's world.

Lastly, my lovely reader, I wrote this book for you. Thank you for being part of my journey.

About the Author

Kristin Ward is an award-winning young adult author living in Connecticut. A science and math teacher for over twenty years, she infuses her geeky passions into stories that meld realism and fantasy.

A lifelong lover of books and writing, she dreamed of becoming an author for thirty years before publishing her award-winning debut in 2018. Her first novel, **After the Green Withered**, is one of many things you should probably read.

~www.kristinwardauthor.com~